THE SOLITUDE OF SOPHIA WHITE

Sophia White wants for nothing. Looks, brains, career, friends and money — she has it all. The last thing she wants is to lose the independence she has so striven to cultivate. But then she meets the brilliant, feckless Thomas, and her well ordered life is turned upside down. On the brink of despair Sophia must decide whether the abandonment of solitude for the love of Thomas is really a recipe for happiness.

Of half-Russian origin, Juliana Abell was born in England. She was educated at Oxford and spent several years working in the City of London, latterly as an investment analyst. Now married with five stepchildren, she lives in the country, where she runs a small thoroughbred stud, and spends much of each winter in Australia.

JULIANA ABELL

THE
SOLITUDE OF
SOPHIA WHITE

Complete and Unabridged

ULVERSCROFT
Leicester

First published in Great Britain in 1998 by
Citron Press
London

First Large Print Edition
published 2000
by arrangement with
Citron Press
Connors Corporation Limited
London

British Library CIP Data

Abell, Juliana
The solitude of Sophia White.—Large print ed.—
Ulverscroft large print series: romance
1. Love stories
2. Large type books
I. Title
823.9'14 [F]

ISBN 0–7089–4274–1

Published by
F. A. Thorpe (Publishing)
Anstey, Leicestershire
Set by Words & Graphics Ltd.
Anstey, Leicestershire
Printed and bound in Great Britain by
T. J. International Ltd., Padstow, Cornwall

This book is printed on acid-free paper

1

Sophia White, highly intelligent, handsome and in her prime, had her life admirably sorted out. Her career was brilliant, her friends compatible, her interests cultural and rewarding. She had learned — not without a struggle — to value her solitude; however, there were certain areas in her life in which she had not enjoyed such success. She decided it was time at last to live dangerously by doing something about this.

The opportunity came when a fascinating man invited her out to dinner a few times. At the end of the fourth dinner, she found herself in a taxi with this man heading for a flat somewhere in the Barbican.

He took her hand. 'You do know, don't you, that I'm married?' he began.

Sophia smiled. 'But of course!'

'I so enjoy being with you. I want to spend what time I can with you. You must understand it's limited . . . '

Sophia squeezed his hand. It was a long, slim hand with little black hairs that contrasted sharply with a white shirt cuff. She found to her astonishment that she wanted to cover it in kisses.

' . . . and it's only fair to tell you I don't plan to get divorced. You must accept that I can't offer you much. It's only fair to tell you right now.'

'It doesn't matter in the very slightest, don't you see? It's not as if I want to get involved. The last thing I want is a big, time-consuming affair. You know I value my independence. If we just see each other when we can it will be perfect for me.' Eager to convince, she rushed to get her words out.

'I can see I haven't misjudged you,' he said with unmistakable self-satisfaction.

Rupert Kingsley had known almost from the day he had met Sophia that he would not find her difficult, even though she had initially impressed him by turning down the prestigious job he had offered her at his merchant bank. Clearly she was too ambitious to have found time to get married and probably, he suspected, too obviously intelligent to be attractive to many men. He found this undisguised intelligence of hers intriguing; she also had large grey eyes, a handsome rather than pretty face and a thin, tense figure that appealed to him. He himself was blessed with good looks, wealth and brilliant connections; most women were so dazzled by him that he was beginning to be slightly bored by it. In Sophia's world, which was the City, he had a formidable reputation as the youngest ever head of a tough, well managed, highly profitable bank; he was said also to be academically outstanding.

The taxi stopped in Gresham Street, well short of their destination. Kingsley led her to one of the anonymous glass and steel towers of the Barbican; they rose in a lift to the fourth floor, where he had an utterly impersonal pied-à-terre. No one had spent much time in it or care over it; the furnishings were comfortable, even expensive, but dull and unconsidered. The warmth of its central heating was somehow obviated by its only colour, which was that of very pale mud. In the kitchen there was not a scrap of food, just wine and champagne in the fridge and cognac in a cupboard. There were large towels set out in the bathroom, which had two of everything, even new toothbrushes. The flat was clean to the point of sterility and obviously specially prepared for the night.

'Do we need another drink?' Kingsley took out the cognac.

'I don't think so.' She laughed — high-pitched — and looked him in the eye, her lips parted, quite unconscious that her breath was sharp with excitement.

There was no question of seduction. She

3

seemed to flow into his arms and thence to his bed, too artless to conceal her eagerness. Kingsley was almost disappointed that his expectations in the ease of wooing Sophia were so exactly fulfilled; he found a little opposition, however manipulative or contrived, titillating. Seduction was one of his less vaunted but not least valued talents. Sophia did away with all such contrivance. Kingsley reached for her under the covers and almost abstractly let his hands take their usual course. She was too thin, of course, and would probably prove to be as interesting to sleep with as a polo mallet. Were four dinners tucked away in Mayfair's discreetest, most expensive restaurant worth such a banal outcome? His body reacted automatically, almost boredly, to Sophia's; his mind more or less switched off.

Sophia, however, was galvanised into action. Free of inhibitions and blissfully unaware of his ennui, she sought his mouth and kissed him almost aggressively. Her hands raced over him. He was momentarily shocked, then excited; abruptly, all his senses and even his mind snapped into gear, becoming totally engaged. The energy of her thin body, now suddenly entwined about his, revealed a frenzied sexuality which was intriguingly at odds with the stern, bookish

4

rationality he had observed in conversation. He hadn't been laid like this in years . . . The image of a polo mallet was replaced by that of thin red chilli peppers of which he was inordinately fond. Afterwards, he snoozed complacently, genuinely spent, half asleep and half awake, reflecting lazily that after all the going might well be good for another few laps. She lay wide awake, her head propped uncomfortably on the crook of his arm, aware only of a wild and tearing happiness and of feeling more alive now than at any other time in her life.

'*Tristan* was never like this,' she murmured, intruding on his incipient snores.

'*What?*' he half exclaimed, turning his head.

'I saw the most amazing production of *Tristan* last year in Bayreuth. The ending was really unbearably moving, the most wonderful thing I had ever experienced in my life.'

'Don't your other lovers find it rather insulting to be compared to Herr Wagner?'

'Maybe I never realised how extraordinarily sexy the music is,' she mused. 'Desperately disturbing though. You wouldn't happen to have it here, would you? It would be just the thing . . . '

He gave her one of his characteristic smiles; his lips twisted and his eyes remained cold. 'We've just fucked each other's brains out, and you lecture me about *classical music*.'

'Oh, it doesn't matter,' Sophia said good naturedly, repressing a comment on classicism versus romanticism. 'It was just my perverse way of saying I enjoyed it . . . well, you.'

Amused despite himself, he moved deliberately to put his arms around her. 'Now,' he said gently, 'it's time, I'm afraid, to go home.'

'Oh.'

'Yes. Now you know I'm married. You do accept that, so that means we have one or two little rules. One is that we always meet here. Not at my house, or at yours. Another is that we don't spend the whole night together. I'm sure it would be very nice, but it can't be done. I hardly need to tell you that in my position I have to be discreet . . . '

Sophia giggled. '*In your position*. You sound like a cabinet minister about to negotiate a naughty.'

Kingsley was not amused. 'Oh come on,' said Sophia. 'You know I understand. It's all right.' She kissed him. He disengaged himself, got out of bed and had a very thorough shower. She toyed with the idea of joining him in it and dropped it. While she had her turn, he dressed in his immaculate

City clothes (his pure white shirts and plain ties gave the impression that he was a man with better things to think about than the frivolity of coloured and patterned ones) and rang for two taxis.

For the first week, Sophia was dazed with joy. At work she was cheerful and expansive. Her job as an investment analyst took her out of the office for several days, so she did not worry when she heard nothing from Kingsley. One day when she had no business lunch she took a taxi to Bond Street and spent a remarkably large sum in a very short time on a dress. The expensive fabric felt wonderful against her skin. In this mood of joyous self-indulgence she next took the time to visit a fashionable hairdresser's. As she was waiting to have her washed and turbaned hair cut, she idly flipped open a *Tatler* and was intrigued to see the picture of a beautiful blonde woman called Lavinia Kingsley. Her husband wasn't in the picture.

In the second week, Sophia had no travelling. She concentrated on her social life, which was full, highly organised and revolved around mostly intellectual friends and classical music; but she grew uneasy. She found another picture of Lavinia Kingsley in her secretary's *Harpers and Queen* from the summer (at Windsor watching Rupert — who had a three handicap — play polo). Friday lunch time found her alone in her office feeling far from hungry.

The telephone rang. It was her outside line.

'Sophie? It's Kev. Kevin. I'm at the Leeds office. I've just been to see Gamma Biotech, and these trains've been cancelled, dunno if I'll make it back to the office tonight. Well I've got these figures, I know you want them, can I give them you over the phone?'

Kevin was Sophia's youngest colleague; he reported to her.

'Have you ever heard of the fax, Kevin?'

'Pardon?'

'The fax, Kevin. It's a remarkably useful machine. If you write all the numbers down in your best handwriting — not your usual scrawl,' she took a deep breath, 'there's every chance it'll be far more accurate than dictating to me — now for Christ's sake — just go and do it — *now*.' She slammed the telephone down, panting slightly.

Sophia wanted to kill Kevin for not being Rupert Kingsley.

Kevin crept into the office at 6.30 p.m. after a terrible afternoon spent between Leeds and King's Cross. He prayed Sophia would have gone home. His prayer was not answered, but his luck had turned.

'Kevin,' Sophia smiled beatifically, 'I'm

8

sorry I bit your head off back there. Thank you for the fax. Did you have a bad time on the trains?'

'Bloody nightmare!' Kevin grinned. 'Signal failure at Newark.'

'You caught me at a bad time. I was expecting quite an important call. Your Gamma Biotech figures look good.'

'Great! Did your call come through OK?'

'Oh no. But it's all right. I'm going home now.'

Kevin didn't see her leave with her briefcase in one hand and a small bunch of white tulips in the other. They had been delivered with a message on a white card bearing an address in the Barbican and the words: '10.30 p.m. Tuesday 30 January. Sorry can't make it earlier.'

Sophia sang along with Schubert on the car stereo all the way home.

'What good exercise you are,' said Kingsley, panting slightly as they disentangled themselves at the next encounter. 'You know, you're very highly sexed.'

Sophia laughed joyously; her mind was blank; she glowed with sensation. Later in her own bed alone that night, she remembered the little scrappy affairs she had had, on and off, over the years from her time at Cambridge up to now. She knew she was falling in love. In the past she had sometimes fancied she might be in love, but this experience was new: she recognised and embraced it.

There was a period then — at least a week — of real happiness. She saw Kingsley again but did not stint either her work or her social life. Everything seemed to be going her way: she was managing an affair with a man whom she regarded as the most glamorous in London, yet she had all the independence she wanted. All the rest of her life was running as perfectly as she could wish. She found another hour one lunch time to visit Bond Street to blow a little more of her large salary and fancied she saw Lavinia Kingsley through the window at Chanel.

'It can't be Lavinia,' she reasoned with herself. 'She would be lunching at this time with another woman at Claridge's, or the Ritz.'

Almost imperceptibly, Sophia began to worry about Lavinia Kingsley as she thought more about her. She ate less and lost weight.

'You're looking dead posh these days, Sophie,' said Kevin.

'Dead thin, too,' added a female colleague. 'You just don't even have to try, I do envy you.'

'Ah well,' said Kevin. 'Got a new man, I bet.'

Sophia looked levelly at him. 'Kevin, when did Reeves Chemicals report its results?'

'Er, day before yesterday?'

'And where is your full report?'

'I was just about to . . .'

'You were just about to. Kevin, when you have done what you were just about to do, am I going to throw it out for being not only late, but also inaccurate, verbose and incomprehensible, like the last three reports? Do you want to go on in this job, Kevin, or would you just prefer to die quietly somewhere, preferably in a deep hole and right out of my sight?'

'God, chill out,' said Kevin. 'What is this . . .'

Sophia turned on her heel and stormed into her office, where the telephone was ringing. It was Kingsley. A little time later, she apologised to Kevin and invited him and a few others out for a drink after work.

'I bet you anything some bloke's giving her the run-around,' he commented to the envious girl.

'Ah well, you never can tell with our Sophie, can you?' said the girl. 'You're probably right, but she's a close one.'

'You're seeing someone, aren't you?' said

her best female friend, Anita.

'Oh, well, sort of, from time to time, you know, just sort of occasionally.'

'Hey, what is this? Sophie, you're a stuttering wreck. You're definitely seeing someone, and he's performed a lobotomy or something, because you've lost your normally alarming ability to speak.'

'My brain is super, thank you. My forecasts for Akzo, whose results were announced today, were absolutely spot on. I'm doing really well, I tell you.'

'Go on, tell me about the man.'

'Look, it's just someone I see very occasionally, OK? It's not as if — not as if it was a big part of my life. I do have a lot on. I haven't stopped. Do you know, I'm going to see the new production of *Lohengrin* tomorrow at the Royal Opera. I can't wait . . . '

She went to *Lohengrin* by herself, having bought one of the best seats in the stalls. To her horror, she saw both Kingsleys in the row in front. During the first interval, she could not resist spying on them. They were drinking champagne with another, older couple. Concealed behind a pillar, she watched Kingsley pour the wine into the four glasses. He was smiling at the other couple. Lavinia Kingsley was motionless and, as far as Sophia could see, almost expressionless, but Sophia was able easily to satisfy herself that she was at least as beautiful as in all the *Tatler* photographs, a perfect match for her husband. She could not hear what they were saying, but she studied the closely knit, confident group they made. She was grateful for the end of the interval, which had dragged on for nearly half an hour, and spent the next one losing herself around Covent Garden.

Sophia also thanked God that the *Lohengrin* production was a good one; otherwise it would not have distracted her from her appalled fascination in Kingsley and his exquisite wife during the second and third acts. She escaped into Lohengrin and Elsa and their doomed marriage, ravished by the music, now silvery and now grand and brassy, and captivated by the girl's breakdown and death. So often, she thought, as she was moved almost to tears at the finale, art was so greatly preferable to real life.

'What did you think of *Lohengrin*?' she asked Kingsley next time they met and were in bed.

'I've decided I don't like Wagner,' he said. 'His late works are insufferable; I can't stand these romantic outpourings; they go much too far and are so self-indulgent. I suppose I can just about put up with the earlier stuff.

How do you know I went to*Lohengrin*?'

'I was there; I saw you at the opera.'

'Well, I'm very glad I didn't see you.'

There was a pause.

'She's very beautiful, your wife,' ventured Sophia.

'Extremely.'

'How do you get on with her?'

Kingsley turned, raised himself up onto his elbow and looked hard at Sophia. 'That's none of your business,' he said.

'I think it is.'

He sighed. 'Oh, Sophia,' he said, quite gently, 'let's leave it. It may be hard, you may not like it, but I'm married, and I'm not going to get unmarried. We've been through this. May we change the subject?'

'I was only mildly curious.'

'Good. Keep it that way, for both our sakes.'

Sophia, trying to bend the rules, said one night to Kingsley, 'How could it possibly do any harm if we went to my house? It's very comfortable.'

'I'm sure it is,' he rejoined. 'You have very high standards. Impossible, I'm afraid.'

'Why should it be impossible? Just think, we could maybe spend a whole night. This flat is a bit gloomy. I know it's difficult, but you once said your wife was in the country

14

sometimes, and you'd be free . . . '

(He hadn't told her anything of the sort; she had conveniently forgotten that she had read about it the other day in someone else's *Hello!* magazine.)

Kingsley sighed. 'I have a constant need for discretion,' he said wearily. 'You *know* that. You're really far too bright for me to have to remind you.'

'Oh, I know, I know — about the discretion, I mean. But wouldn't it be lovely? It's such a bore, having to get up out of bed before midnight. It's just like Cinderella, as if we'd turn into pumpkins if we were late. I'd so love to spend a whole night with you.'

'Come on, Sophie. You know very well this isn't on. I can't be seen near your house, and in the mornings my place is in my home. That's the way it's going to be. You've always known there's a limit to what we can offer each other.'

'There isn't, not for me.'

'Don't push me, Sophie. I like you, you are good company, and I like going to bed with you. But that's it. I've never tried to deceive you that it could be different. If you can't now see it, I'm very sorry. I don't need any grief about it.'

As if to teach her a lesson, he did not

contact her for two or three weeks after this exchange. She sighed with frustration and asked herself why she could not be treated like other mistresses, who apparently accompanied their lovers illicitly on business trips and were far more involved in those lovers' lives. Of course Kingsley would never leave his wife; she thought she had completely accepted that; however, she also thought she had heard of relationships which carried on for years outside marriages. In her case, she never spent more than a few hours on any occasion with Kingsley. If she was lucky, they might have dinner before going to the flat. If she was very lucky, they might leave each other as late as one o'clock in the morning.

So strongly did she feel that when they saw each other again, and she had got over the desperate surge of relief and joy at seeing him after such a long time, she ran the risk of expressing some of these feelings to him.

'*Please* can't we stay a little longer together?' she begged, as he got out of bed.

'No!'

'I'm sorry, it really is hard for me. What's the harm in it?'

He completely ignored her. She was silently furious because she had found it extraordinarily difficult to tell him how she felt; at the same time she felt like crying, which was a thing she absolutely never let herself do in front of other people. He got dressed without speaking while she tried to make herself get out of bed. Unexpectedly, he kissed her on the cheek just before he left the flat.

'Make sure the door stays locked behind you when you go,' he said, and left himself.

A week passed, then another and another. Sophia felt so grim that it began to show.

'Cheer up, it may never happen,' said Kevin at work.

Sophia blanched. Her fists clenched in rage; her hackles rose; half rising behind her desk, she snarled with venom, 'Cut the cliché, punk!'

Kevin beat a retreat.

'Bloody hell,' he said to a colleague. 'She's turning into a Rottweiler.'

Sophia became tired because she wasn't sleeping. Her new clothes hung off her because she also wasn't eating enough. One day she realised she had nothing to lose, so she went home earlier than usual and rang Kingsley's office. He had never trusted her with his direct telephone number. Slightly to her surprise, she got put through.

'Sophie.' The voice was bland. 'What can I do for you?'

'I wondered how you were. We haven't seen each other for a long time.'

'Yes; well,' the voice was still bland, 'all good things come to an end.'

'You're surely not . . . ' She struggled to find the right words.

'There's not much point in carrying on this conversation, is there?'

'You cannot just . . . just drop me like this. You just can't. It's not on . . . '

Now he sounded bored and cross. 'I've moved on, Sophie. You'd better do the same.'

'Now just look.' She became angry, and her spirits soared on the wings of her anger. 'Don't you wheel out these clichés with me. I've done nothing to deserve this sort of thing. How dare you treat me like this! What the hell have I done? Just tell me. Go on. Do you really think . . . '

'Listen to me and listen well.' His words, spoken calmly but very firmly, shot her anger to pieces. 'Everything is over. That's the first thing. Second, you are not to make trouble. I don't care how angry you are, it's not my concern. But make trouble, and I will finish you. You know who I am. You won't have a career. Just remember that.'

She recoiled from the telephone receiver as if it had hit her and replaced it without saying another word. For some time she sat absolutely still by the telephone, her mind blank, aware only of the silence of her house.

When she could no longer stop herself from thinking, her idea was to escape from the mounting horror of her hurt; however, her normal escape routes — her books and music — were mysteriously closed.

She refused to dwell on Rupert Kingsley and what he had just done to her. She could not tolerate being alone with her tears because the pain seemed too enormous for them. Crying was something she only let herself do when she had read or heard a particularly moving book or piece of music.

Then she recalled that in a drawer upstairs was a paperback book. Its title was embossed on the front in large gold letters, and it was a best seller, a big juicy thriller. Her sister had pressed it on her.

'Go on, do read it, Sophie. It's ever so good. I couldn't put it down on holiday. Oh, I know it's not awfully highbrow like your normal books, but I can't imagine anyone not enjoying it, it's riveting.'

Sophia, who did not read best sellers, had forgotten to throw this book out. Now she took it from the drawer and examined it gingerly. She opened it on page one and began to read. It was exactly what she wanted. She read feverishly and very quickly, devouring the pages. Its author was a marvellous story-teller. However, when she had finished it, and it was three o'clock in the morning, she couldn't sleep. Being awake and alone with her thoughts was unbearable. She escaped again, this time into the familiar territory of P.G. Wodehouse, and caught an hour's broken sleep before dawn.

It was a relief to get to work because it distracted her from herself, but she was too tired to be good for much. Kevin and the rest observed her pallor and the dark rings under her eyes, but something about her prevented them from commenting; they left her alone.

In the months that followed, Sophia sometimes wished she could confide in someone, but she isolated herself almost against her will.

'I know something's wrong, Sophie,' said her friend Anita. 'You know I'm not prying, but don't tell me it wouldn't help you if you told me at least a bit about it.'

'I just can't, I'm sorry.'

'Look at you, you're a toast rack on legs, and you're exhausted, completely overdoing your utterly bloody work. Come and spend the night here on Friday, we'll be alone, and we shall have a really good meal which I shall cook, and some really good wine. How can you resist?'

'Oh, watch me,' said Sophia, beyond tears. 'You stupid, stupid woman, I really care about you, I don't know why.' Anita was nearly in tears herself. 'Why can't you give yourself a break?'

'I'm really sorry,' Sophia said sincerely. 'I just can't. Don't ask me why. You're the best friend anyone could have, I don't deserve you.'

'Oh, cut the crap. I know you too well to push you, but I'll never understand. I just wish I could help, that's all.'

Sophia read some more best sellers; by and by she picked up again the difficult, serious literature to which she was accustomed, and began to listen to her kind of music. Art was, as ever, preferable to life. At work she calmed down with her colleagues, resolving never again to take out on them her private disappointments. Her professionalism paid off: towards the end of this harrowing year, she was promoted again, this time to head of research. She was also made a director of her firm.

This was Sophia's first real experience of being in love. For several months its aftermath frequently brought her to the brink of despair and the limit of her self-control. She despised herself; what possible expectations could she have entertained from an affair with a married man? She found the situation banal and herself pathetic; for all her sophistication and success she had behaved with startling naiveté and felt herself to be a fool. The Rupert Kingsley episode had been an unmitigated prat-fall and forced her inescapably to the conclusion that some risks were too great for her.

Of course, the only alternative was solitude. She began to let it enclose her. It was not always a comfortable or even tolerable haven, but it was the only one she knew. It gave her a dangerous and false sense of security.

2

It had been an appalling day. One of the firm's major companies to which it was broker unexpectedly announced disastrous results, having pulled the wool over the eyes of every institution and analyst in the City. As head of the research department that was supposed to know the company better than anyone else, Sophia was in the thick of the scrum. She talked and listened and talked — on the telephone and in meetings, to sales people, market-markers, clients, the company directors, accountants, lawyers, financial journalists, all avid, angry or defensive, some quite stupid, some horribly clever. The company's shares crashed. Millions were lost.

Over twelve hours after she had entered the office, she found herself virtually alone on her floor. Having had to satisfy herself on the quality of the report her department had put out for the firm's clients on the débacle, she had outstayed all her subordinates. She yawned and stretched and looked at her watch. It was eight o'clock and time to go home. The prospect seduced her: she would sit in her warm sitting room with a mug of hot chocolate and listen to her new recording of *Der Freischütz* and have a long hot bath and go to bed with the electric blanket on.

Blinking slightly, she took the lift down to the garage, where hers was the only car remaining. Then she remembered something that completely blew away her vision of a cosy evening alone at home. Her friend Anita was having a small dinner party, and she had promised to be there.

Anita lived in Notting Hill with an actor called Harold who spent a good deal of time resting. He and Sophia had little time for each other; Anita was too easygoing to allow this mutual antipathy to interfere with her friendship with Sophia, which dated back to Cambridge. Although Sophia had never been forthcoming with her own problems, she had been steadfastly loyal to Anita, who was less introverted and confided more. Each of them greatly enjoyed the other's company. They regularly entertained each other with dinners and suppers and overlapping circles of friends.

Now Sophia nearly groaned out loud. Not only was she exhausted, but also she felt sweaty and stale. There was no time to go home and renew herself. She was not self-conscious, but she would have preferred to go out to dinner more suitably dressed, with clean hair and fresh make-up. Had the dinner been given by almost anyone but Anita, she would have been ruthless enough to cancel at the last minute. On the way from the City to Notting Hill, she stopped at an off-licence and bought a bottle of Chablis. Feeling slightly guilty that it had even occurred to her to let her friend down, she made sure it was a premier cru.

'Sorry I'm a mess,' she said as Anita admitted her, 'and late.' It was a quarter to nine; they went into a big, warm, untidy kitchen, where Anita was putting the finishing touches to the dinner.

'You're the first to arrive, don't worry, and Harold's still in the shower.'

'I don't believe this. I killed myself to get here. I didn't even have time to go home and change.'

'What fabulous wine! Come on, let's have a quick glass together before the others get here. It's too good just to chuck around.'

'Sorry, no; I daren't; I'm driving. Put it away and have it when you're on your own. I'd love some orange juice or Perrier or something.'

'Is this what you call a mess, White?' Sophia was wearing a black suit, beautifully cut, a pale pink shirt with white collar and cuffs and no jewellery. 'The trouble with you is, you'd look good in a sack. I don't know why I like you.'

Anita was Sophia's physical opposite. She was slightly overweight and very pretty with it; her hair and her clothes tended to be long and flowing. She exuded comfort.

'I have to tell you this has been the worst day of my life.'

'Sure you don't want a slug of vodka in there? What's up?'

'All hell let loose at work. Have you seen the main headline in the financial bit of the *Evening Standard*? No, of course you haven't. Let's say that if we have another débâcle like this one it could seriously threaten the firm's reputation.'

'The *firm's* reputation, good grief. Don't you dare start losing your sense of humour.'

The doorbell rang; at the same time Harold came downstairs with a damp head. (He had recently, in preparation for an audition, shaved off most of his hair, which Sophia found ugly and irritating.) He opened the door and admitted a friend of his, who worked for the Arts Council, and his wife. The five of them sat in the drawing room over drinks for some time until Anita announced that she was fed up waiting; the food would spoil if they did not eat.

Sophia was seated between Harold and the

Arts Council friend. Her slight antipathy for Harold didn't preclude the enjoyment of a conversation with him. Over soup, they locked horns. She forgot how tired she was and had a lively debate with the actor and Arts Council.

They were just starting the main course when the last guest arrived.

'I'm sorry I'm late,' interrupted the newcomer, almost gabbling. 'But you see I'm so lucky to be alive. Can you believe there was a bomb scare somewhere on the Central Line, and we were stuck between Holborn and Tottenham Court Road for forty minutes, and wouldn't you know there was the most howling drunk in my carriage?'

Sophia looked at him and saw a fairly tall and very thin man with large, dark eyes set in a pale face; he would have looked young had his thick, almost black hair not had a noticeable smattering of grey, unusually all at the front. This grey-black forelock kept falling into his eyes, and he had a mannerism of tossing his head to flick it back which gave him an air of nervousness.

'This is Thomas Avondale,' said Harold. 'Good to see you alive, Thomas. Come in and have an enormous drink and a first course.'

Conversation flowed from the bomb scare to terrorism and current politics. Sophia found it predictable and wanted to talk to Thomas, but she was hemmed in by Harold and Arts Council, and because Thomas had a soft, somewhat indistinct voice, she couldn't hear him properly. She observed him out of the corner of her eye; as far as she could see, he was talking with great charm to Anita and Mrs Arts Council, who seemed mesmerised.

In the drawing room over coffee, she manoeuvred discreetly to sit next to him. He was, she discovered, an artist who had been commissioned to draw a portrait of a niece of Anita's.

'Is it difficult to portray a child?' she asked.

'Can be,' Thomas replied; 'depends on the child. It helps to like children. I do, I love them. But I can't do them a lot younger than Claire, their faces just change too much every time you see them, it's like a sculpture in the sand or something. But so I'm an artist, after a fashion; what do you do?'

'I'm an investment analyst. Probably right over your head.'

'Thank goodness, I can't bear other artists.'

He suddenly and unexpectedly smiled and looked into her eyes, as if he was seeing her properly for the first time.

'What's wrong with other artists?'

'Oh, they're like me. You see, you have to be madly, madly selfish to be an artist. Artists

28

are monsters of selfishness. I don't suppose investment analysts have quite such an enormous selfishness requirement as artists. What investments do you analyse?'

'All sorts.'

'But what do you have to do?'

'Well, I have a lot of colleagues. They go and see the people who run the companies and try to estimate how much money their companies are going to make. They write reports and recommend people to buy or sell the shares. I make sure everything is on the right track.'

'Is it fun? Do you enjoy it?'

She smiled wryly. 'I didn't enjoy it today. One of the companies we're broker to — and a big BUY recommendation — announced terrible results. The shares and our reputation crashed.'

'Oh dear! What happens now?'

'Not much. Perhaps tomorrow another of our BUY recommendations will announce superb results, the shares will soar, and everyone will love us.'

He laughed. 'You must make tons of money — all that insider trading . . . '

Sophia raised her eyebrows. 'You'd be surprised how difficult it is to engage in insider trading these days — quite apart from it being illegal, of course.'

'Oh come on, I thought that was how you people got on? I met a man once, lived in a lovely great pile, and he said, did I imagine he could possibly afford to keep it up just on his salary? He was the most dreadful bore, talking about costs and salaries and things, but the point was, he'd made stacks dealing on the inside track. Actually he got done for it — oh dear,' he laughed, 'you probably think I think you're a wicked miscreant, when I really wouldn't dream of being so rude. I'm so sorry.'

An unexpected reciprocal giggle bubbled up in Sophia. Thomas asked again, 'But *is* it fun, what you do?'

'Fun? Well — it's satisfying.'

'Just *satisfying*? It can't be that boring, surely. It has to be fun too. Life would be quite insupportable if there wasn't lots of fun in it. Satisfying? Take food. Porridge is *satisfying*, I suppose; you feel nicely full when you've eaten it; but it's not *fun*. Now caviar is also satisfying, frightfully rich and filling you know, but it's much, much more fun than porridge. Wouldn't you rather eat caviar than porridge, and wouldn't life be horribly boring if you were only able to eat horribly boring satisfying porridge? No, you've got to have fun. Don't tell me you don't, you look far too nice not to.'

'Ah, but what about you? How much caviar and how much porridge do you get out of being an artist?'

'No porridge, extremely occasional caviar, and the rest's starvation. Yes, of course, at the end of the day it is fun. When it comes right it's unbelievably wonderful. I can't really describe it. When you're working at a picture, and it comes right — oh, it's — it's orgasmic, it's so exciting, you're high as a kite and all the bloody awfulness of everything else is worth it, however bloody the awfulness may have been. It's even more than fun, it's everything.'

'What about the bloody awfulness?'

'You're asking too many questions. We're going to have to continue this conversation another day. I tell you what, will you find me a nice sponsor in the City? All that money has to be spent. Surely one of these rich City creeps needs someone like me to sponsor. Don't they have pictures in those glass buildings of theirs? How would it be if you arranged for me to meet a rich person who would take me out to one of those amazing three hour lunches and commission me to do a lot of wonderful pictures and pay me lots of money?'

Sophia drew back slightly and regarded Thomas with some surprise. 'I don't mean to sound abrasive,' she said, 'but I'm afraid you're quite badly out of touch with reality. Three hour lunches went out with insider trading.'

Thomas stared back. 'How very grim you sound! Haven't you any sense of humour at all?'

'How do you define a sense of humour?'

'I don't trust people who answer questions with questions.'

'In that case, we'd better terminate this conversation; it will get us nowhere. Would you like some more coffee?'

'No, thank you; but to go back to what we were saying, I can't believe you're as prickly as you make out.'

'I don't believe we were saying anything of the sort; I might just as well say I can't believe you're quite as naive as *you* make out.'

Thomas leaned forward, chin in hand, and smiled. 'D'you know, it's rather fun talking to a very intelligent woman for a change. I bet you have got a sense of humour really.'

'You can't know I'm intelligent. I've hardly spoken to you.'

Thomas roared with laughter. 'I should like,' he continued, 'to ring you up, preferably at work?'

'I never give anyone my home telephone number.'

'Really, I do think you are prickly, whatever you mean to be. I was going to ask you for your work — not your home — number. People are never in when you ring them up at home, but even if they aren't in at work they have secretaries and things who will tell you where they are. Actually, you probably won't want to hear from me anyhow. You're awfully good looking and sorry, I *do* think you're intelligent and obviously madly successful anyhow; what would you want with me?'

'On the contrary; I don't see what *you* would want with *me*. We clearly have nothing in common. Anyway, I have to be going now; it's fairly late.' She added, with truth, 'I've really enjoyed meeting you.'

She half rose. He gently but firmly put his hand on her arm, stopping her.

'Don't rush off.' He gave her a beatific smile which lit up his face. 'Please may I have your card?'

'I'm going abroad tomorrow for the rest of the week,' she said, but her smile broke through in response to him, and she fished a card out of her bag.

'You know, you have a very, very nice smile. I shall simply have to ring you up. Ah — your card — a real little rinky-dink engraved jobbie. 'Sophia White, director'. How grand! It's just like a miniature stiffie.'

Presently the dinner party broke up. Eschewing the offer of a lift, Thomas insisted on catching the last tube home; he lived just beyond the City in Wapping. Sophia wondered at his lack of transport; nearly all her acquaintances had cars. Perhaps he had left his car at home so that he could drink tonight. She herself left after him, driving soberly home, having drunk just one glass of white wine.

As she reviewed the dinner party to herself on her way home, she grinned. Thomas Avondale had made her laugh and had provided a good ending to a dreadful day. Whether or not she saw him again was irrelevant; she had deliberately done nothing to encourage him; she did not expect him to ring her up.

3

'In case I said anything particularly stupid at that dinner party, I have to tell you I wasn't drunk,' Thomas told Sophia on the telephone a week later. 'The reason that I'm ringing you up is that I terribly much want you to see some of my pictures. No, don't say anything, I know it's completely beyond the pale. I just feel — I'd really love to have your opinion.'

'Well,' said Sophia carefully, 'you mustn't expect much from me. I don't know very much about visual art.'

Thomas sighed audibly. 'Jesus *Christ*,' he exclaimed. 'I don't care a stuff how little or how much you think you know about visual art, as you call it. I've simply painted some pictures, and I want to see if you like them. I'm not even trying to sell them to you, or anything like that. You do *not* have to 'know' about art to appreciate them or not, as the case may be.'

'This does rather beg the question, why on earth should you then value my opinion?'

'I don't know. Look, I'm sorry I rang. I shouldn't have disturbed you. You obviously don't want to see them, and it was silly and presumptuous of me. I must let you get back to your analysing. I do hope you haven't had any more disasters.'

'Oh no, not at all, but look, I didn't say I didn't want to see your pictures. I should in fact be interested. It was only fair to tell you my opinion wouldn't be worth much.'

'That's for me to decide. I'm so pleased. Come tonight. If you can? You're probably going out to dinner. I wish it was with me. I tell you what, come and see my pictures and I'll take you out to dinner.'

A dreary little voice in Sophia's head told her to put Thomas off, certainly until another day if not altogether. However, there was nothing she had to do that evening; this dinner was sure to be fun, certainly different; she was tempted to disregard the little voice. She hesitated, and Thomas went on:

'Or even if you aren't being taken out somewhere glamorous, you're probably up to your eyeballs in analysing and all that high-powered stuff. I know, I *am* so presumptuous, it's dreadful; but I will bet that my pictures and I are more fun than your satisfying reports.'

'It's all right. I'll come.'

Sophia's dreary voice gave a little whine and shut up.

'Wonderful! Shall we meet in Wapping? You

are mobile, aren't you? I shall be in this pub,' he gave her a street name, 'the Ulcer and Prune. You can't miss it. Seven o'clock.'

'The what?'

'*You* know, the Rose and Crown. I always call it the Ulcer and Prune. It's my local. We've got to meet there, you'd never find my frightful studio, and besides, I shall have to buy you a large drink to prepare you for the studio. Longing to see you.'

Sophia did not normally patronise pubs. At least it's Wapping, she thought as she drove her white sports car in that direction after work, not the real and unknown East End. She had been to a dinner party in a remarkably smart flat in Wapping once. The flat, which had been part of a converted warehouse, had contained a sitting-room the size of a small ballroom. She wondered if Thomas's frightful studio was anything like that and concluded that he must have been joking.

She found the Rose and Crown and opened its door circumspectly. In the murky interior, she could see the bar, some dim lights and a few tables, some of which were unfortunately occupied by people who did not resemble Thomas. All the instincts of her class and sex against going into a pub alone rose up in outrage. She pushed the door only just as wide as necessary and slipped in as discreetly as she could, feeling rather than seeing the landlord and the patrons of the pub turning to stare at her.

'You made it!'

He was sitting alone at a table in a corner with a large sketch pad on his knees. He looked pale and tired, but his eyes were bright, and he was apparently pleased to see her.

'Thank you for meeting me here,' he said, taking her hand. 'I'm rather fond of this pub. It inspires me not to work.'

'But I thought you loved . . . '

'Enough. I don't want to talk about work. What'll you drink? I'm so pleased you came.'

'I should like a glass of white wine, please.'

'No, you wouldn't. Pat!' to the landlady 'the lady would like a large gin and tonic, and may I have another pint please, and please, please would you be an angel and let me pay you tomorrow?'

'It's very kind of you,' Sophia said as they retreated to a table, 'but I don't normally drink spirits.'

'They don't have wine here. This is the East End, you know — no poncy City wine bars here. Besides, you need this drink.'

'I don't need this drink,' she contradicted, sipping it. 'I'm driving.'

'Not immediately; besides, there are always taxis. Anyway, you'll probably smile more if you're slightly drunk, and that would be lovely. Has anyone told you you have a very nice smile? Oh, I probably did before. Silly me. But that's by the by; you see, I get very nervous when I show anyone my pictures.'

'Why? Surely the whole point of painting a picture is to show it to the world?'

'No, not at all. The whole point of painting a picture is that you can't not paint it.'

'No art can be created in a vacuum.'

'What do *you* know about art?'

Sophia took a big swig of gin and tonic and regarded Thomas over the rim of her glass.

'That's a very interesting question.'

'Can you answer it?'

She paused, then pronounced: 'I know nothing about the creation of art. I have certain opinions as to the validity of a work of art. I refer, of course, to art in general, not just the visual arts; as I told you, I know very little of that. I am, however, very interested in music and literature.'

'Did you make that up just now, or did you learn it, parrot-fashion, from a book about literary criticism? How very serious you sound! If I knew you better I'd say it was extremely pompous, but I don't, so I mustn't.' He smiled and touched her hand.

'Now finish your drink, and let's go.'

She felt the drink working through her and, relaxing, acquiesced; she let him help her on with her coat and lead her out of the pub.

It was cold and dark outside; Thomas put on a very old Loden coat and took Sophia's arm. 'Come on,' he said, 'forward. We've got to walk briskly, otherwise we'll seize up with cold, and all the good of the drinks will have gone.'

Sophia found the sensation of being led quite pleasant. It was not normally something that she allowed.

The studio was as difficult to find as Thomas had predicted; they had to walk down a tiny, nearly invisible side alley and climb the steps of a fire escape. Sophia felt stimulated and even a little excited. It would be interesting to see the studio of an artist; she so hoped he would be a good artist, and that his work would be worth seeing. She liked the idea of learning a little about visual art; this had to be an adventure.

The studio itself was not immediately encouraging: it was depressingly obvious that Thomas had not been joking about its frightfulness. He unlocked a battered wooden door at the top of the fire escape and switched on a solitary and dismal light which hung baldly from a high ceiling. She found herself in a large, bare room with a great expanse of dusty floorboards. Right in the middle were a couple of easels, and all around a mess of materials — oil paints, charcoal, pastel crayons, water-colours, brushes in big irregular jars and the like. The place smelt of turpentine and oil paints. Canvasses were stacked against a wall, together with portfolios of drawings and watercolours. On a round table lay a litter of hundreds of photographs and slides. It was very cold.

What drew Sophia's attention first was a blown-up photograph tacked to the wall. It was of a young woman's head, blonde, irregular features, but very pretty.

'That's Allegra,' said Thomas. 'Isn't she beautiful?'

Sophia said, 'Do you think so? Who is she, anyway?'

'Someone. A friend.' She looked sharply at him, but Thomas's mobile face was carefully neutral, as if a shutter had been pulled down over any feelings it might have shown.

Then, suddenly, 'The pictures, the pic-tures,' Thomas chattered, his face reanimated. 'Oh God, I'm *sure* you'll hate them! I shouldn't have put you up to this. Oh well, let's start with something you'll know. Here's Claire.'

Sophia had seen Anita's niece once or twice at weekend lunches. Although she was the favoured relation of her best friend, she hadn't paid her much heed. Children were not part of her world. Claire had appeared an unremarkable, average little girl.

Thomas's portrait was a pencil drawing. You could tell it was this niece of Anita's, but there was far more to it than that. It wasn't just its lively realism; there were two other special qualities. One was light. Sophia found it difficult to understand how such light could have been introduced into a pencil drawing, but there was an almost incandescent quality about the child's face. The other was joy. It was suffused with happiness. Claire may or may not have been a very ordinary child. That was irrelevant. In Thomas's picture, which was utterly unsentimental, she was joyous. She made you want to smile.

Sophia did smile. Then she asked, almost spontaneously, 'Did you enjoy doing that picture?'

'Yes,' said Thomas. 'I like children.'

'And you like doing portraits?'

'It's funny, that. They're my bread and butter. I don't like the idea of doing portraits — some stupid rich person who's making this pathetic attempt to have himself immortal-ised, dreadful sentimental parents trying to get their children done — but when I actually get down to the individuals something just takes over, especially if it's children. You see, they're so beautiful. Don't you think Claire's beautiful?'

'I never used to, but yes, she is in the picture, and at the same time it's unmistakably just Claire.'

'Good, I'm glad. Here, look at this. It's a sketch I did of a friend. I loved doing it, not that I'll get paid, and it's just rough.' He showed her another pencil sketch; and then he showed her picture after picture, oils, watercolours, pastels and drawings in profusion, not letting her pause to consider each one. From time to time she wanted him to stop so that she could look more closely, for some of the pictures were very beautiful. They were mostly of realistic subjects; Thomas was clearly a competent draughtsman. The most successful were country landscapes, simple still lives and portraits. There was an exceptional one of a view through an opened window; the subject was possibly banal, but Sophia found it impressive for the quality of light streaming through the window. Some, however, were too abstract for her, or too highly coloured. Birds were a recurring subject, especially in the more abstract works which seemed to have been created entirely from Thomas's imagination.

'Well?' said Thomas at last, restacking the canvases with their faces to the wall. He looked nervous and ran his fingers several times through his black and grey forelock.

'Thomas,' she said, for the first time using his name, 'I haven't had time really to look at these pictures.'

'You don't have to say nice things about them,' he said seriously. 'You mustn't chatter brightly about them if there's nothing there.'

Sophia did not know how to react and felt an unwonted embarrassment. She looked at Thomas, who was standing expectantly by the pile of pictures, his arms folded.

'Ye — es,' she hesitated, speaking slowly. 'I shall tell you what I liked. The view from the window, the light.'

Thomas scrabbled among the pictures and drew it out. 'This one,' he indicated.

'Why,' Sophia asked uncertainly, 'don't you like it? Don't you think it is good?'

Thomas shrugged. 'I enjoyed painting it.'

'Oh, but that's obvious! It looks like the sort of picture that it must have been great fun to create.'

'Not satisfying, though,' Thomas said gloomily. 'Oh, Christ, I suppose I am in a vacuum. I mean look, here's this picture, this *fun* picture, as you say, and yes, painting it

44

was just a ball, but so what? I can't sell the bloody thing. God, I don't know if it's good or not.'

'But I think it is good,' Sophia ventured with unaccustomed timidity. 'It's joyous, like the Claire picture.' She warmed to her theme. 'I look at this picture, and it brings out a response — the light . . . it actually makes *me* feel good. I am enhanced by it. If I looked through a window and saw heaven, perhaps it would resemble your picture.'

Thomas stood very still and looked at her intently. She finished speaking; there was a silence; then he spoke.

'That is the most wonderful thing to say about my picture. You see, if my pictures can just reach people like that — why, then, they're worth it, and it's all going to be all right, and I'm all right, and what I'm doing is right.'

'But you surely don't need me to tell you that.'

'But what if you're just trying to flatter me? I mean, it would be dreadfully bloody awkward for you to come into this God-awful barn of a place and see all these pictures and hate them and then have the gall to come out with it and say, 'Christ, these absolutely stink, who do you think you are anyway?' P'raps you've just taken a fancy to me and are being nice to me because of that.'

'That's an astonishingly vain and stupid thing to say. It's actually rather insulting. Why on earth should I flatter you? Good God! I've singled out one picture I liked. I haven't even mentioned the ones I didn't like.'

Thomas glared at her. 'You really are incredible, aren't you? So defensive! I'm not totally unreasonable. Surprising numbers of people do flatter. I suppose I ought to be glad you don't. Would you please not jump down my throat? What didn't you like?'

'Oh,' said Sophia airily, feeling a good deal more confident, 'all those abstract birds. I thought they were too brash. I should rather be honest than merely flattering.'

'Hah! Now we hear it. A bit uncomfortable, were you, with all that colour?'

'I just didn't happen to like them.'

'Well, they're just experiments, anyhow. I love the idea of birds. I can tell you hate the idea of colour.'

'How do you mean?'

'I suspect you have very little colour sense.'

'Then why on earth did you seek my opinion?'

'Oh, anyone can be a good judge, they don't have to be geniuses about colour. Because you're intelligent. You're actually quite sensitive. Yes, you are honest. I'm sorry if I say idiotic things.'

'I don't, in any case, see why I have a poor sense of colour.'

'Way you dress,' Thomas said casually, tossing back his forelock; 'I've only seen you twice, but it's clear you wear far too much that's neutral, when bright colours would be much nicer. Get a red dress.' He laughed.

'I think I'd better be going,' Sophia announced.

'No, we're having dinner. Where would you like to go?'

'You had better know that I detest personal comments. If I wish to buy a red dress, I shall not rely on your superior colour sense. I thought I may enjoy having dinner with you tonight when you invited me, but now I have doubts, and besides, I have to get up very early tomorrow.'

Thomas observed that she had drawn her dark brows into an intense frown, and her thin body was tense. She looked almost ugly in her anger, but he was excited by the stifled energy it generated.

I've got to sleep with her, he thought. Out loud, he said, 'You're so prickly it's funny. In the first place, please don't worry about tomorrow. It's not important. Now is important. Secondly, would you please come to dinner if I promise to make no offensive personal comments?'

Sophia relaxed suddenly and turned away to conceal her smile. 'Oh well, I suppose so. Where are we going?'

Thomas moved away from his pictures and stood straight in front of Sophia.

'I have a dreadful confession to make,' he said, looking her in the eye and twiddling his hair.

'What?'

'I'm flat broke. I can't actually afford to take you out to dinner.'

He was not remotely ashamed or awkward. Sophia was temporarily stumped. He smiled rather beguilingly. 'I should *so* like to have dinner with you, though,' he went on; 'it's too boring that a little thing like money should stop me. It's frightful cheek, but would you be an angel and lend me some?'

He had called the landlady in the pub an angel earlier, she remembered, when touching her for credit. Suddenly the laughter bubbled up inside her and spilled out like champagne; she whooped; he looked stunned and then laughed with her.

'Come on,' she said, half out of breath, 'I'll treat you!'

'God, you're so nice! D'you know, I'm so glad I met you. Look, I swear I'm not a total con man, I do have a certain sense of honour.

I really, really won't let you pay for dinner; it will be a proper loan. You are too kind to offer to treat me, I couldn't have it, not until we're the most terrific friends with total trust. Come on, let's get out of this hole. I so hate it sometimes, I can't tell you how much.'

The ice broken, he took her hand; out they went to her little car, and she drove them to Soho, where he knew a small Italian restaurant.

The dinner was a great success. Thomas ordered a bottle of wine, which they began before they had looked at the menu. Sophia, who was seldom interested in food, was not hungry and ate rather lightly, so that as they despatched the first bottle she became a great deal more relaxed than usual. Thomas ate, drank and conversed voraciously.

He told her how he had gone to art school after three unsatisfactory years at Christ Church.

'Oxford was terrific fun really,' he said, 'but I felt it wasn't for me, somehow, that I was wasting my time dreadfully there. In my second year I realised I desperately wanted to go to art school. I'd always been good at art, only it got to be an obsession at Oxford. Father wouldn't hear of it, insisted on me finishing Oxford. I just about scraped a third. But when I was twenty-one I inherited a bit of money, so I could afford to go to art school as soon as I finished Oxford. Father didn't like it, but there wasn't a lot he could do about it.'

'Just like Charles in *Brideshead Revisited*.'

'Oh yes, I suppose so, only the similarity ends there. I haven't been quite so rich and successful.'

'So what happened then?'

'Oh well, after art school I was amazingly lucky and landed a job teaching in a girls' school in Newbury. It was lucky because art school graduates are not famous for their ability to find work, and it's pretty well impossible to make a living off selling art when you're fresh out of art school and unknown. It's pretty bloody impossible even when you aren't fresh out of art school, come to think of it.' He pulled a rueful grimace.

She leaned forward, fascinated, hardly bothering with her food. 'How did you get on with the girls' school?'

'I stuck it out for three years, biding my time. It really wasn't too bad. I lived in a cottage in some beautiful country outside the town, and the children were wonderful, well, not really children as some were A-level standard. I should really have liked to teach very small children, not that you can actually teach them art, but I love very small children.

50

I could have shown them my birds.'

'And why did you leave?'

'I had to come to London. I love the country, but you have to be in London if you're trying to live off art. Also, I wasn't getting anywhere as an artist, living in the country. I needed to be in London to get on. I'll explain it more to you one day. There was also this woman I was with at the time. We went out with each other for a year or so, but she couldn't stay with me in the end. It was my fault really, I was so impossible. You really must never live with an artist, they're dreadful people. Poor Annie. She's married now, and I still see her very occasionally.

'I scrape by now on portraits. There's a little gallery off the beaten track in Kensington where I've had a couple of shows, and they sell bits of my stuff, but you can't imagine how hard it is. Let me tell you, making it as an artist is five per cent talent and ninety-five per cent bloody-mindedness, or possibly lunacy. You don't think I'm mad, do you?' he added facetiously.

'No,' she said seriously, 'I don't think you're at all mad. I'm rather surprised, though, at what you say about talent.'

'Believe me. But in fact I've only really started doing decent stuff recently, over the last six months or so. Before that, life was just — oh, I don't know, hopeless, I suppose, always waiting for something — but we won't go into all that now. Tell me about yourself. I'm twenty-nine, how old are you?'

Sophia started. Not only had it not occurred to her that Thomas might be younger than she, but also it should not have mattered. Suddenly she felt mildly self-conscious.

'Oh dear,' said Thomas. 'I shouldn't have asked that, should I? How indiscreet of me. But you can't be all that old.'

'Well, I am older than you.'

He grinned. 'No! Really? Go on, tell me how much.'

'I'm right on the shelf; I've just had my thirty-third birthday.'

'Well, well, well. I honestly thought you looked younger. But on with the questions. Why the City? Are you — were you married? Oops, another indiscreet question — I'm getting much too personal — sorry.'

'No, that's fine.' She took a large swig of Barolo. 'No, I'm not married.' She gave a flourish. 'No one would have me!'

'Get away. Wrong sort of man probably. Frightened of intelligence. Bloody wimps.'

'Oh no, the men in my life have all had the acutest colour sense, that's what did it.'

'I still say silly buggers, you may not dress

in red, but you're rather good looking you know — no, I know I mustn't flatter, but really. Colour sense. Smashing hair. Must stop being so personal. Why the City? What got you into that?'

'I didn't know what to do when I went down from Cambridge. I read English and loved it. I didn't want to be an academic, so I didn't stay on to do a Ph.D. Oh, the City was different all right. I started by researching chemical companies.'

He raised his eyebrows. 'Chemical companies! Sounds a bit punishing.'

'As I said, it was different. The funny thing is, I got to be very fond of my chemical companies. I learned all sorts of not normally known facts. I could tell you a lot about synthetic pyrethroids.'

'Must you? I'd rather go on asking dangerously personal questions.'

'Ah, but acquiring a certain level of expertise — even just at the layman's level — in synthetic pyrethroids and their ilk is so very useful. If I hadn't learnt about them I wouldn't have made enough money to buy colourless clothes.'

'Do you still do chemical companies? I really can't quite believe it!'

'I still follow two or three, but I haven't got time to do the sector properly. They put me in charge of all research, so I have to make sure all the other sectors are done properly too.'

'My God, so you really are a director, like it says on your card. Are you in charge of lots of people? Isn't it awfully difficult?'

Sophia smiled. 'Yes, and yes. They're a good bunch of people. I believe they call me the Rottweiler on bad days.'

'Blow me. I don't think I've ever met anyone like you. A real career person, as they say.'

'Well, there you go. It's one heck of a conversation stopper. Oops, no more wine, please! I've already had far too much.' She half-heartedly moved her hand to cover her wine glass.

'Oh, don't worry.' He deftly negotiated the wine past her hand. 'You're way over the limit, and so am I. We'll leave the car and get a taxi, OK? Come on, let's have another bottle. God, I'm so enjoying this.'

'You're going on as if you hadn't eaten for a week.'

'Oh, but I haven't. You know all that stuff about artists starving in garrets? It's all true.'

'I bet. You're just looking for a sucker who'll take you home and feed you up.'

'Bingo! Can't wait to see your place. Would I do well, though? You look as if you need feeding up yourself.'

Sophia laughed immoderately. They made short work of the second bottle of wine and progressed to grappa.

'Try it,' Thomas urged. 'It's heaven with this very strong coffee.'

As the wine took hold, she found herself staring into his eyes, as if using them as an anchor for her failing focus. The rims of the irises were particularly dark, and the eyes were fringed with unusually long black lashes. Suddenly she was assailed by the strongest desire for him. It was very similar to the feeling she had had for Rupert Kingsley before she had slept with him for the first time, but now she remembered nothing of that. Fired by an extraordinary determination to get Thomas back to her house and her bed, she swigged the grappa.

She spluttered, gasped and nearly wept. 'Do you know,' she said, recovering herself, 'I do believe I'm getting drunk. I've never been drunk. Let's go home.'

Sophia could not afterwards remember how they left the restaurant, found a taxi and came to her house; nor was she properly aware that she and Thomas pounced on each other in the taxi and spent most of the ride kissing each other hungrily.

Half an hour later, she found herself on the

floor of her neat white sitting-room, half crushed under the apparently dead weight of Thomas, who seemed to be about to pass out on top of her. She felt most peculiar and nearly passed out herself. Her sitting room revolved before her eyes, but just before it clouded over she recalled that the last thirty minutes had been insanely exciting and more fun than anything she had ever know. Now Thomas was suffocating her. She also became quite painfully aware that her soft carpet covered a hard floor. She tried feebly to wriggle.

Thomas's tightly shut eyes opened cautiously. She peered into his face, which was very pale and so close to her own that it appeared blurry. He whispered very faintly, 'Oh God.'

Very slowly, he lifted himself off her. She realised that it was cold, and that both Thomas and she were half naked. Clothes were strewn in puddles about the room. Gloomily Thomas dressed, not looking at her. She began to feel deeply uneasy.

'Might it be more comfortable,' she ventured, 'simply to go to bed?'

'No,' Thomas muttered, 'I've got to go back and work.'

She sat up and pulled some of her clothes and herself into some kind of shape. She didn't feel drunk any more. 'That's ridiculous,' she said.

'Look, I'm sorry, OK?'

'It's very late, you're tired, you won't achieve anything tonight. Why not just stay here?'

Suddenly she very much wanted him to stay. She wanted him to sleep with her through the night and wake up with her in the morning.

'No way,' he said brusquely. 'I'm sorry, I didn't mean this to happen. I simply must go back now.' He stood up.

She saw that he was determined. 'I'll call you a taxi.'

'I'd rather just go, a taxi'll take forever. I need to walk anyway.'

'Oh, really — ' she began.

'Please, would you just leave me alone?'

She said no more to him then but got up, savage with disappointment, walked over to the front door, which opened straight into the sitting room, and opened it.

'Goodnight,' he said. 'I'm sorry.'

'Oh, forget it.'

'Dinner — it really was a loan. I'll pay you back, I promise. I'll send you a cheque!'

'Just go!' She just prevented herself from slamming the door behind him before locking and chaining it.

Quietly she gathered up the rest of her misplaced clothes and went upstairs; having taken two aspirins and drunk as much water as she could, she went to bed.

Just before she passed out in bed, her body gave an unaccustomed little shiver, and the faintest echo of the evening's laughter stirred in her. The episode with Thomas had, of course, been an uncontrolled disgrace. A far deeper instinct, never normally heard or acknowledged, told her it had also been the greatest fun and had brought intense pleasure.

4

Next day Sophia only just arrived for the beginning of her firm's early morning meeting. During it, she was nearly sick. When she at last had to run, white-faced and shaking, to the loo, she was, luckily for her, alone and unobserved. One or two colleagues thought she looked paler than usual, and if she consumed more black coffee and ate even less lunch than on other days, they hardly noticed. Until about four in the afternoon she toyed with the idea of going home and dying quietly there; then she gradually began to realise that the odds on her survival were, however miraculously, shortening. She threw herself into her work and kept at it until eight at night, when she took a taxi to Soho to pick up her car.

At ten o'clock, having had her car removed to the garage for repairs to its door locks, alarm system, windows and paintwork, she returned home. Seldom had she so longed for her warm, bright little house. As the taxi that brought her home gurgled reassuringly on the road outside, she turned the key in her front door lock and entered. All was well; the central heating had come on; the house smelled fresh and looked bright.

However, the first thing Sophia saw was a large, crumpled, brilliant red handkerchief on one of the little tables in her sitting room. Her daily, who had left the house looking and smelling so clean, must have put it there. She knew immediately that it was Thomas's, and she was suddenly furious and upset, because she had wanted to blot Thomas and everything that had happened between them from her mind. She took the handkerchief (it was silk and quite clean) into the kitchen and threw it into the dustbin. Then she made herself a cup of hot chocolate, had a wonderful, long, very hot bath and went to bed.

For the next two weeks Sophia worked even harder than normal. She sometimes had difficulty in keeping the Rottweiler down.

'Kevin!'

'Sophie?'

'*What* is this?'

'Er, my Plexis write-up?'

'Can you do sums, Kevin? Is this a dividend yield, or a figment of your non-existent imagination? Since when have Plexis shares been yielding 52 percent?'

'Jesus, Sophe, ever heard of misprints, like in decimal points?'

She did not feel like seeing anyone, so she cut back on her minutely organised social life. She took to going to bed just too late to get a good night's sleep and became as a result increasingly cranky.

She refused even to think about Thomas because she was furious with herself for what had happened. More than anything else in the world, Sophia hated being out of control. How she could have let herself drink too much and be seduced was beyond her. He had been remarkably charming, of course, and he really had flattered her and made her laugh. She did not expect him to contact her again and persuaded herself that she was relieved when he did not do so; what made her even angrier, and not a little uneasy, was the notion that deep down this silence of his was a serious disappointment.

At the end of these two weeks, she began to feel run down. One day in the office she suddenly felt dizzy and a little sick, and as this had never happened to her before she wondered what the cause might be. Suddenly, she had a terrible thought. She had been too drunk not to be seduced by Thomas; they had both been too drunk to worry about contraception.

Another horrible week passed. She spent a day in the Netherlands and two in Scotland with colleagues, seeing clients. Putting up a professional front took up nearly all her dwindling reserve of energy, but most of the time she felt too tired and overwrought to eat.

On the Saturday at the end of this third week, she woke up at half past five in the morning. Her head ached slightly but nauseously. It occurred to her that she was thinner than usual, and her hip bones were the most prominent feature of her body. She then realised that she really was feeling sick, and that the time had come to face the possible reason for it.

Calmly she got out of bed and put on her dressing gown. In her bag downstairs was a small diary in which she recorded dates that mattered. She found it. It told her she should have started her period ten days ago.

Still calm, she considered and rejected the idea of buying a pregnancy test kit at a chemist's; for some reason she couldn't stand it. Instead, on Monday she would make an appointment with her family planning clinic. She did not let herself consider what she would do next if the result was positive.

At first the worst thing was that she felt like a fool. A woman like her simply did not get pregnant by accident. She felt nothing but amazement and a faint scorn for other single women who, desperate to have a child, deliberately got themselves pregnant. Her life was not intended to allow for accidents like this. She had made another prat-fall, this time with a vengeance.

She made herself some coffee and, drinking it in her immaculate white kitchen, thought about these things. Her feeling of foolishness was presently overtaken by deep depression. Having poured most of the coffee down the sink, she went back to bed.

Sophia was no stranger to depressions, especially since the Rupert Kingsley débacle. They gave her unwelcome reminders that her organised, self-assured way of life was indefinably lacking in something. Occasionally, but nearly always on a Saturday when she had less planned than usual, her being would be taken over by a semi-conscious but profoundly sincere wish to go to sleep and never to wake up again. This wish would be accompanied by a numbing inertia and, by an irritating contradiction, insomnia. She never answered her telephone when in this state and would be tormented by an unwonted indecisiveness about it: should she listen to her hated voice bleating out its message on the answering machine, or should she switch this off and suffer the horrible intrusion of its repeated ringing? However, the best seller she had read after her last telephone conversation with Kingsley had provided her with the beginnings of a tentative short-term solution to this problem. She took to stockpiling these books, which she would buy furtively at odd moments and keep at the back of a certain drawer in her bedroom. They were instant escapism for her deadened brain. She could always tell when she was beginning to feel better, because it would be at this point that she would pick out, with increasing avidity, all the faults she could perceive in their written style. At night she would take a sleeping pill, and next day she would finish the stories. Finally, she would wrap them up in a bag and conceal them carefully in a waste bin. She would feel deeply guilty and ashamed for having read them, but by then the worst would be over. This usually coincided with Sunday evening.

It occurred to her one day after she had emerged from a depression that she was a literary bulimic, gorging on illicit trash and then throwing it up, or rather away. She thought the term literary bulimic was quite witty and regretted that she could never air it, as she would never admit to anyone that she actually read what she thought of as trash.

The current depression differed from the others insofar as it had been brought on by a clearly insoluble problem in Sophia's life. The possibility (probability) of pregnancy lurked on the edge of her mind, a monster round the corner. Like a snail in its shell, she curled up on one of her white sofas and tucked into her latest blockbuster. She had just become interested in the unlikely but very well crafted plot when her telephone began to ring. The plot was too absorbing for her to lift the receiver before the answering machine cut in.

'God, I hate these stupid machines,' said Thomas in reply to her voice. 'I shan't ring you up at home again. I knew I shouldn't have. I'll ring you at your office.'

Sophia resolutely ignored the message and went on reading as if nothing had happened. However, she felt faintly better. By and by she was almost hungry, although depressions were apt to make her even less interested in food than usual, and she padded into the kitchen for a small piece of toast and a cup of coffee (black, no sugar).

The depression continued, but it eased perceptibly to the point that Sophia was able to put on a little music that Saturday evening. Her depressions were normally silent affairs. However, when she had finished listening, she went back to her lowbrow book. At night, she took two sleeping pills to be on the safe side.

The whole of Sunday passed like that, listening to music and reading. After she had finished and thrown away the last best seller, she as usual eased herself back into a more real world by reading excerpts from favourites of hers — P.G. Wodehouse again to start with, then Jane Austen.

Thus, reeling faintly from a mixture of fantasy thrillers and sleeping pills, she presented herself for work at eight o'clock on Monday morning. Her mind was muzzy. She didn't notice that she wasn't feeling sick. Having coasted through the morning meeting, she telephoned the family planning clinic and made an appointment for the day after tomorrow. Then she settled down for a quiet day's desk work and got tremendously involved in the report by one of her subordinates about a fine chemicals conglomerate. Something was badly, suspiciously wrong with the accounts of the conglomerate, and she could not immediately put her finger on it. Miraculously, her mind cleared as she got down to work, with the first real enjoyment she had experienced for weeks.

Thomas rang her up late in the morning.

'Can we talk?' he asked.

'I'm busy.'

'Can you come out to dinner tonight?'

'I'm very busy.'

'I've just been paid for a picture. I want to celebrate. I haven't seen anyone for ages and

I'm desperate and I want to see you. What's your favourite restaurant?'

'I haven't got a favourite restaurant.'

'Oh come on. Look, I'm sorry I haven't been in touch before. I've been maddeningly busy. I know it was rude of me not to ring you up. I really am sorry. I tell you what, let's meet somewhere smart for drinks before dinner. How about the American Bar at the Savoy — seven o'clock?'

'I don't believe we're having this conversation,' Sophia said. She hung up.

During the afternoon, Sophia rang up the finance director of the suspect conglomerate. They were having a wonderful conversation in which he was finding it increasingly difficult to answer her questions, when she was interrupted. A large, thin, oblong parcel, tied up with string and accompanied by one of the company messengers, had entered her office and was standing insistently by her desk. Two amused colleagues hovered not inconspicuously behind the parcel and the messenger.

Sophia tried to ignore the parcel, but her concentration had gone. Determinedly she carried on the conversation, keeping the messenger waiting as long as possible, but the savour had gone out of it. The finance director became evasive; she was irritated to realise that he had stopped squirming. She got rid of him. More colleagues drifted along.

'What on earth have you got there, Sophie?' asked one.

'Go on, open it up,' said another.

'Ooh look,' said a third; 'there's a letter with it.'

Sophia got to her feet and went to stand in front of the parcel. 'You're dear, sweet people,' she said, 'and I love you all. However, you all have work to do. Now run along and mind your own business.'

'Spoilsport.'

She tried to ignore the parcel and worked on for an hour or so. At last her curiosity got the better of her. Having shut her office door, she cut the string and tore off the brown paper. It was Thomas's picture of light through a window.

Sophia's office was austere. She had taken no trouble over it; it had no pictures or ornaments belonging to her; its only redeeming feature was a large weeping fig tree in a corner. She saw immediately that this picture would transform it. The light here was far stronger than in Thomas's studio, and this rendered the picture even more joyous and incandescent. She stood the picture first against one wall, then another; then she rang up the maintenance people to get it hung.

As she was picking up the wrapping paper to throw it away, she noticed the letter.

'You must be so angry with me,' Thomas had written, 'I can only apologise. I would so love to see you again if you felt you could, so I have been really presumptuous and booked a restaurant, a really good one on Thursday. I'll try and ring you up again, but even if you never want to see me again I want you to have this picture. You were sweet to me about it.'

A little later a colleague came to see Sophia about a report.

'Crickey, that's nice,' he said, looking at the picture.

'It's lovely, isn't it?' Sophia smiled.

'It's ever so good. Who's it from?'

'That'd be telling. Do you think the guys might fancy a drink tonight? I think we've earned it, don't you?'

The colleague grinned. 'Oh yes, Sophia. Working for you, we earn it.'

That evening she relaxed. She and her favourite colleagues put away a few bottles of champagne at a wine bar; then they took a taxi to the West End and had a convivial dinner.

As she went to bed, she remembered that she was meant to be pregnant. The day had gone so well that she had almost forgotten this. Now she felt almost unconcerned: there was no need to do anything whatsoever about it until Wednesday, when she would know for sure. Then she would make the decision. She knew she would be up to this. The insoluble problem would be solved.

Thus it was almost with a sense of anti-climax that she greeted the start, early next morning, of her much delayed period.

5

'Tell me more about yourself,' Thomas asked over dinner. 'I bet you're an only child.' They were in a little French seafood restaurant of his choosing in the Covent Garden area.

'Wrong.' She squeezed lemon into a shrinking oyster.

'Seriously? Oh well, that blows up the theory I read in the Daily Express. You don't read the Daily Express.'

'Its theories are clearly half baked.' Sophia laughed and tipped the contents of the oyster-shell delicately into her mouth.

'Well, according to this theory, over-achievers tend to be only children. Lots of frightful tycoons are only children. God, how I love garlic.' He tucked into *soupe de poissons* into which he had dunked *croutons* and dollops of golden *rouille*.

'But I'm not a tycoon. Oddly enough, I'm not the type. I spend quite a lot of my life talking to real tycoons, so I should know.'

'I'm going to honk of garlic. You don't mind, do you? Well anyhow, tell me about your family — brothers and sisters.'

'One younger sister, one brother who's younger still.'

'D'you get on?'

'No.'

'Oh.' Thomas paused, waiting for her to elaborate. When she failed to do so, he carried on: 'I've got a half brother and a half sister. Our family's a bit complex. Father married their mother, and it didn't work, and they split up when they were quite little. Then he married my mother, but she died in a car accident when I was quite little. Now he's married to Hermione, my wicked stepmother, who has a son called Julian from her first marriage. He's my favourite brother. I love her. They all think I'm quite mad.'

Sophia prepared to eat her last oyster. 'Perhaps you and they have nothing in common.'

'They live in the country, in deepest Dorset. Charles manages Father's estate, which is just as well, as he'll inherit it. Victoria's married to a farmer. They all hunt and lead very countrified lives. They've got nice children.'

'You do have nothing in common.'

'Oh no, far more in common than you realise. I love the country. God, I wouldn't live in a hole like London if I didn't have to. My ambition is to become recognised as an artist, so that I can go and live in the country for ever and never have to come back here. But I want to know about you. I've talked too much and haven't finished my soup. Why don't you get on with your brother and sister?'

Sophia surveyed her six empty oyster shells and toyed with some bread. 'I really do have absolutely nothing in common with them. You know, I very much dislike talking about myself.'

Thomas paused. He raised his wine glass, looked at Sophia and put it down again untasted.

'Was I absolute hell the other night?' he asked.

'Must we talk about it? No, not really.'

'But you were cross with me.'

'I was cross with myself.'

'I really was a bastard though. Much worse than you would even believe.'

Sophia looked into his eyes, dark and rimmed with long eyelashes. They and Thomas were out of bounds She smiled rather stiffly. 'Oh really,' she said. 'You're going to tell me . . . ' and she shut up suddenly, because even though she was absolutely determined not to get involved with Thomas she did not want him to tell her that he was seeing someone else, and that he found it unethical to sleep with a second woman outside this relationship.

'I had absolutely promised myself to behave,' Thomas continued.

'Well, your promises to yourself are hardly my concern.'

He could feel her distancing herself; his stare became unfocused, and she seemed to recede before him. He pressed on: 'There's this girl — oh dear, how awful this sounds — and I'm not even seeing her that much. I was — I suppose I am — very interested in her. The hell of it is, she doesn't want to know. Then you came along. You're utterly different from her, couldn't really be more different. You were sort of perverse and incredibly attractive without even knowing it, and you were such *fun* — not in the conventional way, but sort of perversely, d'you see what I mean? . . . and — well, I couldn't resist, I just had to be bad and have a bit much to drink and — you know.'

'No, I don't know.'

Thomas now swigged his wine. 'Christ, you are so difficult. I really mean it, you are.'

'Well, you don't impress me very much. I don't want to know about your other women and your badness, as you call it. Can we just stop talking about it?'

'Are you always this cool? Do you only talk

about what really matters when you've had too much to drink?'

Sophia, having ruthlessly quashed any latent desire in herself, gave Thomas a freezing look. 'Look here,' she said. 'I don't know what really matters to you, and I don't want to know. I didn't come out with you tonight to hear your confessions or to make any myself. I detest that sort of thing. When I'm not at work, I simply want to relax. Do you understand?'

Thomas grinned. 'D'you talk like that to your minions at the office when they get the price-earnings ratio wrong?'

'How on earth do you know about price-earnings ratios?'

'Believe it or not, you're not the first stock broker I've ever met. I tapped a mate's brains the other night. He even knew who you were. He said you were frightfully good. Anyway, he gave me one of your old reports to read. I didn't understand a thing, and I couldn't even follow your recommendation, which was SELL, since I hadn't bought the shares in the first place, but I just couldn't help remembering price-earnings ratios. You burbled on a bit about that. Apparently this one's weren't quite up to speed.'

Sophia laughed. 'I'm hell to work for, if you want to know. I regularly threaten the colleagues with death. I don't know why they put up with me. Who's the girl?'

Thomas wisely gave the appearance of taking this in his stride. 'The gorgeous Allegra. You know, the blown-up photo. She's extremely pretty, utterly self-centred and completely infuriating. I've known her for years and years. My step-mum and her step-mum are bosom pals. They used to hunt together with the Belvoir. Actually she does now, she's absolutely crazy about horses. Apart from that, she's fond of spending money, is outrageously social and does as little work as she can get away with.'

'Why do you like her?'

'Dunno. She's so irritating. She doesn't mind seeing me from time to time, but she doesn't really want to know. I suppose I'm not rich or grand enough. No, it's more than that. I don't know.'

'She sounds gha-' Sophia checked herself in time. 'What are you going to do about it?'

'Nothing.' Thomas raised his head and smiled. 'I'm having dinner with you. It's quite appallingly rude of me to talk about her at all.'

'I did ask.'

'You're honest.'

'*Le feuilleté de saumon — c'est pour madame?*'

They were distracted by the arrival of their main courses. Thomas, who was interested in food, led the conversation onto that subject.

'I never thought I cared,' said Sophia, savouring her salmon. 'I'm so enjoying this.'

'Oh, I knew you'd like it.'

'You couldn't know that. I didn't.'

'It's absolutely obvious. You're very sensual.'

She stiffened as if he had smacked her and frowned so deeply that he followed up: 'Oh God, I shouldn't have said that. Sorry.'

She looked at her plate. 'I do hope yours is good. It's the turbot, isn't it?'

'Wonderful. Hey, relax.' He took her hand. Something flickered in her eyes; he could not be sure if it was pain or frustration. She seemed again to retreat into herself, as if behind a shield.

'I'm all right,' she said brightly, peeping out through her defences.

Thomas looked at her dreamily, his eyes half closed. 'You're so reserved. I like that. I don't know why. Allegra doesn't know what reserve is.'

'That must suit you a little. I should hardly call *you* reserved.'

'Oh, I don't know. I'm not really that open. I'm not all that articulate either, come to that. Funny thing: you're very articulate indeed, and yet you don't say much.'

'Was it very difficult, when you left Oxford and went to art school, to go against your family's wishes?'

Sophia learned quite a lot about Thomas, his family and his background. He seemed to be very fond of his family, despite his earlier quarrels with it, and he went to Dorset as often as he could afford to do so. He described his family Christmases in glowing terms, and, enjoying his description, she smiled and grew animated.

'What do you do for Christmas?' Thomas asked.

'Oh!' Sophia's face fell. 'Nothing like as much fun as yours. Don't remind me.'

Thomas looked at her with a puzzled expression.

'Your Christmases sound so wonderful — a huge family in a big house in the country, log fires, great big tree, church people actually enjoy going to, neighbours you actually enjoy seeing, wonderful meals, hunting on Boxing Day, shooting, all the generations together. I've never enjoyed Christmas like that.'

'You're beginning to sound like a deprived child.'

'Oh, no! We have big meals too, Christmas dinner, neighbours round for drinks, mandatory church, even a tree, not nearly as many relations as you, but I'm not sorry about that — the only difference is, you enjoy it all and I don't.'

'I'm so sorry! I can't tell you how much I love it, and d'you know, almost the best bit is watching the children open their presents.'

'I always go mad wondering what on earth to get them all for Christmas. I don't have time to do the shopping. In the end I always just order things from catalogues.'

'I take lots of silly little presents because I can't afford anything decent. The children like it anyway. Sometimes I do someone a picture. My stepmother, Hermione, likes my pictures.'

The rest of the conversation over dinner was frothy, insubstantial and great fun. Later, when Sophia looked back on it, she was reminded of bubbles, the big brightly coloured ones blown by children, full of shifting colours and charm. She remembered only the laughter, not what they talked about.

She came away from the dinner buoyed up by high spirits and feeling she had made a friend. Very rarely had she had such uncomplicated fun. The silliness of childhood had largely passed her by; she was not used to such straightforward laughter. It acted like a tonic. Next day she rang up Thomas simply to tell him how much she had enjoyed herself. She had no ulterior motive. He sounded surprised and delighted to hear from her.

However, Sophia did not get the opportunity to see her new friend for some weeks, because Christmas intervened.

6

Christmas was good and bad news for Sophia. She enjoyed the run-up to the holiday; there were always parties. Even at work the atmosphere became festive. She and her senior subordinates had the odd boozy lunch with their best clients. With her fellow directors she had a seriously good dinner in one of the best restaurants in London. They weren't busy because very few companies announced their results at that time, and there was hardly any other corporate news worth analysing. Sophia was usually happy in her London world before Christmas.

This left Christmas itself, and this was the bad news. This was one of the rare occasions that Sophia was obliged to visit her family.

Sophia went to work on Christmas Eve, but the day was unusual because there were few people in the office, very little work was done, and it was a half day throughout the City. Like everyone else, Sophia packed it in around midday. She drove out of the City, looking out for the early drunks meandering off the pavements, and headed not for her beloved house, which was locked up like Fort

81

Knox and appropriately alarmed, but further west. Her parents lived in Epsom. Although she had little interest in getting to their house as early as possible, she detested traffic jams, and she wanted to avoid the dreadful traffic that was guaranteed to make the journey a misery from about three o'clock.

Her Christmas present to herself had been a CD player for the car to replace her vandalised cassette deck; to preserve some good temper on the way to Epsom she played *Die Meistersinger* loudly. The traffic was already bad enough for her to get through the whole of the first act and a little of the second by the time she reached her parents' house.

Her parents lived in a large, complacent house within walking distance of the race-course over the downs. It was quiet and secluded, except on Derby and to a lesser extent Oaks days, when all Epsom was invaded. Bernard White had bought it about twenty-five years ago. Now he was a senior partner at a leading firm of solicitors in the west end of London; he had paid the mortgage off; he looked forward to a prosperous and well-earned retirement. Susan White, who had never earned a salary in her life, had nonetheless always worked indefatigably, not only as a mother but also as a highly ambitious wife. They had a happy marriage, the foundation of which was a deal: Mr White provided the house and the money, and Mrs White provided the means whereby they could both enjoy them according to their standards of enjoyment. With remorseless efficiency, she had made the house very comfortable; she had produced three reasonably handsome children whose manners and abilities were unexceptionable; above all, she had been tireless socially, not only as an exemplary hostess to her husband's associates but also as the driving force behind all her husband's professional ambition.

Sophia did not fit into her family. She knew it and was possibly unaware of the extent to which her brother, sister, mother and father all knew it too.

Christmas at Epsom was a bore and a strain for Sophia. The least unsympathetic member of her family was her father, but he was remote. She hardly knew what to say any more to her brother, Edward. Her attitude towards her younger sister, Anthea, bordered on active dislike, and she found Anthea's husband, Andrew, pompous and self-satisfied. Her stays at Epsom might still have given some pleasure, however, were it not for the barely concealed strife that existed between her and her mother.

'Hello darling!' Mrs White gushed as

Sophia entered the house. 'Did you have a *frightful* journey?'

Susan White was small, thin and vivacious. She had immaculately permed hair, and Sophia could remember very few occasions, even in childhood, that she had seen her without make-up. Sophia bent stiffly to kiss her powdery cheek and wondered if her voice had become more tinkly since she had last seen her, the emphasis on the word *frightful* more pronounced.

Bernard White appeared in the background; he was much taller than his wife, but also much greyer, and her liveliness reduced him to a shadow. He pecked Sophia formally on the cheek. She wondered if he was even remotely pleased to see her.

As she entered the house, a faint waft of pipe smoke assailed her. As far back as she could remember, her parents' house had been characterised by this aura of tobacco, which she associated with very earliest childhood; there was the whisper of a memory of a time when she had sat on her father's knee, unrivalled for his affections by Anthea or Edward. Now the tobacco was overlaid by the scent of pine from the small Christmas tree which stood in the drawing room. The Whites had always had a real tree, its trunk pushed into a log. Mrs White had never allowed her children to help to decorate it and festooned it discreetly with red and gold baubles and small silver lights. The effect was tasteful and restrained.

She went to the room that used to be her bedroom. It was a small pink room. The little bed that had been hers from childhood had a pink counterpane; the wallpaper and curtains were in the same rather dated pink rosebud design; even the painted furniture and the skirting boards were pale pink. At least the ceiling was white. The one reason that Sophia had always liked this room, despite its pinkness, was that it was the only one on the third floor and was accordingly the most isolated. She looked out of the window, which had little diamond panes, onto the large garden; even though it was bare and wintry, it was immaculate. She sighed, hung out her clothes and put away her presents.

Later that afternoon, her sister Anthea and her brother-in-law Andrew arrived with their two small children; they were soon followed by her brother Edward and his girlfriend Felicity, whose parents lived locally. Mrs White cooed over the grandchildren and gushed over Andrew and Felicity.

Sophia, having no partner or children, was more free to help her mother with dinner than her brother or sister; thus she found herself alone with her in the kitchen before that meal.

'It's been so long since we last saw you, dear,' Mrs White ventured. 'I suppose you've been frightfully busy, as usual.'

Sophia murmured, 'Yes,' and stirred the white sauce she was making for cauliflower cheese.

'It must be so hard to find a little moment to visit your parents. You do work so hard. Still, as long as there's time for social life; so frightfully important, isn't it? All work and no play . . . '

'I am fairly well organised,' Sophia said.

'I expect more and more of your old friends will be married now.'

'Oh, there's even the odd divorce coming through.'

'I suppose *it all depends* on the sort of friends one has.'

'The sauce has boiled; I hope it's not too early for the cauliflower.'

'It's *perfectly possible* that Edward and Felicity might get engaged, you know.'

'We could always just put it all under the grill until it's ready to be served.'

'She's just twenty-three, but I for one think that is a *very good age* to get married.'

'Shall I warm up these rolls for the soup?'

'I mean, I got married at twenty, and

86

darling Anthea was only twenty-two.'

That night, Sophia, feeling every moment of her thirty-three years, took a sleeping pill.

Christmas Day began dreadfully early with shrieks from James and Camilla, the children, opening their stockings. Sophia clung to her bed and avoided breakfast, taking quick refuge in some black coffee before accompanying the family on one of its biannual visits to the local church. After church, they all opened their big presents under the little tree, following a family tradition. Sophia thought of Thomas enjoying the sight of all his small relations opening their presents and wondered, not for the first time, why she felt so left out of things here.

She always gave very generous presents and agonised over them because she was never sure that their recipients would really like them. She also brought several gifts for the whole household, such as bottles of brandy and expensive chocolates. The fact that she could easily afford to buy these things somehow made it more awkward for her.

They mostly didn't know what to give her, either. There were compact discs she already had or didn't want, there was a silk shirt in a green that she wouldn't feel comfortable wearing, there was a pair of gloves she was meant to wear while driving. The one present that gave her pleasure was a little Victorian antique brooch from her father. She tried to let him know how much she liked it and felt she had failed to do so.

There was too much food for Christmas dinner, which was really a late lunch. James and Camilla attended the meal. They were aged four and two and had not yet learned much about table manners; Sophia was amazed as always at their grandmother's indulgence. Mrs White always had been very strict with her own children. Sophia eyed these horrible grandchildren as she pecked at her food and decided that whatever her feelings about marriage she was not sorry so far to have foregone children. During the meal much was made of Felicity, who was absent, and Edward seemed delighted with his mother's coy questions about her. Toasts were drunk.

When the meal was over, and everything was humming away in the washing-up machine, it was dark outside. Everyone — including Sophia — felt too full of food. The children's quarrels over their new toys died down; most of the grown-ups slumped in front of the television; Sophia retreated to her room with Dostoevsky's *The Possessed*, which she had not yet read and had been promising herself for some years. She found it quite thorny but so fascinating as to provide a serviceable escape.

Hours later, she heard someone calling her. She sat up on her bed and in an instant was transported back to childhood. How many hours, days, weeks had she spent exactly thus, lying on this relentlessly pink bed and engrossed in some wonderful book which was always infinitely more attractive than the world around her? She had always had privacy, having never liked anyone to enter her room, though she had been unable of course to prevent her mother from doing so; Anthea and Edward, who had always been close to each other and not to her, had been strictly forbidden.

Edward now called, 'So-phie! Do you want some supper?'

She stayed back in her childhood, trailing down to family supper, her mind a million miles away, abstracted at the table, lacking in conversation, unable to tear herself away from the book that was currently interesting her.

'Did you hear what I said, Sophie?' her mother asked. 'Honestly, she's not all there.'

Edward and Anthea giggled menacingly, conspiratorially: 'Sophie's going to turn into a bookworm, a bookworm, eeugh, a horrible *worm*, hee hee hee!'

'Now now, children, that's enough,' Mrs

White said, and then, in a sharper voice, 'I said *pass the peas, please*, Sophie. Must I say everything twice?'

Now grown up and on the shelf, Sophia felt the old isolation; as she took her place at the kitchen table for a supper she hardly felt equal to eating she wondered what she was doing there. She brought little pleasure to these people, and they brought equally little to her. Why not be on my own on my own terms, she thought, in my little house, surrounded by the things I like; I could listen to music, do some reading, indulge myself. She knew she had no choice, because these unwanted and unwanting people were her family. All her friends had families who appeared very desirable; they were not lonely. She had always conformed and must continue to do so, but the difference between herself and the rest of the world felt grievous.

Boxing Day brought the traditional White drinks party: achingly boring neighbours, the reappearance of Felicity, numbers of small children of a similar disposition to James and Camilla. The Christmas tobacco-pine-roast turkey aroma of the house were suddenly overlaid by cigarette smoke and the harsh smell of dry and medium sherry. Sophia drank tomato juice and tried not to get irritated with those neighbours who tried to patronise her; a dose of Epsom always brought out the latent feminist in her. Felicity and Edward stood hand in hand, apparently inseparable. Andrew was anything but hand in hand with Anthea; Sophia noticed that he seemed to be making up to every half-way presentable woman in the room and decided, not for the first time, that she detested flirting. She would have liked to talk to her father, but he was in a corner, talking to a good friend and neighbour, probably a fellow solicitor and committee member of the golf club. She avoided her mother, who was making a point of talking to everyone there.

The guests left at around one thirty; the Whites sat down to a late lunch of cold turkey, Anthea, Andrew, James and Camilla having departed for his parents in Dorking. Mrs White made heavy weather of a middle-aged young man who had been at the drinks party with his wife of a few months. He apparently had been interested at one time in Sophia. Sophia was unaware of this and said so. She was counting the minutes to the time that she could decently leave, with the excuse that she was meant to be in the office the next day.

It was bliss to get into her white sports car. One of the few nice things that had happened this Christmas was Edward's frank and unabashed admiration for this car. He loved cars and knew something about them; he really thought Sophia must be very clever to have such a fine company car and was generous in his praise. As she drove out of her parents' quiet road she turned Act Two of *Die Meistersinger* up louder. The car began to warm up. Sophia felt the purest relief; she loved driving the car; for an instant the getaway was so wonderful that the ordeal of Christmas seemed almost worth it, just for that.

There was little traffic, and she got home quickly. Her house was cold; dusk was falling. It smelled of nothing, neutral after her parents' house. She walked briskly in and spent five minutes or so busily switching on lights and heating and putting the kettle on. However, the heat was slow to permeate the house, and it soon occurred to her that it was only five o'clock, yet dark. There was nothing to do. Christmas was over. The remembrance of childhood came back again with the feeling that nothing nice was ever going to happen again after all the excitements. As a child, she may not have been very happy, but Christmas had always been a relatively good time, and the anti-climatic aftermath had always been more or less hideous.

'Nothing nice is ever going to happen

again,' she thought, 'and I haven't even had a good Christmas into the bargain.'

Sophia began to feel very depressed.

She was toying with the idea of going to bed with a bottle of whisky and a hundred Mogadons and wrestling with the fact that she could not stand whisky when the telephone rang. When she had finished speaking to her caller she was coming round to the notion that whisky could taste pretty good if you were in the mood. The caller had been her mother.

'Dad and I so hope you're all *right*, darling. You shouldn't have left so suddenly, really you shouldn't. You hardly spent any time with us at all. It is Christmas, after all. Sometimes I think you just don't care. I suppose you just went back to that cold little house of yours, all by yourself.'

Sophia added guilt to her list of things to be depressed about and began thinking seriously about adding a bottle of gin to the whisky. She then discovered she only had about ten Mogadons, so that put paid to that. Fortunately, however, there was a frightful best seller to hand, swiped from one of the few bookshelves at Epsom against precisely such an eventuality. In the end she compromised and went to bed with a glass of water, a couple of sleeping pills and this novel.

7

The old year drew sluggishly to its close. Sophia went back to the office and tried to work through the twilit days. It was difficult to concentrate; few people were in the City; there was none of the necessary urgency. She longed for the year to be over.

On New Year's Eve she went out to a party. Thomas hadn't rung between Christmas and the New Year; she supposed he had stayed on at his family's Georgian house in Dorset, quite unimaginably far away in another world, and ten to one not suffering as much as she. She missed him, remembering what fun he was. Then it occurred to her that she may be capable of having fun without him. Was he not in the country, and was his availability in any case not circumscribed by the irritating Allegra? Here was a party, and it presented an opportunity. Sophia made a conscious decision to go out on the razzle and even, if the spirit took her, to behave badly.

She dressed with some care in tight-fitting black velvet trousers that showed off her figure, a gold silk satin shirt and a special bra to give her at least the ghost of a cleavage.

Her hair was left loose, and she wore more eye make-up and glossy lipstick than usual.

When she got to the party she took care not to drink too much, because she wanted to be properly aware of everything and in control. She did not know many people, but this did not shake her confidence. By and by she got herself introduced to someone who appeared presentable, and she was delighted to see, on closer scrutiny (the lights were dim), that the individual was even positively attractive, being tall (taller and heavier than Thomas) and possessed of wavy brown hair, blunt, not unhandsome features and a wide smiling mouth. He wasn't at all her usual scene, being a young but senior foreign exchange dealer, originally, and inevitably, from Essex, but she decided this made their meeting even more of an adventure for her. Feeling sexy and brazen in the golden shirt, she gazed up into his eyes and accepted one drink. Mindless music poured into her ears, precluding conversation. Following the example of the writhing, twitching bodies surrounding them, they danced.

Midnight sounded; everyone shrieked 'Happy New Year!' and fell into each other's arms in an orgy of congratulation.

Colin, Sophia's foreign exchange dealer, grabbed Sophia and kissed her thoroughly.

She was quite elated; this was what she had intended. Sophia was pragmatic about sex. She enjoyed it on her own terms; having made up her mind that she wanted Colin she saw no reason to hang about. Accordingly, she ended up in bed with him in his flat somewhere in Islington. It all happened quickly, and it wasn't nearly such fun once they were undressed; arriving was a poor thrill compared to travelling hopefully. The experience was extremely safe. She had an uneasy sense of anti-climax at this tidy act. He immediately went to sleep.

Wide awake, eyes staring in the dark, she remembered the last time she had made love — the drunken tumble with Thomas on her sitting room floor. For the first time she recalled the encounter in detail, down to her last shiver of delight, even after she had slammed the door on him. It had been even more exciting than the imaginative sex she had enjoyed so voraciously with Kingsley. Colin's large body had not pleased her; she shocked herself with the thought that compared to Thomas he was Neanderthal; she bitterly missed Thomas's ardour.

Five or six hours later he woke up. He was delighted to find Sophia still in bed beside him and reached for her. Feeling guilty that she had compared him so unfavourably to

Thomas, she made an effort to respond and even managed to extract a little satisfaction (if not positive enjoyment) from the encounter.

They got up. Sophia had a bath in a dazzling white-and-chrome bathroom and washed off last night's make-up. She felt horrible in last night's party clothes and her colourless, underslept face. Colin, however, was nice to her and told her she still looked great, and then he made them some very good espresso in a fantastically expensive machine in a space-age kitchen. His hi-tech flat had been designed almost to death with expensive modern furniture and carefully neutral colours, but Sophia found it arid. They talked boringly about those of his possessions which most interested him (electronic and costly) and then about the City, which was all they had in common. At last he took Sophia back to her car in his own predictable, silly-money, boy-racer car, and to her surprise (for did she not really look awful this morning, and had she not misbehaved last night?) asked to see her again.

She agreed. After all, why not? Thomas was not only not there, he wasn't even her lover anyway. Colin was not in the same league as Thomas, but he was good-natured and had *something* (success as a foreign exchange dealer? the smiling mouth?); also, he was interested and might even turn out, on closer acquaintance, yet to be interesting. She prided herself on her ability to draw out unpromising subjects; her job required her to be very good at making conversation with people with whom she had nothing in common. There was a fund manager who liked her because he could always tell her about his favourite pursuit, which was caravan holidays, to say nothing of the finance director who really believed she shared his passion for the electric organs, from Yamaha to the mighty Wurlitzer, which he collected. Colin would surely be a pushover compared to these two. Then she was flattered that he had appeared to like her. She was so sick of always being alone.

The following evening Colin turned up at her little house to take her out to dinner. Sophia, having decided to eschew the sexy look and show Colin her real self, wore an austere grey dress of impeccable cut, tied her shiny hair back in an extra severe black bow and tried to appear more than usually cultured and intelligent. Colin took her to an extraordinarily grand restaurant somewhere in Mayfair where the table was hidden under yards of white damask tablecloth, and they sat next to each other on a squashy velvet sofa. They were handed enormous, unwieldy menus with a great deal of very curly writing in them. Self-confessed bon viveur Colin studied his with care and then, having ordered food and champagne (how guilty all that expensive food and drink made Sophia feel) jovially grabbed Sophia's knee under the damask. She was furious but found it amazingly difficult to express this and stop him, because he was being so generous. Again, they talked boringly about the City. Sophia tried to find out Colin's other interests. It turned out he was fond of motor racing as well as electronic possessions, and he supported Arsenal.

Like many a disciplined single woman, Sophia was a trier, but before the evening was half over she knew it was a failure, and that she was a fool to have agreed to it. It seemed to go on for ever. She didn't eat a pudding, but he did. She was relieved when he refused coffee, then despondent because he obviously expected to be asked in for it when he took her home.

Back at her house, Sophia found she only had instant coffee, which was not impressive after Colin's espresso. Colin looked at her tasteful CD collection and remarked that it all looked very highbrow, but didn't she have any rock or pop music, especially Diana Ross who really turned him on? Tempted to lie that she hadn't heard of Diana Ross, she refused to put anything on, expressing a haughty dislike for music as mere background. Then he perused her bookshelves with all her intellectual books and remarked that he'd heard of Evelyn Waugh; was she any good?

Sophia had been ambivalent about sleeping with Colin again. She didn't really want to, but she wasn't averse to trying again; the conversation hadn't been brilliant, but as a last ditch he might be better in bed this time. Now she knew she couldn't possibly go through with it. Her intellectual snobbery was deep-rooted, perhaps in unconscious sympathy with her mother's social snobbery, and could sometimes inspire her to nasty behaviour. She brought the instant coffee and pointedly sat down in one of the armchairs. When Colin patted the seat on the sofa beside him, 'Come on darlin', come and be sociable', she managed to be so cold in her demeanour that he was quite put off and didn't even finish his coffee before leaving, plainly hurt.

Thus Sophia was left alone again in her silent white sitting room. She took the coffee cups with the wasted coffee into her little white kitchen. Her spirits plumbed new depths. She could not remember ever having behaved this badly before. Of course it *was* bad behaviour. She had used the hapless Colin. He was no plug to fill the hole in her life. She didn't like herself for despising his lack of culture. So what if he didn't know Evelyn Waugh was a man? It would have been funny if it hadn't been so awful.

I can't have the man I want, and I can't even have the man I don't want, she thought in despair, and that night she felt so detestable that she hit the Mogadon again.

8

There were four days between the new year holiday and the weekend. Luckily for Sophia, the stock market picked up from its holiday stupor, so work was able to offer a distraction; emotionally, she remained so low that not even the purchase of some exceptionally sexy and exciting new penny shares, which promptly went up thirty percent as soon as she had bought them, gave her a buzz. Nothing seemed to work for her; she was doomed to loneliness; her family didn't like her, and after the way she had behaved to Colin (who didn't ring up) she didn't see much in herself to like.

Saturday, by contrast, dawned fresh, crisp and bright. Sophia was grateful for it. However unpleasant the last two weeks had been, this new day seemed to hold out the promise of a fresh start. It seemed so clean, with the first appearance of the sun this new year — even if she felt herself not to be clean. Suddenly inspired, she drove herself to Hyde Park and walked around it and Kensington Gardens.

Others were abroad that day, also enjoying

the sun. Some were out walking in pairs, in groups and alone, with and without dogs; from time to time a solo runner pounded by. There were mothers and nannies with their children. Groups of horses and ponies were being ridden along Rotten Row. The trees were dark and bare, and the flower beds were bare too, but the grass was a gentle green, and the sun, pale in a pure blue sky, had taken off the frost and seemed almost too warm.

On days such as this in the past Sophia had often felt she was missing out. She might go for a walk, but she had no one to go with. Whatever she was doing (or whatever she was) never seemed quite enough. Today was different. She was not feeling happy, but for the first time she found there was an enjoyment to be had simply from the bright fresh air which could not be denied or exchanged for anything better.

When she got home, she found Thomas had rung and had left a message on her answering machine, asking if she could meet him for lunch. Suddenly her spirits, which had been soothed by her walk, rose positively; she felt excited.

They met at his studio an hour later. She was almost surprised at how pleased she was to see Thomas. The smell of oil paints and turpentine seemed to be crystallised in the cold there, but Thomas had lit a joss stick, the blue scented smoke of which wafted thinly above this; there was also a little old-fashioned electric fire. He looked much better than on the other occasions that Sophia had met him. 'I slept and ate a lot over Christmas,' he explained.

'How was your Christmas?' asked Sophia. Thomas busied himself with making coffee.

'Laid back. Actually it was heaven. All the grown-ups except me went hunting on Boxing Day, then Father and Charlie and Jules went shooting the day after, and generally they were all wrapped up in some kind of sport or other that endangered the life of small animals. I stayed at home and corrupted Charlie and Vicky's children, though Vicky's daughter is pony-mad and insisted on hunting too. I think Father's given up on me, he generally left me alone and rather ignored me. How was your Christmas?'

'Standard White. Exactly as it's always been, except that I'm more aware of the children. Mum dotes on them; they're both very pleased to be grandparents. Little talks from Mum about my myriad shortcomings.'

'Were your people awful?'

Sophia sipped her coffee, which was cheap instant in a cracked mug. 'Do you know, more awful than I had ever realised. It's quite a shock when you suddenly understand that your parents, Mum more than Dad, are not nice people. In fact I think Mum is rather a bully. I don't suppose she's aware of it. Dad's light years away, and Anthea and Edward and their other halves are just smug.'

'Poor Sophia. Did you tell them about me? They'd have had a fit.'

'Not if I'd censored it. If I had gone on about your background — the estate in the country and all that — they would have loved the sound of you. Another interesting little fact about my parents — but especially my mother — is that they are crashing snobs.'

'Oh dear. So you didn't say anything much. But isn't it gorgeous today?'

'It certainly is. I even went for a walk in Hyde Park'

'Feels good to be alive, doesn't it?'

'Well . . . up to a point. Now, are you going to show me some pictures?'

'Yes, right. Now what do you think of this?'

Sophia began to contemplate a landscape that had presumably been painted in Dorset. Suddenly there was a knock on the door, and a high-pitched female voice cried out, 'Thomas! Are you home?'

Sophia knew it was Allegra.

The door burst open, and a golden girl

dressed in a long fur coat clattered in, running across the studio to hug and kiss Thomas. Her heart-shaped face was framed with white-blonde wavy hair which tumbled attractively onto her shoulders; she had a small, up-turned nose, irregular features and large blue eyes. She was smiling engagingly, a curious crooked smile. It was an unusually pretty face, much more alluring than in Thomas's blown-up photo. Sophia had to stop herself staring in fascination.

'Happy new year, darling,' she said. Was that high-pitched, upper-class voice faintly mocking, or was Sophia imagining things?

'Hi petal,' said Thomas. 'Last time I saw you you vowed never to come to my hell-hole again.'

'Don't ever call me petal. Aren't you pleased to see me? Goodness knows, you want to see me often enough!'

'Allegra, I'd like you to meet Sophia White. Sophia, this is Allegra Staveley.'

They shook hands and eyed each other.

'Nice Christmas?' Thomas asked Allegra.

'Not much. Had to spend it with Mummy and Alex. I just cannot get on with Alex, he's so *boring*, and I couldn't wait to go back to Daddy's. Couldn't miss all that hunting, and New Year was fun; what about you? How is your family? Did you see . . . '

106

For the next five minutes Allegra and Thomas talked about people Sophia had never heard of. They lived in the country and pursued field sports. Sophia became bored. When Thomas offered Allegra coffee, she prayed Allegra would not accept.

'Love to, but no time. I've got to meet . . . no, hang on, why not? Let him wait. It'll be good for him.'

Sophia gritted her teeth.

'Who's your latest victim?' Thomas asked.

'No one you know, I don't think. I can't decide if he's a human being or just a stockbroker. He actually lives somewhere near here. He's meant to be taking me out to lunch.'

'Sophia's a human being *and* a stock-broker,' Thomas said.

Allegra inclined her head towards Sophia and giggled. 'Oh dear, how frightfully tactless of me. He'll probably turn out to be heaven. How d'you know Thomas?'

'We met at a dinner party,' Sophia said.

'Oh yes, whose? Yes please, sugar too. You know I always have sugar. I'm the only girl I know who has sugar in coffee. Everyone else has to diet, lucky me. Do you diet?' She turned again to Sophia.

'It has never occurred to me to do so.'

Allegra grinned. 'Just like me, isn't it

lovely? I eat exactly whatever I like, and it never makes the slightest difference. All that food. Don't you just adore it?'

'No, not particularly.'

Allegra seemed not to infer any snub. 'God, Thomas,' she rattled on, 'how can you live with this revolting instant coffee? And don't tell me, *milk powder*. You must do better for yourself than that.'

'Haven't time to faff around with real coffee,' Thomas pointed out, 'and this stuff is a lot cheaper. Come on, I live on it. And I've actually got some real milk — but there's powder too if you like.'

'Oh God, I forgot.' Allegra rolled her eyes. 'You're an impecunious artist. All this art for art's sake is very boring, Thomas.' She finished her coffee. 'Off I go, I shall be ten minutes late.'

'As usual,' Thomas said, rising to kiss her.

'Bye-bye, darling. Lovely meeting you, bye.'

'Ta-ra, blossom.'

Sophia remained seated and had no chance to utter goodbye before Allegra had blown out of the studio, leaving a faint cloud of Hermès' 'Amazone' behind her.

When Thomas had closed the door behind Allegra, Sophia sighed rather more loudly than normally.

'Well,' said Thomas, looking at his most

neutral, 'there goes little Allegra.'

'I suppose you might say she was very attractive.'

Thomas sat down and ran his fingers through his grey and black forelock. 'Oh yes, very. She's very — quicksilver? Never still, so animated.'

'Rather a butterfly, in fact.'

Thomas looked straight at Sophia. 'It's very funny,' he said. 'Allegra is the least bitchy person I know, but she seems to bring out the worst in other females.'

'She's simply not the sort of person you can take at all seriously.'

'Hey!' said Thomas sharply. 'Put your claws *away*. You're in a filthy temper. What's your problem?'

Sophia wrinkled her nose disdainfully. 'Are you seriously interested in her? Oh, of course I appreciate that she's physically attractive — very. But surely . . . '

Thomas drew himself in and said quietly, 'It's none of your bloody business.'

Suddenly feeling treacherously upset, she clenched her fists, took a deep breath and said nothing.

'Anyway, you haven't got any axe to grind. It's not as if you were interested in me. You've made that pretty clear. I mean, damn it, I don't pry into your affairs. I don't know you're not seeing someone, and so what if you were? It's not like that with us.'

A wave of upset abruptly invaded Sophia. It was so completely unexpected that it threatened to overwhelm her. Perilously close to tears, she said in a voice very unlike her normal one, 'Will you stop attacking me? Will you shut up?'

'I'm sorry, I'm sorry,' Thomas said in a far gentler tone. 'I didn't mean to upset you.' He suddenly moved over to her chair, knelt by it and put an arm around her. She began to shake. 'It's all right,' he went on, now very soothing. 'It's all OK, it's all right to cry.'

Not expecting to be comforted, Sophia froze; Thomas could feel her stiffen; she shrank away from him into the chair.

'Not all right,' she muttered. 'Never all right.'

Thomas put his other arm around her, as if he wanted to hug away her stiffness and reserve.

'It doesn't matter,' he went on, 'nothing matters. Relax, it's all right.'

The last time Sophia had been tempted to cry had been with Rupert Kingsley. The memory of this returned to her with such appalling, uncontrolled vividness that the effort to hold back the tears she had never then shed was almost physically painful.

'You look as if you're very upset about something. Would you like to talk about it?'

Sophia stared at Thomas with huge eyes, not trusting herself to speak. The tears were now stinging; she wanted to raise her head to make them run somehow to the back of her eyeballs; one wobbled on her lower eyelashes and spilled down. She tried to stop breathing to control this, and to her unspeakable horror all she could do was to emit a harsh sob.

'Don't you see,' Thomas carried on in the same soothing voice, 'I like you so very much. I think so much of you. I don't think a bit less of you because you're crying.'

Rather like a conjurer, he produced a large, bright pink handkerchief, similar to the red silk one he had once left behind at Sophia's house. The unbidden image of a white rabbit appearing from this handkerchief sprang distractingly and mercifully into Sophia's imagination. She blew her nose.

'Are you going to tell me what's upsetting you?' Thomas went on. 'Tell me who he is, and I might go and kill him.'

'I behaved like a cretin and had an affair with someone wrong,' she said in a rush, and then she really lost control. By and by Thomas's shoulder became fairly damp. He hugged her and stroked her hair softly and regularly.

'He was such — a — bastard,' she said at last, as the first flush of tears passed off. 'In the end, can you imagine, he actually threatened me to get rid of me. I didn't deserve it.'

She cried again. It was horrible and humiliating, but there was also the faintest suspicion of a different feeling which seemed not to be wholly bad, and which she did not recognise as relief.

'Go on,' said Thomas.

'I know I was a cretin, because he was married, but I didn't deserve him to be quite such a bastard.'

'He must have torn you apart.'

'It was so — bloody — painful . . . ' The fresh abundance of tears almost surprised her.

'And you've never told anyone until now,' Thomas guessed. 'You've kept it all bottled up. It must have been so hard.'

'I thought I could cope. I can cope. Then I was awful to someone who wasn't bad at all. Oh God . . . ' She wiped her eyes. 'I didn't mean to do this.'

Thomas shifted, putting his hands on her shoulders so that they were facing each other directly. 'Now look at me,' he said, staring at her straight in the eyes. 'You've got to know I'm really very fond of you. I really mean it,

I'm just as fond of you crying as not crying. I think just as much of you. Do you understand?'

Sophia flinched from his stare and shook her head mutely, seeing in her mind's eye her wet, red, ugly cheeks, her eyes swollen and piggy and her hair tousled and messy. Thomas took her in his arms again, hugging her head to his chest. She was trembling again.

'Talk to me,' Thomas urged.

Sophia sat up and wiped her eyes for the last time. This time her self-discipline succeeded: she refused to let herself go on crying, and she forbade herself to talk about herself.

'You've been very good,' she said stiffly. Tears now stood in Thomas's eyes. 'Don't get emotional with me now!' she added in a shaky voice, with a twisted attempt at a smile.

'I hate seeing how badly you've been hurt,' he said bluntly.

'Please let's leave it.'

'Trust me.'

There was a pause.

'I've got to go,' Sophia announced.

'But we're having lunch.'

'I'm sorry, I can't eat. I'm sorry. Please let's leave it for now. I just — I'm not feeling well.'

'Don't go — please don't go . . . '

113

She got up and, apologising again, took her coat and bag.

'You're running away!' Thomas said sharply. 'Stay with me, Sophia! It'll be all right!'

'No,' she nearly shouted, feeling tears rising unbearably again. She ran out of the flat and scrambled into her car; through a haze of tears she drove quickly away, leaving Thomas cursing and bemused.

In the safety of her house, she retreated to her bedroom and flung herself on her bed to cry unreservedly. The tears squirted out of her eyes, and she shook with loud, unrestrained sobs. She forgot why exactly she was crying as her memory stretched back well beyond Rupert Kingsley. An incident popped into her mind from the time that she had been about eleven: she and three other girls from school with whom she had been superficially friendly had been taken roller-skating. The other three had all done a little skating before and could hold their own on the rink; not so Sophia, who had never worn roller skates in her life and had no aptitude whatever for the activity. While her friends glided effortlessly around the rink, she clutched stiffly and painfully to the side, terrified that any second the little wheels on her feet would betray her and hurl her against the ground. She never did fall, but neither did she roller-skate. In the end she had been exhausted with the effort of being so stiff. It never occurred to her that she too could be like the other children who were not stiff and who could skate. She longed with all her soul not to be different from them, but she was inexorably trapped within herself. The three girls were never friendly with her again after the roller-skating.

There were whispers, real or imagined: ' . . . hopeless . . . clinging to the side . . . no one else like that . . . in front of all the *little* children, too . . . no fun with *her* . . . She's just a stupid bookworm anyway.'

The sensation of crying for herself was quite unlike the tears shed pleasantly at the opera or on reading a good book. Those tears were merely an indulgence; they were almost physically comforting. This was mourning. She wept for herself for the first time, both as an unhappy child and as a heartbroken adult. It was appallingly painful, yet Sophia experienced again — in flashes — that mysterious feeling of relief which was not negative. It mixed confusingly with guilt that she had let herself go and cried in front of Thomas.

As for Thomas himself, she felt at first the painful and confusing stirring of physical attraction; she quelled it and the rise of other, more disturbing feelings, by refusing even to think about him.

9

That night she slept intermittently, but not so badly as she feared. She dreamed that she was pushed into the sea. The part of the dream in which she was pushed was nightmarish: the sea was not rough, but she was mortally afraid of the water. Suddenly, however, she was able to swim. (In real life she was a poor swimmer.) She saw a ship and began swimming towards it, and the sensation of moving through the friendly water was wonderful. The ship turned out not to be a ship at all; at this point she woke up. It took a few seconds for her to realise her waking circumstances. They did not appear propitious, but the utter despair of yesterday was gone.

Somewhat mechanically, Sophia got up. She had been invited to a lunch party this Sunday, but as she did not feel up to it she rang up and cried off on the grounds of ill health. Some work from the office claimed her undivided attention until her doorbell rang. She nearly didn't open the door.

Thomas stood outside, looking paler than ever. 'I can't let you run away,' were his first words. He ran his hand through his forelock.

'You'd better come in.'

'Thanks. It's freezing out here.'

'I've only got lousy instant coffee,' she apologised as he took off his coat. 'No. I lie. I have some very good wine, but it's not in the fridge. I can soon get it cold.'

'You know me, I live on instant coffee. Let's have some.' He sat down, still shivering slightly, wrapping his hands around his coffee mug. 'I love your colourless house. It's so warm. Can I decorate it for you?'

'This coffee is horrible,' Sophia said. 'I gave it to the person I behaved badly to. He gave me wonderful espresso from a special machine, and all I could manage was this stuff.'

'Stop putting yourself down. The coffee's fine. It's hot and wet. You ran away yesterday.'

'So you keep saying. I don't want to talk about it.'

'I'm sorry. You see, I care about you.'

She refused to look at him and concentrated on her own coffee mug, sipping the over-hot liquid gingerly.

'I care about you a lot,' Thomas ploughed on. 'I only realised yesterday. After you ran away — I was devastated — I couldn't work or do anything. I had a rotten night last night.' He twiddled his hair.

118

Sophia continued to stare at her coffee. Thomas abruptly put his hands down.

'Oh, for Christ's sake,' he burst out angrily. 'Do you think this is easy?'

She looked up. 'I don't want you to feel sorry for me.'

'Why the hell not? You wouldn't want your worst enemy to go through what you went through. Why shouldn't I feel sorry for you? Anyway, it's not a question of that. I'm not here to tell you how sorry I feel for you.'

'Oh, let's leave it, shall we? I wish I could offer you something to eat, but I don't think I have anything in the house.'

'I don't *want* anything to eat! I only want you! Do you understand? You! You're the one!'

He had got up and was pacing up and down her sitting room. She sat as if glued to her armchair.

'Can't you say anything?' he demanded, stopping at the end of the room with his back to her.

'I don't know what to say,' she said truthfully. 'This is all going a bit fast for me.'

'The thing is, you see,' he carried on, 'it's not Allegra any more. I do like her, don't get me wrong. I'm actually really fond of her. We go back a long way. I didn't actually think you

119

were very nice to her yesterday — but, oh shit, you see, I understood suddenly: it's not her, it's you.'

Sophia gazed mutely at him, her grey eyes very large. He approached her and stood over her armchair, glaring down at her. 'Do you like me at all?' he asked aggressively.

She hesitated and cleared her throat. 'Yes,' she said loudly, surprising herself with the unaccustomed tone of her voice. 'Yes, I do. Very much.' Then she looked up at him as he stood over her, his hair dishevelled and his dark eyes very intense. As if by lightning, the impulse *I love you* flashed through her; for an instant she was flooded by light; he just caught the sudden radiance. He dropped down by her chair and reached out for her, but the impulse had passed too quickly for her to make anything of it. Half shocked, she shrank away.

'What is this, Sophia?' he demanded. 'Can't I even touch you?'

Sophia firmly rejected the light. 'For God's sake, leave me alone just for a bit! It's all too much for me. I just don't know. I don't know if that's what I want. I'm fed up. Every time I get remotely involved with someone, it's a disaster. I can't take it — '

'Oh come on, I'm not married like that bastard who threatened you.'

'That's nothing,' Sophia said, rather confusingly. 'It's just that last time I got a bit
involved with someone I was so awful to him.'

'Well, we've all behaved badly, surely? I've
been terrible, honestly, a real shocker. You're
different.'

'I just don't feel up to being involved any
more, don't you see?' Sophia said with more
conviction.

'You *do*,' Thomas contradicted, having
seen the light in her face. 'You — you can't
tell me you don't want me. I just don't believe
it.'

'I'm not going to argue,' she pointed out
tiredly. 'Look, I'm sorry, you'd better go. I'm
not feeling all that well, I've got work to do, I
really want to be on my own.'

Thomas lost his temper. 'You are so
screwed up,' he shouted, 'you know? *So
screwed up*. God, why did it have to be you?
All the girls I've had — and let me tell you,
there've been *dozens*,' (he spat the word) 'and
you . . . I don't even *want* to be involved,
either. I just don't need it at this stage. Life's
difficult enough as it is . . . '

'Then why the devil are you going on at me
now?'

'You just don't see, do you? God, Sophia!
I'm getting out of here. You know what?
You're hooked on loneliness, that's what you

are. You're so into being alone, you'll just shrivel up and die all by yourself one day. All this running away . . . I think I'll take a leaf out of your book. I'm off. I don't know when I'll see you again . . . '

He swept out of the little white sitting room in mid-speech and slammed the front door.

Again there was absolute silence in Sophia's little white sitting-room. For a moment she sat quite still in the armchair where he had left her; then she bit her lip, took up her Sunday newspapers and deliberately began to read a business section. Presently she rang up one of her musical friends and arranged to go out that night to hear a Beethoven string quartet at the Purcell Rooms.

The music was rigorous. If she had let it, it would have revived the light in her, but she restrained her emotions and used her head, thus turning a superb concert from high enjoyment to an intellectual exercise. Her companion was an ascetic young man who was probably gay; he was even more cerebral than Sophia and thus not an exacting companion. They had supper together after the concert in a little restaurant near Waterloo and discussed chamber music seriously. Later, when she came home that night, she gave herself another small indulgence. Tucked up in bed, before switching the light out, she began to re-read *To the Lighthouse*. How admirably Virginia Woolf wrote! How right she had been to go to the Beethoven! Sated with culture if not joy, Sophia went to sleep.

★   ★   ★

Next day, Sophia took a few extra minutes to organise her social life for the next few weeks. She contacted Anita and other friends; she had her secretary book tickets for the theatre and opera; she invited seven friends to a dinner party and arranged to have it catered. There was no business lunch that day, so she popped out to a bookshop in the City and bought herself some books to which she had been planning to treat herself. Her work also hummed along, and she kept at it until late; she rewarded herself by going home and starting the most tempting book over a cup of hot chocolate.

However, after a week or so hitches occurred in this order of life. One afternoon she was alone in her office considering a rights issue for one of the firm's clients. Her concentration suddenly wandered: although she did not stop reading the words on the draft prospectus, their meaning went out of her control and altogether eluded her.

'Senior management resources are being substantially concentrated on optimising the key subsidiaries in niche markets,' she read. Her red pen hovered, but instead of striking with it she unconsciously laid it down. She remembered that on Sunday she had been furious with Thomas. He had said she would shrivel up and die. She frowned and read on: ' . . . in order to fully realise the benefits to be had in the growing European market for circular and straight mill blades for the engineering industry . . . ' Thomas had been very angry too. She saw him in her mind's eye trying to take her hands as she sat mutely in her armchair. His physical image was terribly vivid. He cared for her; he preferred her to Allegra. *She loved him.* She stopped reading the prospectus. When a buzz from one of her screens, indicating a share price movement, broke her reverie she was shocked and for a split second almost forgot where she was.

One of Sophia's brighter young members of staff commented later, 'Sophie must be losing her touch. I deliberately put in the most clichés and crap English I could in the middle of that prospectus and she never squeaked.'

That night she woke up at three, surfacing gradually from uneasy sleep. For a long time she lay with her eyes shut, unwilling to admit to herself how wide awake she was. She was restless, yet her body felt like lead. Her bedroom, when she opened her eyes at last, was very dark except for a dim yellow light from a street lamp outside, which sent the faintest sulphurous ray through a narrow gap between the curtains and the wall by the window. The four corners of the room were just discernible as she peeped out from her blankets. Her bed seemed extraordinarily large; she was in the middle of it, with lots of room on either side; she began to get the feeling that the bed and the room contained too much space, and that beyond the room there was even more space in the house, not to mention the impossible black world outside with its false yellow light. In all the space, in all the darkness and all the world she was absolutely alone.

She shivered under all her covers; her head ached dreadfully. She felt massively weary and knew that she was not to sleep again that night, even if the night lasted for ever. The memory of light inside herself which she had so successfully extinguished in the past several days came back to mock her.

He wants me, he cares for me, he probably really loves me, said one side of herself.

So much the worse when you screw up,

came the response from the darkness. *He'll reject you in the end, just like everyone else.*

Couldn't I at least give it a try!

Oh come on, how often have you said that before? They all turn you down, you know. They always have and they always will.

But he didn't mind when I cried . . .

Believe that and you'll believe anything. You know you pushed your luck there. He won't put up with that sort of thing really. He won't put up with you. No one will put up with you. As you know very well, no one ever has. Well, you remember how Thomas put it. 'Shrivel up and die' — those were the words he used, isn't that right? That's what he really thinks of you.

It's what I really think of myself . . .

All around her, the darkness was absolutely silent. Normally she could hear a clock ticking and the faint sound of London traffic, even in the small hours. Tonight it was different: she wondered if she was sleeping or waking. At one point the yellow light seemed to go out; perhaps she was dreaming, or the street lamp had failed. The darkness and silence oppressed her; they were in her as well as around her. She was possessed of a profound revulsion and a nameless dread which was deeper than fear; her soul was exhausted and craved oblivion.

Dawn came. Its light was grey and tired, but it was stronger than the darkness. It brought a certain relief: Sophia slept dreamlessly.

Many hours later, towards midday, Sophia dragged herself up and to the City. She was as white as a sheet and felt numb. The physical effort was so enormous that she nearly gave up before she got there. Having told the people at work she was unwell and closed the door of her office, she sat at her desk with her head in her hands and wondered seriously how she was to cope with her life.

Dispassionately she considered how quickly she could get her hands on a large quantity of sleeping pills or tranquillisers. Once she had got them, she would take them, with plenty of alcohol and maybe a bottle of Paracetamol, on a Friday night. It would be necessary to cancel all engagements for the ensuing weekend, because she would have to ensure that she would not be missed for the longest possible period. No one must suspect anything, so she must go on working just as usual, even though this would be extremely difficult. There would be no messing around with notes. It was the only logical thing to do.

Sophia's telephone began to ring.

10

Automatically, unconsciously, she lifted the receiver. 'Sophia White.'

'Hello, you don't know me,' said a faintly hesitant yet determined woman's voice. 'My name is Hermione Avondale. I'm Thomas Avondale's stepmother.'

Sophia sat bolt upright; the words were like a smack in the face. For a second she could not speak.

'Hello, are you there?' asked Hermione Avondale.

'Yes, yes, of course — I'm so sorry.'

'I'm sorry to ring you up so abruptly, but you see Thomas isn't well.'

'Oh dear? What's happened to him?'

'He had a heart attack; he's still in intensive care — '

'A heart attack,' Sophia repeated stupidly.

'Apparently he collapsed in a pub. He's never been strong.'

'But he's so young! I never knew — I'm sorry — I'm so sorry it happened. It must be desperately worrying for you?'

'He wanted to see you. He gave me your name and telephone number. He would have rung from the hospital, but he's not up to much at the moment.'

'I'd love to see him. Where is he? When can he see visitors?'

Hermione Avondale told her. Her despair evaporated almost as if it had never been; she felt her heartbeat quicken. For a few moments she stared into space and thought about Thomas. It did not seriously occur to her that Thomas's life might be threatened; his heart attack was so inconceivable that she could hardly think about it; all she could do was to summon her memories of him. She suddenly wanted fiercely to see him, and this stirred her into action. There was work to be done before she could go to him.

Having left her office as early as was decently possible, she drove to the hospital. The cardiac ward was at the end of miles of wide, dim corridors lined with soft green linoleum. When she arrived it was barely lit, with only two or three of its eight beds occupied. She found Thomas in a pool of light set in a limbo of darkness; on seeing him, she had to stifle a gasp.

He was lying nearly flat, his head and shoulders propped up with pillows. Several wires seemed to be attached to him; there was a drip and a heart monitor; it looked like a computer screen with a green moving graph which was Thomas's heartbeat. His face under the electric light had never looked so thin, its extreme pallor accentuated by deep shadows. His smile when he saw her transformed it.

'I'm very glad you came,' he said in a surprisingly thin voice.

The table by his bed was covered with vases of flowers. She wished she had brought some.

'I'm so pleased to see you. How are you feeling?' she asked, almost at a loss for words in shock at her reaction to seeing him.

'Weak.'

'What happened?'

'I was in a pub; feeling very low. Somewhere in the East End, don't know why. Didn't know anyone there, had some beer. Then I got this pain, thought it was stomach ache; then it was just huge, unbelievable. I wanted to pass out and couldn't. I fell over. All these people stood over me. The ambulance people came and here I am.'

'Wailing sirens?'

'The whole bit. It's my second day. Hermione and Father came at once. They were really good. People are lovely . . . ' His voice faded.

'I'm so sorry,' Sophia said.

'Not your fault. I do love you,' he added.

Oblivious to herself, Sophia smiled, took his hand and stroked it. She wanted to hug him. Around his wrist was a plastic bracelet giving his name and religion.

'Church of England,' she read.

He raised a smile. 'Just in case.'

He was too tired to talk, but his face now radiated calm and happiness. She sat on, holding his hand, absorbed by his presence, deeply tired and conscious for those moments only of a curious contentment. Presently a nurse came up and whispered to her, 'Lady Avondale is here. He's allowed two visitors at a time, so it's OK.'

'You never told me your stepmother was Lady Avondale,' Sophia said in a low voice to Thomas.

'Things you learn. I'm a Christian, and Daddy's a lord.' He smiled again. She went on stroking his hand.

Her first impression of Lady Avondale was that she was small, neat and apprehensive. She had round blue lost eyes in a round ageless face with very fine skin and no make-up. Sophia stood up as she approached and immediately felt tall and gawky by her.

'You must be Sophia White,' said Lady Avondale in a low, anxious voice. 'Hermione Avondale. How very kind of you to come so soon.'

'But of course — I had to come.'

'Hello, Tom.'

'Hi, Herm.' He grinned. 'Sophia. It's my wicked stepmother.'

'How is my evil stepson?' The apprehension in Hermione's eyes was replaced by a spark of humour. She bent to kiss him, and a voice in Sophia's head suddenly screamed, *Why didn't you kiss him too?*

'Plotting against you. What have you done to Father?'

'House of Lords.'

'Why are we whispering?' whispered Thomas. 'Can't hear a thing.'

Hermione giggled softly. Sophia suddenly felt like crying. By and by the nurse came up and told them their time was up; the patient was too exhausted to receive visitors for more than a few minutes at a time.

Sophia and Hermione had cups of unpleasant coffee in a cafeteria in the hospital.

'He's very, very ill, isn't he?' asked Sophia.

'It was fairly touch and go. Poor Thomas, he's so *hopeless*.' The round eyes now reflected concern, but Hermione smiled. 'He's always had a weak heart. There was something very nasty when he was about three, and then at Oxford, but there's never been anything else up to now. He's always

132

known he must be careful. I bet he never told you. The idea of Thomas being careful is a joke.'

'You're right, he didn't tell me.'

'How long have you known Thomas?' Hermione's face was open and guileless.

'Not long. A few months. We don't know each other all that well.'

'I think he cares a lot for you. You were the only one he asked for, you know. Not Allegra.'

Sophia looked away. 'Poor Thomas.' There was a silence; they took distasteful sips. 'How long is he expected to be in hospital?'

'With luck, only a day or so more in intensive care — the cardiac ward; then we've got a private room for him; a few days there. They don't keep them so long these days. You wouldn't believe how much better he is today; he was more or less unconscious yesterday. Will you be able to see him again?'

'Of course. I really want to do so — only please tell me if it's too much. Should I come back tomorrow?'

'Every evening, as much as you can. Oh, it would be wonderful if you did. He really did ask for you very specially.'

'But what will happen to him when he has to leave hospital? He surely can't go back to his flat?'

'Oh no. We'll take him home.'

'Home?'

'To the country — you know; we live in Dorset. I believe Thomas would be very much happier in the country. Sometimes I think he doesn't like London very much. I must say I don't. He'll be better off with us.' She spoke softly still but with an authority Sophia noticed now for the first time.

The next day, Hermione got out of London, returning to the country to run her house and her yard (she was a horse-breeder) and to hunt. Lord Avondale, however, would not leave as long as Thomas was in hospital. His attendance there was sparing, because he detested hospitals and found visiting painful, but he could not bear to be far from it. Sophia never met him there. When Thomas, who made a quick and satisfactory recovery, was allowed to leave it a week after admittance, it was Lord Avondale who, having gathered together whatever he could find in the chaos of Thomas's flat, was there to take him away to the country.

11

Thomas rang Sophia at work from the country.

'Would you be an angel and come and see me next weekend?' he asked.

'I'd love to. You're sure your father and step-mother won't mind?'

'Don't be silly. Hermione likes you, and Father's longing to meet you.'

'How are you feeling?'

'Absolutely terrific. You wouldn't know anything had gone wrong. I've begun riding; I'm meant to take exercise, you know, and eat sensible food. I can't wait to start painting.'

'I thought you had all your things?'

'No; that's the trouble. Father didn't know what to bring. Look, would you really be an angel and get the stuff I need? Can I give you a list? You can get the key to my flat . . . '

'Oh, I see. You don't really want to see me, you just want your art supplies.'

'*That's it*. Did I ever tell you what a cynic you are? Today's Tuesday, isn't it? I can't wait for Friday. I shall count the hours. I'll ring you up every day to make it go quicker.'

Sophia prepared for her journey. Avondale

House was well over a hundred miles from London in another world. She had seen very little of the country and knew nothing about it. The people she was to visit might almost have been from another planet. She longed wholeheartedly to see Thomas but worried about little things, such as the clothes she might be expected to wear and the present she might take to Hermione.

The journey began in the conventional way: there were serious traffic jams all the way to the start of the M3. Sophia had picked on Mozart to see her to Avondale; the first act of *Le Nozze di Figaro* kept her sane as her little white sports car crawled past Knightsbridge, down the Cromwell Road and over the Hammersmith flyover. The third act was under way by the time she reached the M3 and the open road beyond the M25. She turned up the sound; the car roared along the motorway at ninety miles an hour; the drive became fun. Anticipation of seeing Thomas again mingled with the enjoyment of the music.

At nine o'clock she telephoned the number of Avondale House on her car telephone; it would be polite to let them know how late she was. The telephone rang and rang. There was no reply. The seeming emptiness of the ringing made her uneasy. A little after that time, she began paying attention to the instructions she had written out and turned off the main road.

Sophia was an efficient navigator. Whenever she had to go to a new place, she obtained directions and made sure they corresponded to her road map. She wrote them out in large letters and easy steps, so that she could drive herself without continually stopping. There had been plenty of practice during her years as an investment analyst; many were the industrial estates and head offices she had discovered, hidden in or behind provincial cities with labyrinthine one-way systems. Her pride in this ability matched her self-satisfaction at her success in drawing out diffident, untalkative or simply boring industrialists. On this occasion, in the night and in the country, her navigational talent seemed mysteriously to desert her.

At first the road was broad, and when she reached her first turning it was lit. Then the way became increasingly dark and narrow. At one point it seemed to her that there was room only for her little car on the road. She was blinded by the very occasional approaching headlight and had to shrink into the side, terrified of driving into a ditch. She missed a crucial left turn and carried on hopelessly for what seemed miles. Suddenly, *Le Nozze di*

Figaro came to an end, and she became aware of being surrounded by a profound silence that the roar of her car's engine could not completely mask. Her body became tense without her being aware of it as she hunched herself over the wheel.

A village appeared. Not recognising its name, she stopped under one of its few street lamps and studied the map. It was miles away from Avondale, which was separated from it by an apparent tangle of tiny roads. Panic began to rise; she forced herself to calm down. She was never going to get there; this foreign and unfriendly country was leading her irretrievably astray. *Why did Thomas have to go back here?* She must force logic to prevail. She switched off the engine and was now really overwhelmed by the silence. The engine gave one or two ticks. An owl hooted. She knew without opening the door that it was freezing outside and getting colder all the time. She summoned her strength to study the map, find her way and write herself some new instructions.

She plunged back into the dark and, by dint of driving incredibly slowly, managed to overcome her difficulties. Once or twice there was the need to reverse to take a turn that had nearly been missed. She refused to look at the car's clock. The CD player and radio remained silent. At last she saw in her headlights the village name Avondale. Avondale House was half a mile beyond the village on the same road.

It was easy enough now to find the house. There were gates which she had to open, drive through and shut; a friendly security light came on. The drive was impressively long and led to a large house. Light peeped out of tall windows from behind drawn curtains. As there were no cars parked in front of it, she drove on round its corner and stopped in a paved yard by a Range Rover. For the second time that night she switched off the engine.

For a moment there was, again, that absolute silence which she found uncanny. Barks — volleys of them — shattered it. She had been just about to open her door; she withdrew her arm in an instinctive reaction as a pack of dogs hurled itself towards the car, their noise crashing around it. Canine heads bobbed in the window, the eyes wild in the light of the house beside them, the teeth terribly white and visible. Sophia froze.

Suddenly Thomas's head became visible behind the leaping dogs. He was shouting something and appeared to be laughing at the same time. He strode through the dogs, grabbed Sophia's car door and opened it.

'You made it! I thought you'd got totally lost! Oh, it's fantastic to see you — '

He bent down, very awkwardly put his arms around her and kissed her strongly on the mouth. The dogs continued to bark senselessly.

'Come on then. Out you get. Is your luggage in the boot?'

He moved back. The dogs closed in on Sophia. An apparently gigantic black Doberman bounded at her, tearing her tights with an enormous paw. Sophia did not see that the dog's stump of a tail was wagging frantically. She shrank in near panic as the dog thrust forward its rather sharp brown muzzle, put out an incredibly long, pink tongue and tried to lick her face.

'Thomas,' Sophia tried to scream, but all that came out was a strangled 'Argh.' The barking took on a nightmare quality.

'Super flowers for Herm, she'll love that,' said Thomas meanwhile, extracting an azalea and Sophia's suitcase from the boot. 'Come on. What are you waiting for?'

'Argh,' said Sophia again, leaning back desperately and nearly impaling herself on the gear lever in a futile effort to escape from the Doberman. The barking was driving her mad.

'Come on, Bella, you silly dog,' said Thomas, seizing the Doberman's collar. 'Let her out. Come *on*. Christ, you're strong. Shut up, you others.'

He managed to drag Bella off. The barking stopped, but the cold air was alive with panting and scuffling as the Doberman, a Labrador and two small terriers sniffed eagerly around Sophia's car.

Sophia tentatively stuck her head out of the car, her eyes enormous. 'Is it safe?' she asked.

Thomas shouted with laughter. 'Safe! I don't think so. They might love you to death.' He stretched out a hand and pulled her out of the car. Then he hugged her. 'Oh, it's so, so brilliant to see you.'

Sophia looked at him properly for the first time. 'You're looking fantastic,' she said. 'I've never seen you like this.'

'Country always does this to me. Aren't you pleased to see me?'

She smiled. 'Of course I am.' She kissed him impulsively.

'Come in. It's freezing! Let's go and see Father and Hermione.'

Accompanied by all four dogs, they entered the house by a back door, went up a passage and entered a large, warm, stone-flagged kitchen. Hermione and a tall, handsome man with dark, slightly greying hair got up from the table, where they had been eating pudding. Hermione greeted Sophia very warmly, kissing her.

'Heavenly azalea! You are sweet, you shouldn't have. Now at last you get to meet my husband, Tom's father.'

'How do you do,' said Lord Avondale, wreathed in smiles and holding out his hand. 'I've been longing to meet you.'

She could see the likeness between him and Thomas, but if she had not known their relationship she might have failed to do so. Lord Avondale had, like Hermione, intensely blue eyes. They were surrounded by laughter wrinkles.

'We're very rude, I'm afraid,' said Hermione. 'We've started dinner. Come and sit down and have some casserole. It's pheasant, I hope that's all right? Did you get lost?'

'Were you stuck in your horrible office?' asked Thomas. 'I told you she worked too hard,' he added for his parents' benefit.

'I did get slightly lost, but I rang to warn I'd be late. I didn't get a reply — it must have been a wrong number.'

'Oh no, we wouldn't have heard it,' said Hermione. 'Darling,' (to Lord Avondale) 'we simply must get a telephone extension in the kitchen. We never hear it, and I'm here all the time.'

'But that's the whole point,' he countered. 'You know I hate telephones. Why have them

142

where they're in the way? One in my office is quite enough. You really didn't need to ring,' he added, to Sophia. 'Do you like burgundy? I've got some rather nice stuff here which goes quite well with the pheasant.'

She found the wine delicious and was just about to tuck into the food when she felt something brush against her leg. She stiffened. Next moment something warm and furry jumped into her lap. She dropped her knife and fork.

'Whatever's the matter?' asked Thomas.

Sophia looked down apprehensively at a grey cat, which in turn looked up coolly at her. It had four white paws and a white bib. Settling down, purring, it stretched and dug its claws experimentally into Sophia's thighs, to the detriment of her expensive skirt.

'Hello, there's Alice the cat,' said Thomas benignly.

'Might it be possible to remove Alice the cat?' Sophia said through clenched teeth.

'Why? She's paying you a great compliment. Oh well, I suppose it's difficult to eat with Alice like that. Come on sweetheart, come to Uncle Thomas.' He picked the cat up from Sophia's lap and put it on his own.

Sophia felt the three Avondales looking at her. In that instant, even despite Thomas, she was as foreign as a Martian in this warm, quiet kitchen full of cats, dogs and humans who all understood and liked each other. She sat in silence, unwilling to explain that owing to her mother's hatred of mess they had never had dogs or cats at home when she was little. She recalled suddenly and with dislike a small hamster Anthea had once been allowed because there had been a craze for them in Anthea's form at school.

The Avondales quickly broke the spell. They chattered animatedly, discussing the difficulty of finding their house and praising Sophia's cleverness in only getting lost once.

'That's why we didn't wait for you to eat,' Lord Avondale said. 'We knew you'd be late. Once someone came to dinner here for the first time and only just arrived in time for the port.'

'Oh come on darling,' Hermione remonstrated, 'that was only what's his name from Beaminster. He was several cucumber sandwiches short of a picnic.'

'Well, we always have to invite people early if they haven't been before, because we know they will be late. His wife had the little moustache.'

'No, no — that was Thingy whose horse rolled on him in the point-to-point. *You* know. It was desperate. Crushed pelvis. Everyone in the county knows the way here by heart by now,' Hermione said.

'My parents like parties,' Thomas explained. 'It's open house here.'

'But we're very quiet this weekend, I'm afraid,' Lord Avondale said. 'I hope you won't be bored.'

Sophia ate, drank and listened to them, more at ease as an observer than as a participant in their conversation. Soon she began to feel overwhelmingly tired.

Thomas took her suitcase and showed her up to her room. Outside the kitchen the house felt cold; upstairs the temperature was even lower. It was a large bedroom with a high ceiling, a double bed, good antique furniture and an old-fashioned, lukewarm radiator. There was a vase of flowers on the chest of drawers.

He put the suitcase on the bed. 'The best room,' he said, putting his arms around her. 'I can't believe you're really here. Thank you for coming.' He kissed her.

She felt warm and comfortable with him despite the surrounding cold; almost instinctively she kissed him back. 'I'm glad I'm here,' she said, the strangeness of everything momentarily forgotten.

'I want to spend the night with you,' he went on. 'I want to be close to you.'

She had not dared to expect this, imagining

he must still be too unwell; cautiously she held herself back. 'Not tonight. Your father and Hermione — '

'Nothing to do with them. They never bother about things like that.'

'Give me time. Give yourself time. You aren't well yet.'

'Don't you worry about me. I'm not going to push you, I can wait.' He grinned. 'I know how prickly you are.'

In that instant she wanted him suddenly so badly that she nearly flung her arms around him, but she still held back, as if on the brink of something far bigger than anything she had ever experienced before. Without understanding the reason, she sensed strongly that she should wait. They had time, and she had to see out this first night here on her own. Quickly she unpacked her case, hanging clothes in a wardrobe that was nearly full of long dresses and mothballs. They rustled secretively in the silence as she moved their hangers to one side. Next door was a huge bathroom. The bath stood in the centre of the room on claw feet; it had enormous brass taps and a venerable rust mark. To one side was a massive washbasin and a magnificent oak chair with a high back and arms which resembled a small throne.

Suddenly feeling desperate, she tiptoed out

of her room to find a lavatory, wondering at the eccentricity of a country house bedroom and bathroom without one. Finding herself in a broad corridor, she examined with rising panic the closed doors along it; they all looked too large to open into what she sought. At last she found a little white loo up some back stairs. It was freezing there, and the loo did not appear to have been used for some time.

Back in her room, she was very dismayed to find Alice the cat lying in the middle of her bed. An irrational vision of the cat sitting on her head while she slept and suffocating her sprang into her imagination. The cat became a huge obstacle between her and her night's rest, and she was deeply, painfully tired. Having opened her door, she determinedly took hold of the counterpane and shook it to get rid of the cat. It meowed reproachfully, jumped off the bed and ran into the bathroom. Sophia crossly shut it in; then, beset by thoughts of a distressed cat and an even more distressed bathroom in the morning, she opened the door again, hoping to shoo the cat through her bedroom and out into the corridor. However, Alice was nowhere to be seen. Sophia gave up.

The sheets on her bed were heavy linen and icy cold. Sleep was impossible. She switched on her light and examined the books on the bedside table. There were a prewar book about shotgun maintenance, another on the breeding of foxhounds, an account of deer stalking in the Highlands. She also discovered *Diary of a Provincial Lady* and took it up. Half an hour later, charmed and diverted, warm and calm, she fell asleep.

12

Meowing and scratching woke Sophia up before dawn. A shock of cold attacked her as she scrambled out of bed. She ran shivering to her bathroom door and opened it. A furious Alice dashed out and across the bedroom. Sophia opened the door to the corridor a crack; Alice was gone. Sophia crawled back into her warm bed and tried to go back to sleep.

A few minutes later the radiator in her room began to clank and groan, as a faint roar from far away in the innards of the house signalled that the central heating system had just woken up. The bedroom stirred gradually to life as floorboards creaked in response to the heat seeping into the metal above them. In the corridor, a door opened and closed. A bright strip of electric light appeared beneath the bedroom door. Footsteps progressed past the bedroom, onto the main staircase and down. Dim grey daylight filtered past the drawn curtains.

Sophia consulted her travel clock; it was half past seven — later than her usual getting-up time in London, except at weekends. She realised with dismay that she wanted the loo again and that she had not brought a dressing-gown. However, a morning inspection of her bathroom brought the discovery that the throne had hinges on its seat, a basket containing several rolls of paper beside it and, high above, a chain. She ran a bath; the water was boiling to the height of about six inches, then abruptly turned freezing.

She dressed with care in black wool trousers, a warm shirt and a cashmere jumper that had been bought for the occasion. Her apprehension having been overcome by curiosity, she opened her curtains and, through the large frozen panes of her high, broad window, surveyed a big garden, walled on two sides, its magnificent lawn lined with wide flower beds. Beyond it were rolling hills. Under a heavy grey sky, everything looked extremely wintry, browns and greens blanched by frost. The black Doberman and the Labrador were pattering about the flower beds. Hermione's small, neat figure, attired in an indeterminate sludgy green outer garment and a headscarf, appeared from nowhere and shooed them off.

Sophia made her way down a broad oak staircase into a large entrance hall. It was warm, with a polished wooden floor and splendid panelling. Dark oil paintings — a still life with dead game, a hunting scene, a portrait — decorated it. It smelled very faintly of polish and pot-pourri and had, for Sophia, a freshly awakened and expectant air. She found her way to the kitchen.

Thomas's father was sitting at the table, eating bacon and eggs. Hermione was making toast at the Aga. They were both dressed for hunting in breeches, long socks, white shirts and waistcoats; Lord Avondale had imitation tiger slippers with little pink felt claws. He rose as she entered; they greeted her warmly. Thomas was not yet up. Hermione began cooking eggs and bacon for Sophia, who never normally ate breakfast.

She was just beginning to enjoy her meal with some excellent freshly made black coffee when Hermione cooed indulgently, 'There, Alice! What have you got to show me?'

'Oh really, darling,' said Lord Avondale, 'that bloody cat.'

Sophia glanced over at her little grey adversary and nearly spat out her food. Alice had in her mouth a large, dead mouse with a remarkably long, thin tail.

'You'd rather have the bloody cat than the bloody mice, Richard,' Hermione remonstrated. 'Not in here, darling,' she said to the cat. 'You've shown me, good girl, now go and eat it all up *outside*.'

Sophia stopped enjoying her eggs and bacon.

'It's the cold, you know,' Lord Avondale explained. 'Brings 'em in. I say it against myself, but that cat has her uses.'

'I think it's going to snow today,' Hermione commented.

'Not this morning. What a pity you and Tom aren't coming out with us today. I really should have thought of it. Silly of me.'

'Come out with you?' Sophia asked.

'You know, hunting. They're meeting in the next village, too. Should be a good day.'

'Tom isn't really ready,' Hermione pointed out.

'Nonsense, he wouldn't have to stay out all day. He could come home at second horses if he had to. Do him good. Never mind, he'll certainly be hunting next time you come,' he smiled at Sophia, 'and then we'll sort something out for you.'

Sophia smiled back. 'I'm afraid I don't ride.'

The Avondales looked momentarily stumped, as if the idea of someone who couldn't ride had never seriously occurred to them.

'Why don't you and Tom walk over to the meet,' Hermione suggested. 'He's meant to do some exercise every day. Perhaps you'd enjoy it?'

Sophia smiled her assent. The Avondales fussed gently about her dressing up warmly and then went out to the stable yard. Left to herself, she drank another cup of coffee and surveyed the newspapers, which were the *Daily Telegraph* and the *Racing Post*. Bella the Doberman came into the kitchen, made for the table and put her chin on Sophia's thigh. She looked appealingly up at Sophia with unblinking brown eyes. Sophia was just deciding that this animal was less unacceptable than the cat when Bella put an enormous brown forepaw, with rough pads and long claws, on her thigh. As she watched frozenly, Bella brought her other forepaw up to join its companion on her leg and rose onto her hind legs, so that she seemed to be rearing over Sophia and the remains of her breakfast. Paralysis set in. Wagging her stump, Bella licked Sophia's plate.

'Morning!' Thomas announced cheerfully. 'What's Bella up to? Come on, you evil dog.' He dragged her down. 'She's not really allowed to do that, you know. Hermione's awfully strict about not feeding them at the table.'

Sophia glared at him. 'I didn't invite her. She just climbed over me and helped herself.'

Thomas laughed. 'I can see. Just look at her paw prints on your legs! Jesus, you're a bit smart, aren't you? You really should have worn jeans.'

'I don't possess jeans.'

'Only you could possibly not ... You mustn't mind Bella. She's beyond redemption. Yob dog. Hermione rescued her when she was a puppy. One of the villagers had her and couldn't cope.' He began frying eggs and bacon. 'I can't wait to get at my art supplies.'

'Your parents suggested we should go to the meet.'

'Oh! We could, I suppose. Do you want to? What do you want to do, anyway?'

Sophia wanted to say, 'Make love.' What she did say was, 'Don't mind me, I'm very good at looking after myself.'

'But I'm longing to show you everything. It's so beautiful here.'

Well wrapped up, they went outside, and she saw that the house, which had been built two centuries ago of soft golden stone, really was beautiful. They walked around the garden, accompanied by various dogs, where he showed her the trees he used to climb as a child. Behind it were fields on the rolling hills; the Avondales farmed about three thousand acres. To the side was a stable yard with about fifteen looseboxes; they were all occupied except the two with the Avondales' first horses for hunting that morning. They saw them set off for the meet. Lord Avondale looked most impressive in a red coat. 'He used to be Master,' Thomas explained. Hermione was immaculate in black.

They fetched the art supplies from the small boot of Sophia's car and took them to a big, empty room on the top floor of the house which Thomas was to use as his studio. The cold here was peculiarly intense, but he had the use of an electric fire.

'I've had a lot of time to think,' Thomas told her. 'I've been doing some drawings, but I've been so impatient to start painting. You know, it's funny, but in a way what happened to me — with you and my heart and all that — was rather a good thing. I can't tell you how, but it's given me ideas for things.'

'What kinds of things?'

'Oh, just things I want to paint which I never thought of before,' he said vaguely. 'It's going to be a lot better than just my birds. I tell you what, I'm going to paint Allegra. Not a portrait. I never could do her before. I can now. I could really use her in a picture. I just know I can do it. It could be really good.'

'You ought to get several pictures together and have an exhibition.'

'*Exactly*. That's *exactly* what I'm going to

do. I've got a friend who knows someone with a posh gallery in Bond Street. We can fix it up. I never wanted to before, you know. I was scared. I've *got* to do it.'

Again Sophia began to feel warm and at home; talking to Thomas about his painting, she was on familiar ground. They spent the rest of the morning in this way, but the spell was broken at lunch. As they were eating bread and cheese in the kitchen, a groom came in and suggested that Thomas should ride one of his parents' fresh hunters to the place where the hunt was to change horses and hack the tired one home.

'It'll be good exercise,' Thomas decided 'and we didn't walk to the meet. Why don't you take the other hunter?'

'I don't ride. This might be difficult for you to understand, but I really don't.'

'Didn't you once tell me you had lessons when you were a child?'

'They were a nightmare. I wasn't just bad, I was the worst pupil the riding school had ever seen. I only went because Mummy forced me. She only forced me because she thought it was the done thing to have a daughter who rode.'

'But it means you've done some riding. You'll love it now you're grown up. Go on, come out with me. It's only about three miles there, and we won't even go faster than a trot. You'd really love it.'

'Oh no I wouldn't. I shall watch you get up on your horse, and I may even walk a very short way with you as you ride it, but I am not even going to touch the other horse, let alone get up on its back. I don't actually like horses very much. They are completely terrifying. Anyway I'm physically incapable and loathe and detest all forms of exercise.'

'Don't tell Father and Herm, whatever you do. They seem to like you so far.'

In the stable yard, Thomas and the groom led out the two fresh hunters. Their coats were gleaming and their manes plaited. The groom told Thomas to look out for his horse, a bright chestnut gelding which, at seventeen hands, dwarfed Hermione's mount. Lord Avondale had recently bought it as a five-year-old in Ireland, and this was its first season with hounds. It began misbehaving as soon as Thomas was in the saddle, careering around the yard in series of rabbit-hops. Thomas sat still in the saddle and impressed Sophia deeply by bringing it quickly under control. He laughed and told the groom he didn't envy his father. The groom, having told of the trouble Lord Avondale had already had with this unruly subject, got up on Hermione's mare, and the two set out at a sober walk.

Left alone, Sophia went into the house and found the drawing room, a huge, graceful, fading room. Almost every available surface was occupied by silver salvers, small bronzes of horses, cups, cut glass, photographs in silver frames and other ornaments; closer examination revealed that most of these were prizes for winning racehorses. The remains of a fire were smoking in a wide grate; tentatively she put on a couple of logs, not hoping for any result, and was surprised and gratified when they caught fire. She settled on an old chintz sofa in which the springs had more or less gone and took up some reading she had to do for the office. Outside, a few snowflakes fluttered down.

An hour or so later, Thomas and the groom reappeared on tired, sweating horses. Their legs were splashed with mud, and some of the plaits in their manes were undone. Thomas was glowing with the exercise.

'I wish I had gone hunting,' he declared.

'I thought you didn't hunt?' she enquired.

'I haven't for ages, but yes, I do. I can't tell you how exciting it is. You don't know exactly where you're going to go, you only know you've got to follow. Sometimes it's really scary, and you feel like shutting your eyes in

158

front of some of the jumps, but it's fantastic if you've got a good horse you can trust. You just sit there and go and go.'

She sighed; it sounded unimaginable. 'Just like roller-skating,' she murmured.

'What?'

'Oh, nothing. It's so sad in a way. I'll never be able to do things like that.'

'How silly! I don't see why not. Sophia?'

'What?'

'I never apologised to you for shouting at you.'

'It doesn't matter.'

'That day, when I came to see you and got angry.' He took her hand and squeezed it.

'I know.'

'I feel terribly happy with you. The only things I really want are to paint and to be with you.'

'In that order.' She smiled.

'Don't you remember me telling you artists are very selfish people?'

'Vividly.'

'I do so love it here too, of course. I hope you will too.'

'It's all rather strange to me. I've never lived in the country or known it. Your parents are terribly kind.'

'Don't worry about it. Try to relax with the animals. They're very friendly, you know. And you're fine with Father and Herm. They love everyone. They're good like that.'

They drank tea companionably in the kitchen, the cat sitting on his lap. Outside, it grew dark. The Avondales returned from hunting, bringing in blasts of fresh, cold air. They looked as tired and muddy as the first horses that Thomas and the groom had brought back earlier. Having consumed several mugs of tea, they went upstairs to hot baths, while Sophia and Thomas continued to sit in the kitchen and to talk indefatigably, mostly about Thomas's past and present life in the country.

That evening, Lord Avondale took them out to dinner in a local restaurant. 'I'm afraid it's been very dull for you, my dear,' he said to Sophia; 'just the three of us. I hope Tom's been looking after you.'

'Oh, he has,' she responded, 'and it hasn't been remotely boring. You see, this is all very new to me. I'm not familiar with the country.'

'She's a Londoner,' said Thomas.

'Well, we'll just have to convert you to the country,' Hermione said.

'I like London in small doses,' said Lord Avondale, 'but I find it gets awfully irritating after a few days. I'm too old for it. Far too many people.'

'We had a little flat in London years ago,' Hermione commented. 'It just wouldn't do, though; we were never there often enough. It never felt like home. We felt we had to go there to use it.'

'Great relief when we got rid of it,' Lord Avondale added.

'Thank you very much,' Thomas said. 'I'd have loved that flat.'

'You were one of the reasons we sold it, ghastly step-son,' Hermione explained.

'Quite right. You'd have wrecked it,' said Lord Avondale.

'Total trust, you see,' Thomas pointed out to Sophia.

'Anyhow,' Hermione followed up, 'you couldn't have done any painting there. Far too small. Whereabouts in London do you live, Sophia?'

'I have a little house on the south bank, quite near the river.'

'You'd better mind Tom in it, then,' said Lord Avondale. 'He's quite desperately untidy.'

'He wants to redecorate it,' Sophia said, smiling.

'The mind boggles,' said Hermione.

'I just want to give it a little colour,' Thomas said. 'I tell you what, though, I'm going to have a show at a grand gallery.'

'What!' exclaimed Hermione. 'No more portraits?'

'Oh, sure, enough of them to keep body and soul together. It's time for me to — I don't know — to branch out a little. Expand.'

'Well,' said his father, 'I'll drink to that.'

The rest of the conversation centred almost exclusively on horses. The Avondales not only went hunting on them but also bred them for both flat and National Hunt racing. Sophia quickly learned that they were passionately, not to say obsessively, fond of racing and was surprised to find that Thomas's knowledge and interest in the subject almost matched their own.

It was snowing heavily when they left the restaurant; fortunately, it was not late, it was only five miles from Avondale, and they were in a Range Rover. On the way back, Thomas fell soundly asleep. On their return, he was almost asleep on his feet and stumbled off to bed at once, leaving his parents and Sophia to brandy and Armagnac.

Sophia was deeply tired herself when, shortly afterwards, she went to bed. Alone in her room, she suddenly woke up. She was all alone, and she had been yearning to spend the night with Thomas for the first time. For an instant she felt like screaming. 'What a waste of a night!' she spat furiously; however, she had scarcely reopened *Diary of a Provincial Lady* when sleep claimed her.

★　★　★

Next day, when she drew the curtains, the view from her window had been transformed. Everything was white and grey, and snow was continuing to fall. Dogs' footprints already had a covering of more snow on them. She couldn't tell how deep it was.

Thomas was delighted. 'We'll go sledging,' he said. 'Do we still have the old sled?'

'Try the garden shed,' said Hermione. 'This weather is an absolute curse, we can't turn the horses out.'

'The yearlings must go out, even just for five minutes,' contradicted Lord Avondale. 'In fact they all must. They've already been in too long because of hunting yesterday.'

They all helped with the horses. Thomas sorted Sophia out, so that she found herself, much to her astonishment, dressed in old and shapeless corduroy jeans that had once belonged to Thomas's half sister, and on one end of a lead rope. The other end was attached to a head collar, which was upon the head of a large, pregnant mare. She had to lead this mare out of her stable, down a lane and through a gate; then she had to unclip

163

the lead rope and let her go. The mare seemed, as far as she was concerned, utterly neutral, walking when she walked and stopping when she stopped. She was not visibly upset by Sophia's fear, which, Sophia was convinced, travelled down lead ropes and reins into the tiny minds of all horses, causing them to misbehave in an alarming and destructive fashion. It was all so easy and reassuring that she gave the mare a light pat on the neck before she unclipped the lead rope. The performance was repeated with another equally benign mare.

Back at the stables, they quickly mucked out the vacated stables. Sophia wasn't much good at it, never having held a fork in her hands in her life. At the riding school which had been the scene of so many childhood torments, other small girls had performed this task with what had appeared to her pathetic eagerness. Now she was aware of trying to do her best to help the others, even though the groom had to take time to show her what to do. There was only one groom on a Sunday, and they needed to muck out the fifteen boxes quickly so as to get the horses back in again out of the cold. When they were finished, they went back to the fields and led in all the horses, Sophia again being responsible for the two placid mares.

Next, Thomas took the dogs, Sophia and the sled out for a walk. It was a very old wooden sled which had been in the family for decades. Thomas sailed down a steep hill on it, his scarf flying; he gave a loud yell as it bounced over a bump and crash landed at the bottom, spilling out into the deep snow. He pulled it up the hill and insisted that Sophia should have a go.

'No, really,' she protested feebly, disliking the idea.

'Go on, it's fun. It's even fun when you fall off. It's terrific snow.' He overrode her, making her sit on the sled and pushing her hard from behind. Down she slid, the snow crunching beneath the metal runners, gathering speed; she wavered, got her balance and suddenly began to enjoy the descent. The snowflakes blew in her face. The sled bounced; she sat it out, straightened it and ended her ride gently on the flat, a good way away from the bottom of the slope.

'That was fantastic!' she shouted, getting up and running towards the hill, pulling the sled. She puffed and panted her way up.

'My turn!' said Thomas, grabbing the sled.

They played like children for over an hour. The dogs ran around them, rolling joyously in the snow. They had snowball fights and knocked each other down. By lunch time they were both physically exhausted. They came in to find Hermione had cooked a Sunday roast.

'I'm so sorry,' Sophia said. 'I didn't even help.'

Hermione laughed. 'Don't worry about it. I'm no good with help. I know just where everything is; it's easier on my own. Anyway, you helped with the stables this morning.'

Lord Avondale, who knew about wine, produced a remarkable claret to drink with the roast beef. Sophia was not ignorant about wine herself, and after lunch he had great pleasure in showing her his wine cellar. Thomas, tired out after his energetic morning, went to bed for a nap.

When they had come back up from the wine cellar, they sat down to coffee in the drawing room. The fire blazed. The small dogs and Alice dozed in front of it.

'Now tell me,' Lord Avondale asked Sophia, 'is Tom really any good at what he does?'

Sophia carefully placed her tiny, ancient coffee cup and saucer in a minute space on a little table between a heavy glass urn (Winner: Molecombe Stakes Group Three, Goodwood 1981) and a bronze horse and jockey (Winner: Woodhouse Novice Steeplechase, Chepstow 1992). 'You must understand I really know very little. I do believe he's very good indeed. I know I'm biased, but there's no doubt that his portraits are first class, and they sell. I think his pictures are better than that.'

'We've been worried. Tom was always so bright, and he seemed to throw it all away. He's much the cleverest in the family, you know.' Lord Avondale's face, which had been serious, lit up with a smile. 'I came down with a fourth! Charlie never even got near Oxford. Tom really wasted his time there. I was so angry.'

'Tom didn't find it easy, though,' Hermione said.

'His mother died when he was only four.' Lord Avondale's face assumed a neutrality very much like Thomas's. 'We met' (looking at Hermione) 'when he was seven. It got better then.'

'He was an incredibly beautiful child,' Hermione said, 'and so easy to get on with. They say being a step-parent is fraught with difficulties. I never saw it myself.'

'He came a bit unstuck at Oxford,' Lord Avondale continued. 'Had a sort of break-down in his first year. Something also to do with the heart.'

'That wouldn't have helped with his degree,' Sophia observed.

'No, possibly not. He always said he could

have done better, though.'

'His life in London, though,' Hermione said. 'It seems so — well, precarious. We do worry about him, you know.' The round eyes focused on Sophia, again with a hint of the apprehension she had first seen in them.

'Thomas is a risk-taker,' said Sophia. 'His life *is* precarious. But he has no alternative; it's the way he is. He has to go it alone. He's also a very dedicated artist. In a sense he cannot give himself choices.'

Lord Avondale half smiled. 'Sounds a bit clever for me.'

'We only want him to be happy,' said Hermione.

'Seems all right at the moment,' said Lord Avondale.

'To tell you the truth,' Hermione told Sophia, 'we're dreading him going back to London.'

'I don't think he'll rush to get back. He so loves it here. You're right, Lord Avondale, he is very happy at the moment.'

'Richard.'

'Sorry?'

'Don't call me Lord Avondale. I very much hope we'll see more of you.' He smiled his son's brilliant smile.

'Thank you.' Sophia smiled back.

Presently Thomas came down. 'I don't

know if you'll get very far to London tonight,' he said to Sophia. 'I was looking out of my window just now. It's still snowing; I don't believe it's stopped. Your car's just a white mound. I bet the roads are closed. We're probably snowed in.'

Sophia's heart leaped.

'Do you remember,' said Hermione, 'when we were snowed in for three days, and the whole village went to the pub?'

'Really?' said Sophia.

'But that was years ago. It's easier now. If the worst comes to the worst, we'll be able to get you out in the Range Rover, but I'm afraid it'll only be tomorrow. It's dark now.'

Sophia thought about missing her work tomorrow. 'If they can't do without me for a day in the office,' she said, 'they're sillier than I thought. I'd love to be snowed in for three days, but I'd outstay my welcome.'

'Nonsense,' said Hermione.

'Stop us from getting bored,' said Richard. 'No hunting, no racing — we'll die of dullness.'

'I've had such a wonderful time,' said Sophia. She thought back to the things she had done with Thomas — leading the brood mares, the sledging and the snowball fights — and she felt deeply contented.

Thomas taught her to play backgammon.

She quickly picked it up and became rather irritated when Thomas, an instinctive player who was brilliant with the doubling dice, consistently scored more highly.

'Give yourself a chance, you're good for a beginner,' he said.

'I'm too numerate not to do better than that,' she complained.

'Goodness, you're competitive.'

'You can say that again.'

They dined that night off scrambled eggs on toast and spent the evening watching television in a little room next to the drawing room which contained a few more ancient, unsprung sofas and armchairs, dozens of framed photographs of winning racehorses covering the walls and a huge television set.

Sophia retired early to bed. This time, when Thomas followed her into her room, she welcomed him with open arms. When they awoke next morning, the snow on the garden was dazzling in the sun, which shone out of a clear blue sky. She and Thomas blinked in the brilliance of the light, hugged each other, kissed and surveyed the beauty of it through her bedroom window. She wondered when she had ever felt so happy.

13

Thomas spent a month in the country, convalescing. Every Friday evening, Sophia caught a train to Dorchester, where Thomas would meet her; she travelled back to London on Sunday night. She began to get fond of Avondale, the beauty of which — even in winter — was beguiling. Richard and Hermione had been well disposed to her from the start because of Thomas; for her part, she was drawn to them by their unaffected kindness and hospitality. It did not seem to matter that she did not share their passions for hunting and racing, or that they scarcely read books and were almost totally ignorant of the opera. She also learned sooner than she had expected to relax with all the animals.

However, Sophia never began to feel she could belong at Avondale. Despite the growing affection in which she and Thomas's parents held each other, she knew she was an outsider. The knowledge hardly perturbed her; she was used to it. She met Julian, Hermione's son and Thomas's best loved relation. As with Thomas's parents, she found both that she had nothing in common with him, and that she could not help liking him. Her first clash with country life came one Friday evening when she arrived to a dinner party given by Richard and Hermione. Here she met Thomas's half sister and several local people.

'That dinner put me in my place,' she told Anita the following week, when they were having supper together.

'Whatever do you mean?' asked Anita.

'People in the country! They're so unlike us.'

'Oh well,' said Anita, leaning back and looking appraisingly at Sophia over her wine glass, 'you're right, of course. Country people of that sort are incredibly clannish. You have to have been born into their society.'

'They must be pretty inbred, then. Certainly this lot didn't seem very bright.'

'You clearly make an exception for Thomas — and didn't you say you liked his parents?'

'Oh yes, I do. They've been very kind to me. You can't help liking them. As for Thomas, perhaps he's the exception that proves the rule. He's not like them.'

'I don't know him nearly as well as you do, but are you really so sure he's not like them?'

Sophia made an impatient gesture. 'Really! He's a *serious artist*.'

'I'm not saying he isn't, but I've got this

memory of him saying once he didn't like London and wanted to go back to the country.'

Sophia, shying away from this turn in the conversation, deftly changed the subject.

The only thing this country dinner had in common with a typical dinner party of Sophia's in London was that at each — owing to Richard's and Sophia's particular interest in that matter — the wines were carefully chosen and very good. Sophia always had her dinners catered and invited people whose conversation she enjoyed. She never tried to match people or to strive for a balance between the sexes; on the whole her parties were overweight on men. They were usually for six, occasionally for eight; she did not entertain more at one sitting because she felt she would not have a chance to converse properly with more than seven guests, and her dining room was too small. Hermione's dinner was for twelve; the party fitted around the enormous, ancient Avondale dining table with ease. Hermione had done most of the cooking, but the serving and clearing away were down to a couple of women from the village. The Avondales were lavish hosts; champagne was drunk before dinner, and there was a great mass of food.

The first major difference Sophia noticed was in dress.

'I felt,' she explained to Anita, 'like a beautiful swan among a lot of ugly ducklings. No, don't get me wrong. It wasn't at all a nice feeling. I was wearing a regular dress, but I stuck out like a sore thumb. They were dressed in God knows what.'

Anita snorted with laughter. 'A regular dress. God, White, I know your regular dresses. I just can't, my dear, keep up with your favourite designers. Yeah, your little London number by St Laurent must have gone down really well in the sticks.'

'It wasn't as if the label showed.'

'It didn't need to. I can just imagine all the men — *London tottie.*'

At dinner she had been flattered to find herself on Richard's right hand side; on her right was a florid middle-aged man with small twinkling eyes. He looked her up and down unambiguously and settled down for a cosy chat by asking her which part of the world she came from. On being made to realise that she was simply from London and moreover had a serious career there, he began to lose interest in her because he had no idea how to conduct a conversation with such a foreigner; however, she managed to find out from him that he was the local MFH, and with her normal professional charm she asked him so many questions about his pursuit and displayed such apparent interest in his replies that he thought she was rather sweet and had a very fine figure, even if she wasn't one of them.

More culture shock awaited Sophia when Hermione took all the women into the drawing room after dinner, leaving the men in the dining room. Sophia tried to talk to Victoria and the wife of her neighbour at dinner and found it heavy going. Both women were cold, the former owing to shyness and the latter to resentment; Sophia's exquisite dress had made its impression, and her success with the MFH had not gone unnoticed. Soon they were drawn into a different conversation and gradually abandoned Sophia, whose attempts to keep up with them weakened rapidly. She sank further and further back into the comfort of the sofa and, to begin with, listened. They talked about children's ponies, the training of gundogs and local charity fund raising.

' . . . she *won't* let us have the dance there unless half the proceeds go to the Conservatives . . . '

' . . . completely unsuitable . . . how can you expect a show pony to do a day's hunting . . . ?'

'... Pony Club meet's a surprisingly hard day ...'

'... ran a fourteen mile point, I must say I was proud of Emily ...'

'... we began training Blossom at six weeks, and it's certainly done her no harm ...'

By and by, as the depths of the sofa claimed her, the women's conversation resolved itself into a gentle, soporific hum, and by the time the men came into the drawing room she was struggling to stay awake.

She opened her eyes and smiled gratefully up at Thomas as he entered, but he was engrossed in a conversation about shooting and hardly noticed her. Victoria's husband Henry, a local farmer, sat next to her, and she woke up sufficiently to find out about his interests. He gave her exhaustive accounts of the sport they were enjoying on his land this season and decided she was very nice, charming really.

Most of the Avondales' guests had got up at least as early as Sophia; unfortunately for her, however, they had better stamina, probably because they were enjoying themselves. She was almost fainting with tiredness and boredom by 2 a.m., when they began to leave. On retreating at last to bed she woke up in anticipation of Thomas, but he, having been animated from beginning to end at dinner, fell asleep the moment his head touched the pillow.

'There are things in the country I like,' said Sophia to Anita, 'but I will never deceive myself that I could ever belong there.'

Anita shrugged. 'I shouldn't worry about the people. Can't you just enjoy the bits of the country you do like?'

Sophia grinned. 'Well, I do like Thomas. And I've even made friends with the family Doberman.'

★ ★ ★

Towards the end of that month, Thomas began to work seriously at Avondale in the cold top floor room with the little electric fire. He did a little work that pleased him, but he began to get uneasy. The last time Sophia went there, he asked her: 'Would it be all right for me to stay with you in London?'

'How very formal you sound,' she replied. 'Doesn't it go without saying?'

'You're very sweet, but I couldn't just assume . . . '

However, it was Sophia, not Thomas, who had misgivings. She told no one of this. It was due to the fact that since leaving her parents' house she had never shared any house or flat. Even when she had come, fresh from Cambridge, to London she had deliberately chosen to live on her own; she could have gone into a flat, but she had not wanted to do so; her fellow graduates led less private but more sociable lives in overcrowded, scruffy flats in Fulham and Camden Town which resounded to their laughter and parties, while she rented a tiny bed-sitter just north of Oxford Street. Soon she had saved enough money to buy a one-bedroomed flat in Battersea; then she progressed to the house in Kennington. She had never stinted on invitations to the places where she lived, even at the start; however, the idea of sharing with anyone, whether a friend or a lover, had never seriously occurred to her.

The week after Thomas had asked her if he could come to stay with her, she had a free evening which she spent alone in her house. Intending to indulge herself, she brought home no work. She had two boiled eggs for supper, caught up with correspondence and other small personal affairs and listened to an opera before going to bed early with a book.

Sitting up in her large white bed, she imagined how it might be with Thomas there. The bedroom was uncompromisingly femi-nine with white broderie anglaise cushions and blue and white curtains. She had very rarely asked anyone into it. There were always flowers on the dressing-table, which had a white lacy skirt. The wardrobe and chest of drawers were full of her clothes. She got out of bed and looked into them, wondering how they might accommodate someone else's. She wandered into her blue and white bathroom, which was, like the bedroom, spotlessly clean and feminine, with big fluffy pale towels and a discreet small green plant on a shelf by the washbasin. Such was her love of privacy that there was another, smaller bathroom attached to the seldom-used spare bedroom. She even pictured the clutter his things — his razor, his toothbrush — would make on her washbasin. The thought of these foreign objects — in the bathroom, in the bedroom, in the sitting room, right throughout the house — repelled and attracted her. Apprehension tickled the edge of her consciousness.

'Perhaps I'm really not going to be alone any more,' she said uncertainly to herself.

The evening Thomas was due to arrive found her nervously awaiting him at home, longing to see him yet obscurely dreading his invasion. She sat in her sitting room trying to read a newspaper; there was silence, no music. The room had a calm, unexpectant air, although she had filled it with arrangements of unseasonable flowers. *It doesn't know what's going to hit it,* she thought. She had white wine in the fridge (champagne had seemed over the top) and the ingredients for a luxurious but very simple meal for two people. The house was warm; she felt cold and edgy.

Time ticked by; Thomas was late. She thought his father was bringing him, the Range Rover full of art supplies and luggage. Quarter of an hour passed, a half hour and more. She was getting uneasy when a battered Land Rover drew up outside. Loud rock music spilled out of it and stopped suddenly, doors banged, there was a tremendous rat-tat at her door. She jumped up.

Thomas and his step-brother, Julian, stood outside, grinning inanely. Rain dripped onto them.

Sophia's nervous reserve melted away like a snowball in the sun. She hugged Thomas and Julian, suddenly delighted to see not only the one but also the other.

'Come in, come in and have a drink,' she urged, hustling them in out of the rain. Like large dogs, they shook raindrops onto her carpet. Although they had wiped their feet on the doormat they still left footprints.

'This cretin doesn't deserve a drink,' Thomas said, kissing Sophia. 'I'm desperately sorry we're so late. It's entirely his fault.'

'Total crap,' said Julian, removing a mildewed Barbour. 'You, Tom, are the world's worst navigator bar none. What utter, utter bliss this warm house is.' He hugged Sophia.

'Oh yeah? So why did you turn left when I said right and get us into a completely impossible one way system — with road works! — which got *even me* lost?'

Julian had crinkly hair, round blue eyes like his mother's and a broken front tooth which was evident when he smiled.

'Because normally when you say left you mean right. Honestly, Sophia, you mustn't believe him, he is the most ghastly liar.'

'Have some of this.' Sophia handed him a glass of Sancerre. 'It's rather good.'

'Oh you star. God, you're too good for him. D'you know,' he took her arm confidentially, 'he's been *hell* all the way here. I was seriously tempted to throw him out of the Land Rover.'

Thomas went up to Sophia, kissed her again and took his wine. 'You're just jealous,' he told Julian. 'You sad person.'

'Shouldn't you get your things?' said Sophia.

'God, his junk'll ruin this nice room,' Julian cackled gleefully. 'Are you sure you know what you're letting yourself in for, Sophia?'

'Um, Jules,' Thomas ventured. 'You did ring Sophia, didn't you?'

Julian grinned. He looked Sophia in the eye. 'Oops,' he said.

'You've really done it now, haven't you, Jules? You prat. You double-digit-IQ gnat-brained toss-pot. You forgot, didn't you. This is *Sophia* you're dealing with here, not some pea-brained sloanette from Gloucestershire. Sophia, don't listen to him. There's only one place for him, that's out on the streets. With luck, the rain'll turn to sleet, then snow.'

'I couldn't kip on your sofa tonight, could I?' Julian begged. 'I'll be very good. I'll try not to leave any muddy paw-marks.'

For dinner they ate pâté de foie gras and divided two fillet steaks between three; then they sent out for pizzas because Julian and Thomas were still hungry. They disposed of two bottles of Sancerre and two of claret. Sophia barely noticed as Thomas's luggage, mostly in lurid nylon holdalls tied up with bailer twine, made its appearance in her house. She welcomed the noise of chatter and laughter; the bright colours of the holdalls accentuated it. The high spirits of Thomas and Julian combined with the effects of the wine to make her feel awash with happiness.

'You see,' said Thomas drowsily, cuddling her before he went to sleep, 'we're going to be so happy here — even though it's London.'

However, Sophia was overexcited and, with her as yet unaccustomed lover in her bed, slept badly.

Julian left the next morning after Sophia, having left Thomas her spare keys, had gone to work. Thomas spent the day partly in Wapping, sorting out his materials, and partly settling down quietly in Sophia's house. She was very busy in the office and had to send her secretary out to buy more luxurious food from Leadenhall Market; she had a strange vision of doing, for the first time in her life, the sort of mundane things that people in couples did, such as driving to Sainsbury's on Saturday morning and doing a big weekly shop.

When she came home tired and late that evening, she found Thomas lying on a sofa, shoes off, in the sitting room, reading the *Sun*. Her immediate reaction on seeing him was of joy; then she heard the music emanating from her stereo and noticed that most of his luggage was still making loud colour statements in her discreetly white room.

'Good God,' she exclaimed, 'what on earth is this?'

'I just brought a few of my CDs,' Thomas said innocently.

'It's unbelievable trash,' she suddenly hissed, her temper rising out of nothing.

'Oh come on, you need lightening up. Your music is just too much. I can't believe you actually have three versions *in full* of the Ring cycle. Do you try to listen to all of them at the same time? And your books . . . Did you actually finish Gibbons' *Decline and Fall of the Roman Empire?* Oh, and I found *The World of Industrial Chemicals* . . . wonderful . . . I really must borrow that, I can hardly wait. Hey, I even discovered you have a telly, only it's behind that armchair. Clever, eh? Hiding the telly so no one suspects you occasionally stoop to watching it.'

Sophia stalked over to the CD player, kicking a bright orange haversack out of the way, and abruptly turned off the music.

'God, you're intolerant,' said Thomas.

'I can't stand it,' Sophia pointed out in a tight voice. 'It's mindless rubbish.'

'Says you. What's your problem, anyway? Get beaten up at the office?'

She ignored this and marched through to the kitchen with her Leadenhall Market bags. He followed her.

'What's for supper?' he asked. 'God, I'm a bum. I never even offered to get any, and I could have. Sorry. Mmm, this looks good.

What is it?' He took a couple of boned, stuffed quail out of a bag.

She responded stiffly in monosyllables and set about preparing the meal with a deliberate air of busyness.

'Oh come on,' said Thomas, 'let's have a drink. You wouldn't have any more of that Sancerre, would you?'

'Look in the fridge. No, not for me, thank you.'

'Oh, for Christ's sake,' said Thomas, uncorking an Australian semillon chardonnay, 'put the prickles away. What on earth's wrong with you?'

She found it impossible to explain and involved herself closely in tiny, thin green beans.

'Sophia,' said Thomas, 'will you kindly explain exactly what's going on?'

He sounded unusually stern; she turned to face him. 'If you imagine,' she said in a rush, 'that it's going to be easy to live with me you've got another think coming. I'm probably impossible. It's the way I am.'

'Hey. I thought I was meant to be the selfish one around here.'

'Besides, I've never lived with anyone before.' She began to wash some minuscule new potatoes which were already perfectly clean. Thomas poured himself some wine;

then he got another glass and gave her some as well.

'Then here's where you start. Come on, let's drink to it. Mind you,' he laughed, 'I'm a bit advanced.'

She frowned unbecomingly. 'Advanced? What d'you mean?'

'I've never pretended to be easy to live with. Anyway, here's to us.'

Her wine tasted of nothing. It suddenly occurred to her that she wanted to sit by herself and listen to Bach, who was usually very good for her when she was upset. Then she looked at Thomas. His face was open and smiling, his eyes kind and concerned. He moved close to her and put his arms around her.

He felt her stiffen and nearly let go of her in a rush of anger and disappointment; but then she clutched at him and fiercely sought his mouth with her tongue, entwining her fingers in his hair and forcing his face down on hers. Fury against her recalcitrance swept through him. He felt her teeth clash against his; there was biting; beside himself, he pinned her against a wall and tore into her clothes. He wanted to rape her, to impale her body on the wall and to beat all the evil out of her, but as their bodies crashed into each other her fever-pitch aggression at least

186

matched his own; in the next instant, he was enveloped in her and felt her contracting violently around him. He was powerless to hold back; he was drowning in her; he cried out, seized her convulsively and was lost.

They came apart and retreated a few inches. Sophia's eyes were unfocused, her mouth slack. Thomas, recovering first, straightened out his clothes, put his hands on her shoulders and kissed her smackingly on the forehead, all anger evaporated. 'Wow,' he said. 'I haven't come so quickly since I was sixteen.'

'You *bastard*,' she spat.

'Hey, we ought to have rows more often. That was the most brilliant sex. You went off like an alarm clock!'

'Oh, for Christ's sake, Thomas — ' She stopped suddenly and looked over his shoulder into the sitting room. 'Oh, God.'

'What is it?'

'We only left the curtains open.'

He looked round and then back at her. Her face had acquired an almost mundane expression of worry and irritation. Unable to stop himself, he whooped with laughter.

'Oh brilliant, marvellous,' he gasped, 'hope we gave the neighbours something to talk about.'

'Shut *up!*'

'We'll have the police around here in a minute on a rape charge . . . '

She marched over and yanked the curtains shut, forgetting the tidy string she was meant to pull for this purpose.

'D'you know,' Thomas continued, 'I've always had the most wonderful fantasies about doing it in public.'

Sophia flopped down on a sofa in an attitude of despair. 'Come on, cheer up,' said Thomas, sitting by her and putting an arm around her. 'We may not be very compatible, but at least the sex is good.'

'We aren't incompatible,' Sophia said reluctantly. 'It's my fault.'

Thomas gave an almighty stretch, yawning and extending all four limbs.

'What crap people talk,' he said.

'What d'you mean?'

'All this about being sad after sex — '

'*Post coitum omne animal triste est.*'

'There's nothing I like so much after a good bonk as a good meal. It makes me ravenous. Wouldn't it be heaven to have a little fridge by the bed, and a little oven. Just think, we'd never really have to get out of bed.'

The corners of Sophia's mouth twitched.

'Let's eat,' continued Thomas. 'Tell you what, you sit, I'll cook.' He leaped to his feet and fetched the wine. 'You've been at work and I haven't. Besides, I like cooking.' He thrust the wine glass in her hand and went through to the kitchen.

For the rest of that evening guilt over her intolerance and aggression lurked on the edge of her conscience. Thomas had forgotten all his anger and chattered brightly to her as he prepared their supper. He wouldn't let her do anything. By and by the wine made her relax, and warmth that Thomas was cooking her dinner and even clearing it all up crept over her, nearly eclipsing the guilt. She made herself overlook the fact that when he had finished clearing up there was a puddle of water on the kitchen floor, and the pans were left to dry on the draining board in a welter of suds. It worried her that she even noticed the suds.

In the days that followed Thomas found it hard to get back to work. He liked Sophia's warm house. It was easy to lie back on the sofa and watch television, read tabloid newspapers and listen to Radio One. However, he made efforts not to be doing any of these things when she returned home; it helped him that he discovered a new hobby in cooking. He bought cookery books and tried new recipes with varying degrees of success. The failures might have irritated Sophia had she also been interested in food; as it was, his efforts touched her. They gave her the unprecedented feeling that she was being looked after; she found it an unsought luxury.

After a week or so of avoiding his studio, Thomas brought home a portfolio of about twenty pictures to show Sophia. Most of them were from the period before his heart attack; three or four had been done recently in Avondale. He invaded the house with them, propping them up against sofas, chairs, walls, banisters and anything else he could find; then he awaited her return from work.

She came in and nearly tripped over the picture standing at the foot of the staircase. He just managed to save another from being assaulted by her briefcase.

'It certainly beats brightly coloured knapsacks,' Sophia commented.

'Seriously,' said Thomas, 'what do you think?' He twiddled his forelock.

'They're so beautiful,' said Sophia with some awe. 'All the colour.'

'Yeah, well, they're a contrast to your house, sure. In the same way they'll be a contrast to the gallery. Galleries tend to be pretty white too.'

'So this is what you're going to show to the gallery?'

'That's right. I thought I'd go tomorrow

— I mean, I have an appointment at eleven — provided, of course, you think they're all right.'

Sophia stepped around the pictures, entranced. 'No question. You *know* you don't need to ask me. Oh, I wish I could keep them here. They transform this place.'

'Some of them might be a bit strong.'

'They're wonderful. I love them. They're welcome here,' she paused awkwardly, then found courage, 'as you are.'

'Even though you tried to attack them just now?'

She smiled broadly. 'Even though you're ruining my carefully ordered life here.'

Next day they drank a bottle of champagne. The gallery, which was just off Bond Street, had agreed to give Thomas a show in early December.

'I'll be off to work tomorrow,' said Thomas. 'I may be some time. I just can't wait to get going again.'

However, some time turned out to be several increasingly fretful days for Sophia.

14

Alone in his studio, Thomas painted frenziedly, pausing occasionally to snatch at some food and sleeping whenever he became too tired to carry on. He forgot everything in the world except his pictures. He hardly knew how many days passed when he was painting like this. Towards the end of the fifth day or so, it came to him that he had had enough for the time being. In the past on such occasions he had launched himself on his many friends in London; now he thought only of Sophia and was desperate to see her. Abruptly he left his painting — doing the bare minimum of cleaning brushes and putting away paints — and sallied forth. On his way to Sophia's house, he bought the ingredients for dinner. He thought he would get to her house early and surprise her on her return from work with a delicious cooked dinner. He had no idea what she had been doing because he not only never contacted anyone when he was working, but also always had his telephone off the hook.

To his astonishment, she was in when he arrived shortly after six. He found her in the sitting room, and his heart leaped to see her looking beautiful in a black velvet suit with a yellow silk shirt, a little gold jewellery and more make-up than usual.

'Mmm, you look gorgeous,' Thomas said, holding his arms out to hug her. 'Don't tell me, you guessed I was coming today.'

'Thomas, how naive can you get?' Sophia exclaimed, crossly stepping back from him. 'Where have you *been* for the last God knows how many days?'

'Working,' Thomas said blankly. 'I told you I'd be some time.'

'I tried to ring you, but you were permanently engaged.'

'Didn't I tell you I never answer the phone when I'm really working? Come on, hug. It's such bliss to see you. Look what I've got for dinner.'

'But I'm going out!'

Thomas's arms dropped to his sides. Sophia would have laughed at his bewildered expression if she had not been cross. 'Oh come on,' he said. 'Can't you chuck this date? What is it, anyway? It's really early, just drinks surely. You can come back for dinner afterwards at least, you wait till you see what . . . '

'I'm going to the opera. My managing director and I are taking out an important

193

client. There's absolutely no question of chucking this date, as you put it. Business entertainment is part of my job.'

Thomas's mouth fell open. He gaped like a fish. '*Bugger*,' he said.

'Still,' said Sophia, smiling without humour, 'I must admit I have been looking forward to it. We're going to hear *Arabella*. I love Strauss.'

'Oh, sod Strauss!'

'My taxi's here. Oh, Thomas,' for a moment she looked stricken, 'why didn't you *think*?'

'I've got to see someone, I can't stand being on my own any more. Well, you don't want me, so I'll find someone who does. Am I allowed to use your telephone?'

'Whatever. I'll be pretty late. I have to have dinner after the opera.'

'I'll see if I can get Allegra,' said Thomas.

Sophia seized her coat and swept out of the house without kissing him goodbye.

Left to himself, Thomas dumped the bag of food in the kitchen and began to ring up his friends. He was frantic for company. A few minutes later, he too left the house. He just had time to catch the tail end of a drinks party. With socialite friends, he went on to dinner at a fashionable restaurant. To begin with, he drank and chatted eagerly both to people he knew and to comparative strangers, but he was petulant and out of sorts. Before dinner was over he was feeling tired and bored. Instead of going on to a night club with the party, he cried off and went back to his studio; there was an idea in his head that he suddenly had to try out in water colours.

As for Sophia, the opera followed by dinner was normally her favourite entertainment. She had been looking forward to this occasion; the client, who was the chairman of one of the biggest companies in the country, loved opera, was an erudite, interesting dinner companion and had a cordial relationship with her and her managing director. The production of Arabella was first class, but for once the great opera failed to absorb her. At dinner she felt *distraite* and had to make an effort to contribute intelligently to the conversation; she hoped she was not too obviously lacking in form. Increasingly fretful, she longed to get home to Thomas.

It was one in the morning before she turned the key in her door. Softly she called Thomas's name as she mounted the stairs to her bedroom and supposed he must be asleep when he did not reply. When she found the bed empty she almost gasped and immediately rang his studio, although she was sure he would not be there. The telephone was engaged. She went to bed and did not sleep.

The following evening he turned up again at her house just after she had returned from work. It was after eight o'clock.

'It's too bad, Thomas,' she complained. 'Can't you warn me about anything? I haven't got anything to eat, and I'm exhausted after last night. I didn't know where you were and couldn't sleep. The last thing I want to do is eat out.'

'We do have things to eat. What about the stuff I brought back last night?'

'I didn't know you'd brought anything back.'

Thomas's bag of food was still sitting on the floor in front of the fridge.

'Why didn't you put it away?' asked Sophia.

'I went out, didn't I? Why didn't *you* put it away?' He opened the fridge. 'Good God, your fridge is completely empty.'

'I don't eat much here when I'm on my own. I didn't need to go into the kitchen.'

'It's too late to cook. I'm ravenous. Where can we eat around here?'

A pub round the corner provided a meal of sorts.

'This isn't frightfully good, is it?' Thomas

commented between mouthfuls of micro-waved pie.

'It's fuel,' Sophia said indifferently.

'You'd never have come here if I hadn't turned up. What were you going to eat?'

'I told you, I wouldn't have bothered. I don't usually eat much when I'm tired.'

'Will you *stop*making me feel guilty!'

'I'm *not*. What did you do last night, anyway?' She looked at her plate as she asked.

'Went to something of some friends of Allegra.' Thomas said, twiddling his fork.

She stared at him intently; he drew back under the stare.

'Oh yes? And?'

'Rather a bore, actually.'

'What thing was it?'

'Oh, some drinks party. How was your opera?'

'All right. What happened after the drinks party?'

'Dinner. Where did you . . . ?'

'And then what?'

Thomas put down his knife and fork. 'What is this?' he asked. 'The third degree?'

Sophia, who had given up on her meal, backed off. 'Oh, forget it.'

'Yes, let's.' He stood up. 'I'm getting out of here.'

Rather later, he cuddled her in bed. The

lights were off, and they were about to go to sleep.

'Didn't have much of a dinner last night either,' he said.

'What's that?'

He tightened his arms around her. 'I just went back to the studio and did some work. I felt like it. Got bored at dinner anyway.'

She said nothing.

'Oh sweet Sophia, you didn't think I'd gone off with one of them, did you?'

'I thought nothing.' Her voice was muffled by the pillow.

'Liar.' He kissed the back of her neck through her hair. 'I so longed, you know, to get back to you. Goodnight.'

15

Thomas went back to the studio next day and tried to establish more regular working habits for Sophia's sake. His work in the wake of his creative burst was less exacting, consisting mainly of the refining and finishing of the pictures he had painted in those frenzied days; accordingly, it gave him time to think. He was mildly surprised to find his thoughts turning to Sophia and an almost involuntary consideration of things that she might appreciate, such as being consulted about plans for the evenings to come.

Previously he had lived for the moment, interspersing work with play whenever he felt like it. Play was often a party; Thomas nearly always had at any time a small stack of smart invitations, as he was still on the lists of society hostesses for the season. Shortly before meeting Sophia, he had begun to tire of débutantes and to narrow the circle of his friends. However, the younger and sillier members of society had still been able to provide him with a facile diversion if he was pushed for company and feeling, as he put it, particularly spare. The girls were almost without exception easy to seduce. During his latest excursion he had been mildly tempted by the pretty girl he had sat next to at dinner, but after a short time he had found her intolerably vapid. All her talk had been about parties and fashion; then he had found, not altogether to his surprise, that he didn't want to sleep with her because he only wanted Sophia. Society was no longer enough for Thomas; however, he saw he might have to work harder to maintain his relationship with Sophia than to keep up his position in that small, bright and brittle world.

Sophia, for her part, didn't know what to do. The day after her reconciliation with Thomas, she went as usual to the office and wondered how to plan her life for the immediate future. She had temporarily suspended her own social life since his return to London and now felt she must resume it at least in part. The thought of this slightly dismayed her; the appeal of her cerebral friends and cultured pursuits had almost overnight become hollow. More than anything she simply wanted to spend her leisure time with Thomas. It occurred to her to make herself available by simply not going out at all in case she should miss him again, but this brought painful memories of hours wasted in fruitless waiting on the telephone when she had been in the grip of one of her more spectacularly unsuccessful adolescent passions.

When he rang her up that morning to ask if she was free that evening, she was delighted. She put her shallow plans out of her head and resolved to speak to Thomas about the immediate future: there was a performance of *Die Zauberflöte* for which she had tickets. She wanted to see how he would react to it.

He was tickled by her invitation. 'I'd love to go,' he said. 'Do you know, I've never been to the opera. Allegra put me off. Someone invited her to *Siegfried* or something, she nearly died of it, she said it lasted seven hours.'

'Five, actually.'

'This thing isn't that long, is it? And then my parents! Didn't Father ever tell you they got invited to Glyndebourne, and he fell asleep and snored and apparently everyone could hear, and the people who invited them would never even *talk* to them again?'

Sophia roared — rather to her surprise — with laughter. She was constantly surprised these days at her amused reaction to Thomas. In day-to-day matters, she was beginning to find his feats of untidiness funny rather than not. Her early feelings of unease at Thomas's attempts to wash up in the kitchen had been superseded by simple laughter. There was really no other line to take. Thomas was not merely untidy, he was massively, elementally disorganised and possessed a talent for chaos which was unique in Sophia's experience. Clothes were left in puddles not only all over the bedroom and bathroom, but also over a remarkable square footage of downstairs floor and occasionally even the staircase. She nearly cut herself on the razor-blades he would leave rusting in viscous puddles of water on the side of the washbasin, and she marvelled at his ability to make soap, even her expensive, fragrant French soap, look dirty. Piles of papers, photographs, cuttings, magazines and general junk began to appear in piles in nearly all the rooms in the house. Thomas refused to throw anything away.

'My God, Sophie,' exclaimed Anita when she and Harold came over one evening for dinner, 'whatever's happened to your bijou housette?'

'I think I did,' said Thomas, grinning.

Sophia could not understand how the artistic Thomas could get by without loving music or literature. Although he professed to enjoy reading books and was actually quite well read, the vast majority of his reading matter consisted of tabloid newspapers and the sporting press. On the rare occasions that his creative drive deserted him he would watch racing, game shows or *(faute de mieux)* day-time soap operas on television, either at her house or in his studio. He quite liked classical music, but for him it was on exactly the same level as rock music or advertising jingles.

His comment on *Die Zauberflöte* was, 'I thought the scenery and costumes were terrific, and I rather liked the story even though it was totally mad, and Covent Garden is heaven, how could I not have gone before? The surtitles saved me, of course.'

'What do you mean?' asked Sophia.

'I'd have died without them. It wasn't just the music (which went on forever) but all those talkie bits — in *German* — in between the songs.'

They soon found a major difference, however: it was over Sophia's family. Thomas fretted about it and tackled her over dinner one night.

'When am I going to meet them?' he asked.

'I cannot understand,' she said, 'how you of all people could possibly want to do so.'

'Me *of all people?* What the hell d'you mean by that? They're your *family*, for Christ's sake. I've got close to you, it's natural for me to want to meet them.'

'They have absolutely nothing in common with me. I've *told* you.' She laid down her knife and fork.

'Look, I'm longing to meet them. I'm very curious, OK?'

Sophia's grey eyes were cold. 'You *know* I don't get on with them. Now let's just drop the subject.' She began to eat again.

'You sound as if you actually dislike them,' Thomas persisted. 'God, I don't like all my family that much. Victoria's a bit of a bore at times. But I don't know where I'd be without them really.'

Sophia, sensing safer ground, relaxed. 'Your family's wonderful. They're so genuine, everything one could ever wish for in a family.'

'Don't you see, they mean so much to me, how can yours not to you?'

'Oh Thomas.' She looked at him almost appealingly. 'You know how I hate to talk about it! Why do you keep on about it?'

'Because,' Thomas persisted, his voice rising, 'here I am, I'm living with you, you're a big part of my life, and it's just really hard to be kept at arm's length the whole time.'

Sophia's hands gripped the edge of the table; her eyes narrowed. 'Will you get it into your head for once and for all,' she hissed, 'that I *don't like my family*. Do. Not. Like. It has nothing to do with you. If I did like them, I'd probably introduce you. Now I don't want to talk about it any more — or ever again.'

Thomas frowned. 'The trouble with you is, I sometimes just don't know where I am with you. You're so cold sometimes.'

Sophia got up, took her plate, threw away her uneaten food, tidied up and left the kitchen. Then she sat down at her computer and worked all the rest of the evening. Thomas was almost irresistibly tempted to shake her until her teeth rattled and dithered for some time about going off in a huff to his own flat. In the end he took the television up to the bedroom and watched it in bed, since she refused to have it on in the sitting room while she was working.

This row resolved itself in the most unexpected way in late April, when Thomas was beginning to relax the pace of his work.

16

In the morning of this day in April Thomas rang Sophia up at work and announced he was not working that evening; accordingly, she bought steak, mushrooms, other vegetables and cheese for supper. She had everything prepared and was just about to sit down to await Thomas when the telephone rang.

A female voice said, 'Sophie? Hi.'

'Hello?' said Sophia uncertainly, not immediately recognising the voice.

There was a pause. Sophia felt it was a hurt pause. The voice said, subdued, 'It's Anthea.'

'Anthea.'

'Um, Sophie, look, I know it's a bit odd, but may I come and see you?'

'What, see me — God, yes, of course, I mean why not — ' Sophia gabbled. 'When?'

'Can I come right now — please?' The person talking to Sophia could not be Anthea: she sounded as if she was about to burst into tears.

'But where are you?'

'I've left home. I'm at Waterloo Station.' Anthea began to sound desperate. 'Look, please, Sophie, let me come, I'll take a taxi.'

'Of course — but what about the children, are they with you?'

'With Mum. I'll be with you in ten minutes.'

Sophia's immediate reaction was that again she was caught with only two steaks for three people. Getting pizza in had been fun with Julian; with Anthea there could be no such happy informality. Then she cursed herself for the unworthy thought and let the questions flood in: had Anthea left Andrew? Did her mother know? Would she dislike a distressed sister as much as she had the smug one in the past?

A few minutes later, she opened the front door to Anthea, who was carrying a suitcase and looking shabby. Gone was the neat, pussy-cat complacency that had always been part of her persona: this Anthea looked frayed, pale and overweight. Sophia felt instant, unaccustomed pity.

'Would you like to come in and sit down and have a drink?' she asked.

Dishevelled Anthea produced the ghost of a smile. 'Yes, please. Gin and tonic.' She dumped her suitcase on the floor, sat down on the sofa and looked around herself. Sophia went for ice, lemon and tonic, having sloshed plenty of gin into a large glass. For herself she took some white wine.

'Thanks.' Anthea took a swig at her drink. 'Gosh, you look wonderful. And your house.' She burst into tears.

Sophia jumped up, went over and sat down by her sister on the sofa. She put her arms around her. Anthea cried. In Sophia's arms she felt soft and juddery; her hair tickled Sophia's nostrils; Sophia held her gingerly, suspended between pity and sheer wonder at the unaccustomed.

Neither sister heard the key turning in the door. As Thomas walked in, he called out 'Hi!' in such a cheerful voice that Sophia and Anthea almost literally jumped. He walked into the middle of the room and stopped there, goggling at the pair. Sophia said, 'Thomas, this is my sister Anthea. She's come to stay.'

Anthea scrabbled frantically in her bag for a handkerchief, evidently embarrassed. 'Here ... please ... let me — ' Thomas started forward, drawing one of his large, bright hankies out of his jeans pocket. Anthea looked up at him gratefully through narrowed red eyes and blew her nose. 'Tha-thank you,' she gasped; Thomas's attention helped her easily to master her tears.

'There's some wine open in the fridge.' Sophia said, 'or will you get yourself something stronger?'

'Look, perhaps you two just want to talk for a bit together,' Thomas offered.

'It's all right,' Anthea said with a watery smile. 'I'm sorry about this disaster. I haven't even explained to Sophie yet. No, don't worry, I'm not going to cry again. You see, I've left Andrew.'

She gulped down some more gin and tonic.

Sophia, who still had her arm around her, said, 'Oh, Anthea. Do you want to talk about it?'

'I expect I will at some point.' She looked up at Thomas. Her eyes were large, like Sophia's; unlike her sister's, they were slightly protuberant and pale blue. 'I'm sorry, we haven't met?'

'Thomas Avondale,' said Thomas before Sophia could jump in. He smiled at Anthea and raised his glass. 'Well, here's to you, Anthea,' he said. 'I'm glad you've come here and I've met you, though I'm not glad you're so unhappy.'

Sophia said impulsively, 'Yes, you must stay as long as you like and relax as much as you can. I'll take tomorrow off — '

'No, no,' Anthea said. 'You mustn't worry about me. I've got to see a solicitor — someone in Dad's firm. The children are all right, they were meant to be staying with

209

Mum and Dad anyway. We were meant to have been on holiday.'

She turned her gaze on Thomas and gave a helpless shrug.

'I'll go and cook dinner,' said Thomas tactfully, and disappeared into the kitchen.

Anthea could no longer restrain herself from telling her story, even without the audience of Thomas. She and Andrew were to have had a long weekend — four days — away together, without the children. She had longed for this break not for months, but for years; since the children had been born they had had hardly any time alone together. Andrew had seemed content as father and husband, but Anthea felt he had become increasingly remote from her. Of course he was ambitious and worked hard; indeed he was beginning to make quite a lot of money, and last year they had moved into a large, expensive house in Wimbledon. Anthea was a good mother and a conscientious housewife; following her mother's example, she tried hard — and willingly — to be the sort of wife Andrew needed and was largely successful in this. She produced good meals and always looked groomed and pretty; as a hostess she never let him down, and she accompanied him happily to what he called 'functions' — business dinners, the occasional dance, parties of his friends and acquaintances. They made an attractive couple in their circle. She enjoyed her life in Wimbledon and had plenty of girlfriends, young women like herself.

This morning she had taken the children to her parents' house, as arranged, and had left them there; then she had gone home to prepare for the weekend. Andrew had been due to get home early from work, and they were to drive to Devon, where he had at last, after much persuading, booked them into a very good hotel. Having packed for herself, she began to do the same for him. In a zippered side pocket of his suitcase she discovered a letter on pink writing-paper which turned out to be a love letter to Andrew, only it wasn't from her.

'It was obvious it had been going on for ages,' she said, her blue eyes filling with tears. 'She even went on about how she wished they could be together more, and how she longed for him to get divorced — oh God!'

Sophia had never liked Andrew; if Anthea had been complacent, he was insufferable, the cat who had got every last drop of the best cream, and pompous with it. He was a blond, sleek young man, rather handsome in a bluff way, with small eyes; already at thirty-two he was showing signs of the heaviness which would make him a prime candidate for heart

211

disease in ten years' time. Shrewd but not especially intelligent, he had firm, very right-wing views which Sophia found boringly, depressingly predictable.

'I just can't bear the idea — ' Anthea went on, and was interrupted by the telephone. 'Sophie, please get it, will you. It's sure to be Andrew. I can't face talking to him.'

It was their mother, very much worried. Apparently Andrew had come home a short time ago and had found his clothes all laid out and the suitcase empty on his bed. Anthea had left no note; she had apparently disappeared. She had also removed the pink letter, so he could not have realised what she had found and what she might have done. He had telephoned to Mrs White, who had in turn telephoned to Edward before trying Sophia.

'Yes, she's here,' Sophia said. 'Can you hang on a minute, Mum? No, sorry, I must ask you to *hang on* — '

She turned to Anthea and whispered, 'What shall I tell her? Do you want to talk?'

Anthea hissed back, 'No! Just tell her — oh, dear, I don't know, I just don't know . . . ' she trailed off.

'Look, Mum,' Sophia said firmly, 'Anthea has had a disagreement with Andrew, and it's serious enough for her to have to cancel their break. She is very much upset and is going to stay with me for the time being.'

Mrs White's' voice squawked through the telephone receiver: 'But I don't understand. Why didn't she come home to me? What is going on?'

'I'd better have a word,' Anthea murmured, coming up to the telephone. 'Mum, hello. Are the children all right?'

Sophia heard a tinny stream of chatter down the receiver.

'I'm sorry about this muddle,' said Anthea, regaining most of her composure. 'I can't really talk about it now, Mum ... no, tomorrow, I promise. I'm really not feeling all that well. No, it's not that bad. I'll be better tomorrow ... I'll ring you then ... OK ... 'bye, then.'

She put down the receiver.

'Oh, Sophie, I'm glad I'm here with you,' she said warmly.

Sophia smiled. 'But seriously,' she said, 'why didn't you go to Mum, or Edward?'

'Because I'm closer to them, you mean? I don't know ... they wouldn't have expected it; they'd have been so shocked. Such secure lives, d'you know what I mean? All those questions; it would have been so difficult.'

'Perhaps they wouldn't understand about break-ups,' Sophia offered.

'No, they wouldn't. But you — '

'Oh yes, I know all about breaking up, even if I haven't been married.'

'What about Thomas? Are you — is he living here, or something?'

'Yes, most of the time. He's an artist. He has his own place where he has a studio, but this one is more comfortable.'

'He seems awfully nice.'

'Thank you. He is.'

Thomas chose this moment to enter the drawing room. 'Would you like something to eat?' he asked. 'I've made boeuf stroganoff. I used up some cream in the fridge and did some rice and a salad. I've opened that nice claret, Sophia.'

At dinner, Anthea drank a good deal. The more she drank, the more she talked. At the same time, she managed to eat plentifully, too. She did all her drinking, talking and eating extraordinarily fast. At first, Sophia was glad that she seemed to be unwinding and relaxing enough to tell them everything; later she realised that Anthea had not been relaxed at all. All her actions seemed to be compulsive and unnatural.

Anthea rattled on almost non-stop over coffee and a very large brandy.

'So funny, me coming to you, Sophie . . . you know, it would have been quite impossible to go to Edward and Felicity. I said that already, didn't I? Anyhow, they live together now, did you know? I suppose you never see them. We don't, not that much, they live in central London you know, but we get on quite well. She's quite sweet actually. Oh well, they wouldn't understand . . . not about Andrew and me. They're as good as married, so settled, it'd upset them too much, do you know what I mean? Bound to get married soon, just a matter of time. Andrew — I always call him Andy, did you know that? I'm the only one who does. No, I suppose that cow does, I mean that woman, you know, that one he's gone off with — no, he hasn't gone off with her, perhaps he will now, now that I've left home — anyway, as I was saying, it wouldn't have done, going to Edward and Felicity, they wouldn't know what it's like, separating, it wouldn't have done at all. Not Mum either; couldn't go to Mum. Know what I mean? Funny really. Never felt I really knew you, always so superior, but, well, I suppose you know lots more in a way than Mum and Edward, the bottom line is you're the right one to come to. You've never been married, you haven't lived with anyone, you wouldn't be so shocked, if you see what I mean. You know all about living alone . . . living alone . . . Oh God, will I have to live alone, what will I do with the kids? Don't want to live alone. Oh God, I think I've had too much to bloody drink — oh hell, I never swear, Andy doesn't like it, ladies shouldn't swear he says. Ohhh . . . '

She began to cry messily. Sophia put her arm around her again and said, 'Wouldn't you like to go to bed? Come on.'

Gently she persuaded her to come upstairs. Anthea was just sober enough to undress herself. Sophia unpacked a few necessaries for her and left her sound asleep.

'Hard drinking lady, your sister,' Thomas commented as they cleared away the supper things. 'Do you know we had three bottles of wine at dinner, and I swear you and I had less than one between us.'

'I had no idea she could put away that much,' Sophia said. 'Poor thing! I never did like Andrew.'

'We've only heard her side of it.'

'Thomas, what am I going to do? I've never known her like this. She's drinking too much.'

'Hold on, tonight could be a one-off. Though she did put away a lot — all that gin as well as the wine, and the brandy; you and I wouldn't have been on our feet. She's probably just used to drinking a bit more than we are.'

'That's just the point. Maybe she's been

216

unhappy for ages. Perhaps she didn't realise it and has begun drinking a bit too much, almost imperceptibly. I know her so little.'

'But that doesn't matter now — your not knowing her. Anyway, you didn't know she isn't happy. The thing is, you're the only one that can help her now. She won't get a lot of joy out of your brother or parents.'

'I *will* take tomorrow off. She said I mustn't, but I think I'd better spend some time with her. God knows what's going to happen. I can't think why that prat Andrew hasn't rung here. They'll have to meet. I've no idea if it'll end in divorce . . . '

'Don't guess ahead. I don't know much about this sort of thing, but I believe these things mostly don't end in divorce. They've got the children after all. Just be around, be kind, be a nice sister.'

When had she ever been a nice sister? Sophia wondered. When had she started disliking Anthea? Anthea had been a pretty child. She had also displayed — almost before she could talk — a talent for getting what she wanted — a manipulative little girl. Sophia had seldom trusted people who tried to manipulate her. Anthea had always seemed to have an easy life. Whatever she wanted, she got. On growing up, she had wanted marriage, security, Andrew. Sophia had never even admitted to herself either at the time of her sister's wedding or after that she might want marriage too; however, it had been unattainable, forever round the corner, because she had had no idea how to set about getting married. Anthea knew it all by instinct. She had set her cap at Andrew when she was only twenty-one and had got him to the altar before she was even twenty-two. Her wedding day had presented Sophia with one of the all-time lows of her whole life. She had only been twenty-four herself then and had never met anyone she had remotely wanted to marry. At the same time it had been impossible not to envy Anthea from the heart, not to feel humiliated to be the older unmarried sister at the pretty younger sister's wedding. Worse, she had not been able to quell the feeling that such a wedding was simply not for her; not for her the attentions of a loving husband, the joys of starting a new life with a beloved person. Such treats were the preserve of those who got what they wanted, like Anthea.

Notwithstanding all this, Anthea had resented her. She had never suspected it. 'You're so superior,' Anthea had said. She had not felt superior. Her academic achievements had not appeared so tremendous to her; they had been comparatively easy. Getting a man, persuading him to do what she wanted — that was so difficult as to be impossible. It had never occurred to her that Anthea might actually look up to her. She had always assumed, more or less unconsciously, that her family despised her for failing in everything in which they had succeeded. She never thought that they might admire her for her own achievements.

Next day Anthea, who was used to getting up early for the children, took a few seconds to remember where she was and what had happened. As she was rested (she had no hangover) she felt far calmer than the day before. She liked being in bed alone, and it was wonderful not to have the responsibility of the children for once. She lay in bed for a long time, thinking.

By and by she came downstairs, wearing a dressing-gown Sophia had laid out for her. Thomas had left for his studio. Sophia was alone and at a loose end; with her weekday routine of going to the office upset, she didn't know what to do with herself. There wasn't even any housework to be done, as her twice-weekly help came today. Anthea found her reading a novel in her sitting-room; she had finished the *Financial Times* and had no office work.

'Morning!' Anthea said brightly. 'That *was*

a good sleep. I must have needed that. I was so tired I can't even remember going to bed last night. Oh well, may I have a coffee, please?'

'Yes, of course, I'll just make some.'

'I was meant to be away with Andy now. But do you know, it feels good just to be here. It's such a holiday not to have the kids here, if you see what I mean. I don't know when I last lay in until nine in the morning. Heaven!'

'Oh, good. I'm so pleased. I really am. Now what shall we have for breakfast? I haven't had any yet. I was waiting for you.'

'Breakfast!' said Anthea greedily. 'I never get round to having it properly at home. I get Andy's and the kids', and then he's off to work and I have to take Camilla to school and Jamie to nursery school, and I just grab what I can, you know? I never end up having a proper meal at all, and then it's pick, pick, pick all morning, and that's how I keep putting on weight.'

Sophia made a cooked breakfast. She couldn't help noticing that sobriety in no way inhibited Anthea's flow of words.

'So when do you go off to work?' she asked Sophia over bacon and eggs.

'Oh goodness,' Sophia laughed, 'normally I'd have been at work for ages! It's nine thirty now — about an hour and a half.'

'So you have taken time off for me. Really, you shouldn't have. I'd have been fine. I'd have found where everything is for breakfast, and I'd have left everything neat and tidy. I'm really good at home, you know. Of course I have Mrs Jennings who comes in four times a week, but obviously everything has to be nice before she comes, she's there to clean, not clear up, if you see what I mean. Oh no, you wouldn't have to worry about *me* making a mess here. Definitely not.'

'What would you normally do on a weekday like this?' Sophia asked, genuinely curious.

Anthea described it to her at length — the school run shared with other mums, clearing up before Mrs Jennings, shopping, seeing a friend for coffee mid-morning (it occurred to Sophia that they probably had a few glasses of sherry as well as coffee, or was it martini they drank in Wimbledon?), lunch that she never seemed to have time for, going to the hair-dresser's, attending committee meetings for the local Conservative party, going to the tennis club in summer, sewing, knitting, fetching the children back from school, children's tea, cooking dinner for Andrew, going out to a 'function' with Andrew in the evening — all the minutiae of prosperous suburban life.

She enjoyed lingering over breakfast. Sophia made piece after piece of toast for her and refilled her coffee cup many times.

Andrew rang up during breakfast.

'I know she's with you,' he said, his voice coming across in a peculiar mixture of hurt and affront. 'I don't understand what's got into her. Can I have a word?'

Sophia, inclined to be judgmental against this disliked brother-in-law, remembered Thomas saying, 'We've only heard her side of it.' He almost certainly did have a girl friend, but he would still, after all, have no idea why Anthea, the utterly reliable, perfect wife, should do a bunk on him like this. It must have been a shock.

'I won't speak to him,' Anthea said primly.

Sophia put Andrew off as best she could. The fact that she and Andrew had always disliked each other made this difficult.

'Anthea, you're going to have to face up to him at some point,' she warned.

'I *might* — *in* my own good time. He doesn't deserve it, me just rushing back to him the moment he misses me. I haven't completely decided what to do yet. Obviously I'll ring up Mum and sort out the kids. Does he honestly think that he can get away with this?'

She went on like this for some time. Sophia

decided she had been more likeable last night, when she had been in distress. Anthea's instinct for self-preservation, getting what she wanted and being manipulative was surfacing strongly. She was going to get Andrew back all right, but on her own terms.

'Don't you think I'm right?' she demanded at last.

'Are you sure,' Sophia asked carefully, 'that it's what you want? Do you really want him back?'

Anthea paused. She frowned as this dangerous doubt crossed her mind. Then her brow cleared, and she stuck out her chin a little and said, 'Well, what's the alternative?'

Sophia did not take this as a rhetorical question.

'Start out again on your own, with the children. You'd have enough money. You don't have to live with him after what he's done to you. Do you really love him? If you don't, you should give yourself another chance. Perhaps he isn't right for you. You were awfully young when you married.'

'Be a single parent? Ugh! It's not as if I had anyone else up my sleeve. You couldn't understand, Sophie, you wouldn't know, not being a parent, that it's very difficult for a single parent — especially a mother — to find someone else, if you see what I mean. I'd never give up the kids, but I couldn't live on my *own* with them, you know?'

'I'm sure it would be hard,' Sophia warmed to her theme, 'but wouldn't it be worth it? How could you live with Andrew, if you don't really love him?'

'Oh, being married isn't just about love, you know,' said Anthea. 'Of course I was awfully upset when I discovered about Andrew and that *person*. But it's not as if it doesn't happen to other people, you know. My friend Denise had a terrible time, her husband Arthur has such a reputation. Andrew's very discreet — at least' (she frowned again) 'I'm *pretty* sure he is. The main thing is that as few people as possible should know about it. But at the end of the day, I can't not live with Andrew. I mean, I'm *married* to him. There's the house and everything — if you see what I mean. You don't just give all that up, do you?'

Sophia tried again. 'But are you sure you're really happy with Andrew?'

'*I'm* not prepared to give up things, just because *he's* done something wrong,' Anthea pointed out with immutable logic. 'I'm very angry with him, mind. Besides, it wouldn't be right to deprive the children of their father. He *is* a good father, you know? When he's home, that is. He does work very hard. I'll just have to take the rough with the smooth.'

'Are you really going to see a solicitor today?' asked Sophia.

'Mmmm . . . I don't think so,' Anthea said slowly. 'I *do* need to go to the West End to do some shopping, though. Do you think we could go together? We could have lunch. There's South Molton Street. I've always wanted to go to South Molton Street. I think I'll buy myself a nice outfit to cheer myself up, if you see what I mean. It's the least Andrew can do. If I can't have a holiday with him, I'll have one by myself. Do come. Do please say you will. It'll be ever such fun!'

She smiled appealingly at Sophia, putting her head to one side. It was a way she had. She used to do it when she was very small, an act she put on whenever she wanted something badly from someone. It had usually worked on their father.

Sophia understood exactly what was going on. Anthea didn't like doing things by herself. She preferred to have an audience. As a child she had always had friends round, impressionable small girls. Sophia imagined her at the centre of her circle of friends in Wimbledon as they drank their coffee and martinis, demanding admiration, calling attention to her status and person.

She gave in, even though she knew she

ought to go to the office where her time was far more in demand.

At last, after Anthea had indulged in a long, hot bath and had taken as much time as she liked over her hair and face, she appeared fully dressed and made up, looking every inch the old pussy-cat Anthea, well in command of herself and of every situation. She was wearing a bright, immaculate costume, the red jacket and skirt neatly pressed, the ruffled blouse spotlessly white. She mysteriously didn't look overweight today; the clothes fitted her well. Her hair was washed and curled, her make-up perfect. Her hands sparkled with the finery of rings, in particular engagement and wedding. She was ready to face the world.

Sophia was, as usual, well turned out herself, her hair shiny as ever, her clothes dark and beautifully tailored. She was a contrast to the aggressively vivid and blooming Anthea. Anthea paused before they went out and said almost wistfully, 'I do love your outfit. You are lucky, what a figure!'

Without thinking, Sophia said, 'Thomas says I ought to wear brighter colours — like that lovely suit you've got on.'

'He could be right, actually — though you look good in dark things,' Anthea said as they walked away from the house. 'I did like him,' she added.

Sophia smiled.

'How long have you known him?'

'Some ten months. We met before last Christmas.'

'And you never told any of us! You *are* a dark horse.'

'Oh, don't tell Mum or Dad or Edward yet, please,' Sophia urged with some anxiety.

'Why ever not? I mean, he really is super, isn't he? Ever such romantic looks. How did you meet him? Where's he from?'

'At a dinner party. Dorset.'

'*Dorset!* I don't think we know anyone from there.'

'Neither did I, until I met his parents.'

Anthea leaped on this. 'You've actually met his parents! Well, really, I do think you ought to bring him home, you know? It isn't right, surely. Mum and Dad ought to meet him. It isn't fair. You must be really involved with him.'

Sophia said distantly, 'I should rather you didn't mention Thomas to them until I do so.'

'Oh, all right,' Anthea grumbled.

'Oh, I won't leave it forever.'

They went by tube to Leicester Square, changed and went on to Bond Street. Anthea tried to chatter above the roar of the underground trains and gave up. Out on

Oxford Street, she began again.

'Andy's not going to get away with this,' she repeated with satisfaction. 'I'm going to insist on twin beds.'

'*What?*' said Sophia, not sure if she had heard right.

'Now I won't have to sleep with him, and I'll have a good excuse,' Anthea went on.

'But you *can't*,' Sophia protested. 'That's a terrible thing to do. He may go off again . . . '

'Oh no he won't. I'm definitely not going to let him get away with it, you know. You don't have the first clue about marriage, Sophie. Heaps of people — well, stray, if you see what I mean. It's not the end of the world. Not that *I* ever have, of course. I've never wanted to go all the way. I couldn't be bothered with all that going to bed, and Andy gets jealous if I just *talk* to someone. It's rather good, that. It means he can't take me for granted. But now — ! So funny, last night I was all upset, today I'm just really angry.'

She grinned. Then she was diverted by a shop window, and she had to go into the shop and spend a long time trying on clothes and eliciting Sophia's opinion.

Sophia soon got painfully bored. She felt she had outlived her usefulness for Anthea. It was sad to admit, but Anthea had been more likeable when she had been unhappy last night, even when she had got drunk. Now she was beginning to think that if marriage was all Anthea said it was, she would happily remain a spinster for ever.

Anthea dipped and swooped into the shops, every now and again emerging with paper bags containing articles of clothing or accessories. When she had spent about eight hundred pounds, she stopped.

'That's what Andy would have spent on this weekend,' she explained.

She insisted on taking Sophia to lunch. They found a bistro, where Anthea wanted a three-course meal with wine. After they had ordered, Sophia felt trapped and fretful. She wondered how she could put up with any more of Anthea. The wine came and loosened her tongue a little.

She became strict and elder-sisterly. 'Your proposed behaviour towards Andrew sounds quite disastrous to me,' she began. 'Surely you ought to ask yourself why he went off with that girl, and try and make things better. Not sleeping with him will only send him away. It's just using him. You can't love him very much. I think what you want to do is very wrong.'

'Well!' said Anthea, leaning back and raising her eyebrows. 'I must say, Sophie, for someone who doesn't know the first thing about marriage you're taking a very moral tone. I do think that's a bit thick, coming from you. You aren't exactly whiter than white, are you?'

'I'm not going to argue,' Sophia said wearily. 'You will never in a thousand years understand my viewpoint, nor I yours.'

'No, well, I do think you might mind your own business, then.'

'Good heavens, you've rather made it my business, haven't you? The last thing I ever wanted to know was the details of your projected sex life — or lack of it — with your husband. I'm amazed you can even talk about these things.'

'Ohh . . . *come on*, Sophie,' said Anthea appealingly. 'Don't be so grumpy. Don't you think I'm being brave? Most girls I know would just go to pieces in my position, you know? You *are* unfair.'

'But why stay on with Andrew, if you don't like him?'

'I never said I didn't like him. And why break up my home and cause me a lot of grief for something *he's* done?'

'Oh well, we'll have to agree to disagree.'

Anthea, who was enjoying her lunch too much to want to fight, changed the subject. 'Tell me more about Thomas. Will you get married?'

'Good heavens — I never thought about it,' said Sophia, stony-faced.

'*I* would have. He's far too good to let go.'

'Really, it's not a point of letting him go or not.'

'Hasn't he asked you then?'

'Look here, it's not all that important to us. Do you understand? He's a successful artist, I have my own career, we don't need this. That's the end of it.'

'Well,' said Anthea, twirling spaghetti into a spoon, 'he's certainly the most serious boyfriend *you*'ve ever had.'

'Maybe.'

'Oh, don't be *cross*.' Her head went to one side. 'I'm only curious because I liked him so much. He's ever so nice.'

'Thank you.' Sophia's voice softened perceptibly. 'What are you going to do after lunch?'

'Oh please — ' Anthea turned on her persuasive skills, 'may I stay another night with you? It's so lovely to have all this space to myself, if you see what I mean. I wouldn't be a nuisance, honestly. You could give me your key, and I'd go back to your house and you could go to work for the afternoon — though I wouldn't if I were you, you know! — and would you mind dreadfully?'

'When are you planning to go home?'

'Oh, don't *worry*.' Anthea rolled her eyes and pouted. 'I'm not about to desert my kids. Anyway, they'll be all right, they were expecting me to be away for four days, weren't they? Just one more little night, it's not too much to ask, is it?'

'No, of course not. I'll let Thomas know. I don't know what his plans are. We might have dinner out somewhere. I'll think of something.'

Anthea clasped her hands theatrically. 'Oh, that would be *lovely*. I do hope Thomas comes.'

After lunch, Sophia escaped to her office. Anthea went back to the little house in Kennington and spent the afternoon reading a Mills & Boon novel. That evening, Sophia enlisted Thomas, and they took Anthea out to a restaurant in Covent Garden which she thought would amuse Anthea. Anthea ate and drank as if she had been starving, oblivious of the large lunch she had downed a few hours earlier. She flirted unashamedly with Thomas and succeeded in irritating her sister nearly — but not quite — to screaming point.

'*God!*' Sophia whispered to Thomas in bed that night. 'I deserve a medal.'

'Oh come on, she was quite sweet really.'

'She didn't get disgustingly drunk, you mean. Thank heaven for that small mercy.

Unfortunately this just meant she had all her wits about her — all two of them, she's not got many — and she applied them as she always has, flirting.'

'Oh darling, you're such a bitch, you know.'

'You'd have been a bitch if you'd grown up with her. Do you realise she hardly spoke to me all evening and addressed herself almost exclusively to you? I really thought her eyes would pop right out of her head at one point. No wonder that husband of hers gets jealous — though he's a bastard, too.'

Thomas ruffled her hair. 'Flirting's all right. I think it's fun.'

She turned away from him. 'You should know me better than that.'

Silence.

'You must understand now,' said Sophia eventually in a muffled voice, 'why I don't want to introduce you to my family.'

'At least your parents . . .'

She turned to lie flat on her back, so that she was staring up at the ceiling. 'Whose daughter do you think Anthea is? Believe me, there's a lot of them in her, and extraordinarily little in me. When I was little I sometimes thought the leprechauns had brought me. Thomas, for once and for all, I don't get on with them. You've seen what she's like, you've got to understand why.'

'Just don't leave me out of things, OK?' He put his arms around her. 'You know I love you. I want to know you love me.'

She kissed him; they went to sleep.

17

Around this time Allegra, answering the call of spring, fell in love. They met for a drink in a remorselessly fashionable bar, recently opened in Soho, to catch up with each other's news.

It was a fine evening, and the bar, which was illuminated with orange and red lights and had black walls and furniture, seemed unnaturally dark. Allegra's pale hair gleamed orange and pink. Thomas and Allegra had large, babyish cocktails with straws and little paper umbrellas, and persuaded Sophia to have one too.

'You've got a new victim,' Thomas said to her. 'Don't you dare pretend you haven't, I know you too well.'

Allegra tossed her head in a sparkle of red and orange. 'Rat. He's not a victim.'

'Go on, petal, tell us who he is, then. Who's the lucky man?'

'Shut up. I'll tell Sophia, not you. Come here, Sophia — '

'You can't do that, it's rude to whisper.'

'Well, he's no one *you* know.'

Allegra's victim turned out to be an

immensely rich but slightly enigmatic American born of an Armenian immigrant and the daughter of an English duke. He was nearly twice Allegra's age and already divorced; there was a teenage son who lived in New York. Sophia had heard of him because he was famous in international financial circles for buying and selling companies. As a young man he had begun his fortune in the futures markets.

Thomas and Sophia discussed Allegra and the victim, whose name was Emil Edilian, with interest.

'I think she's absolutely hooked this time,' said Thomas.

'She never struck me as the sort that would go for money,' said Sophia.

'She's not. She's worth quite a bit herself. Oh no, this guy's something else — different from all the people she knows here. She's twenty-six, time to settle down.'

'You'd have thought she'd have found a nice English landowner by now.'

'Too mundane. She'll probably marry this Emil.'

'You can't tell that.'

'Oh yes I can. If Allegra wants something badly enough, she always gets it.'

'Just like my awful sister. But why,' Sophia frowned, 'do I not mind Allegra? I even quite like her.'

'You don't know her nearly as well as Anthea. You haven't had to live with her.'

'Yes, obviously, but I usually shy away from the type. I can recognise it so easily. I suppose it's that Allegra's generous. Anthea isn't. Allegra really seems to like people.'

A few days later, Allegra invited Sophia and Thomas to come racing at Newmarket on the Saturday of the Guineas meeting. Emil, who not only owned racehorses but also had one good enough to have a live chance in the 2000 Guineas, had a box at Newmarket to which he was inviting a large party; he let Allegra have a few of her own friends. Allegra asked Thomas and Sophia because Thomas was an old friend who was very fond of racing, while Sophia would be sure to have something in common with Emil.

The 2000 Guineas Saturday was one of those rare, near perfect spring days. Both Thomas and Sophia rejoiced to be leaving London for the day and drove to Newmarket in her little car with its sun roof open for the first time that year. Because Sophia was a stickler for punctuality, they arrived slightly too early.

'We can't possibly go up yet,' Thomas said.

'Are you really sure I shouldn't have worn a hat?' Sophia asked. She was feeling a little unsure of herself, never having attended a race meeting in her life.

'I told you it was optional. You look absolutely fine.'

'Come on, let's find this box of Emil's. This place is huge.'

'No. Let's explore. No, we don't need race cards. They'll have them in the box. I'll buy a Timeform.' (He bought a form guide.) 'Oh! look, Emil's horse is third top rated.'

'What on earth do you mean? This is foreign territory to me.'

'You haven't lived. Come on, I'll show you round. Here's where they saddle the horses . . . this is the parade ring . . . did I ever tell you about Father and Hermione's Guineas filly?'

They managed not to be the first to arrive at Emil's box, where a waitress in uniform offered them champagne. Allegra introduced her to Emil.

'Emil thinks all my friends are silly, like me,' she chattered, 'so I'm going to prove him wrong with you.'

Sophia was quite touched that Allegra considered her to be among her friends.

Emil was ageless, a dark, handsome man with surprising green eyes and thick, smooth black hair. His origins were masked by a transatlantic accent of utter neutrality. His eyes gave the impression that he stared and that he was mesmerised by every word spoken to him. Sophia was reminded of Bagheera in the *Jungle Book*. She decided deliberately not to talk to him about business.

'Are you nervous about having a runner in the 2000 Guineas?' she asked.

Emil smiled, a proper smile that reached his eyes and Sophia, reassuring her. 'Yes, more nervous than about anything.'

They began a conversation about Emil's horse which she was enjoying when more guests came. She had to move on to other people as Emil fulfilled his duties as a host. The party consisted mostly of serious racing people — a couple of major Newmarket trainers, the proprietor of a stud, other racehorse owners — and younger people, all friends of Allegra's, bright, upper class and a little vapid.

Just before they sat down to lunch, someone introduced her to the last couple to arrive. Happy and relaxed from the champagne, she smiled into two unsmiling faces.

'Rupert and Lavinia Kingsley,' said the man introducing them.

For a split second, the brightness of the surroundings, the women's hats and clothes, the sunshine pouring in over the balcony and through the open glass doors vanished. All the colours faded. The sunshine became mere pallor. Kingsley himself was dark and infinitely menacing. In that frantic moment he brought to Sophia an echo of that deep revulsion she had experienced in the night of her solitude.

She paled very slightly, and as she caught her breath the colours and the sunshine slipped back into focus. Automatically she said, 'How do you do' and held out her hand to be shaken. She focused first on Lavinia Kingsley. The woman had huge dark blue, empty eyes; she was ash blonde and as beautiful as Sophia remembered. If she had not looked so vacuous Sophia would have thought she was simply bored. She shook Sophia's hand limply and looked through and past her, barely managing to force her mouth into a polite smile which would not threaten her unlined skin with the ghosts of wrinkles.

Almost instinctively, Sophia drew back from shaking hands with Kingsley. His eyes were like flints. She hesitated. She opened her mouth to say something and shut it again; encouraged by the champagne, she smiled; as she waited for Kingsley to take the initiative she looked at him. For the first time she noticed how cold he appeared. There was no doubt he was good looking; in his way he was far more handsome than Thomas; however, his lips were dreadfully thin. There was a mean-spiritedness about him she had never seen before. Her smile broadened and became radiant.

Why, those two are a match for each other, she thought. Lavinia gazed past her left shoulder.

'Please excuse me,' she said to Sophia, 'but I simply must say hello to an old friend.' She brushed past Sophia, making for a very grand old lady, the wife of a venerable (and again seriously rich) peer who was famous chiefly for having over sixty horses in training.

Kingsley began to say something to Sophia. She looked again into his eyes and deliberately cut him dead, moving past him towards Thomas.

'Wonderful mixed bag of guests here,' she murmured to him. She took his arm, more grateful at that moment for the familiar and much loved feel of him than he could know.

'You can say that again. That ash blonde you were introduced just now, it's not Lavinia Kingsley, is it?'

'That's the one.'

'Well well. Allegra's mama knows her. I wonder if that's why she's here? No, it can't be. *He* must be someone of Emil's. She's got a bit of history, has Lavinia.'

'No! Do tell.'

'It's not so much her, it's him. He's some frightful banker. He's said to play away from home a lot.'

'Go on.'

'Oh, I don't know much. Evil gossip, you know. He must be mad; she's gorgeous.'

'Cold fish, if you ask me.'

'*Claws*. You women are amazing.'

Twenty-four of them sat down to lunch at three tables; the party was highly organised, so place cards had been set. Emil sat between the venerable peeress and Lavinia Kingsley. Sophia had a moment's dread that Allegra and Emil, supposing that they would have the City in common, would seat her next to Rupert Kingsley. She was grateful to find herself between one of Allegra's decorative young men and the stud owner. She applied her usual chat-up lines for industrialists to the stud owner and soon discovered there was a whole world of horse-breeding, the existence of which she had never suspected.

The sun seemed to intensify; outside it grew very warm. Chatting to her neighbours at lunch, Sophia felt radiant. When the racing began, she was active, trotting to the parade ring from the box, to the Tote and back to the box again. She betted on the horses whose appearance caught her eye; she had beginner's luck and backed an outsider to win in the second race. When Emil's horse came second in the Classic, out-performing expectations but just failing to snatch victory, she eagerly joined the cheers and commiseration in the winner's enclosure. Rupert Kingsley had slipped quite out of her focus, having been reduced to a thin-lipped non-entity.

'You've been extra happy today,' Thomas commented as they were driving home.

'Why, didn't you enjoy it too?'

'Of course I did, I absolutely loved it. You know racing is food and drink to me. But I've never seen you quite like this. You seemed to glow . . . '

Sophia smiled but looked straight at the road ahead, feeling and not seeing Thomas's eyes on her.

'I had the most wonderful, wonderful time,' she said. 'Oh, Thomas . . . '

'What?'

'Nothing. You're right. I am feeling good.'

It was on the tip of her tongue to tell him she loved him, but she still lacked the confidence.

18

As spring turned to summer, Thomas got through the burst of post-convalescent creativity and slowed down. He worked more steadily, carrying on with his bread-and-butter portraits as well as with pictures for the exhibition; he spent fewer and fewer nights at his studio. However, his were seven day weeks; except for their day out at Newmarket, they never left London at weekends.

One early June evening he asked her to come to the studio, as he was ready to show her what he had done so far for the exhibition.

Sophia had not visited the studio since before Thomas's heart attack. Now, in the long summer evening, it was bathed in light she had not seen there before; the evening sun shone through huge, dusty windows. Thomas showed her an oil painting propped against a wall.

'Look!' he said. 'One of the dread birds.'

The bird was flying to the sun. It had brilliant plumage tipped with the sun's gold, but what was more striking was the movement in the picture. The bird seemed to be moving incredibly quickly, and it almost appeared as if the sun — an incandescent source of light in the top right hand corner of the canvas — was pulling it towards itself and accelerating its flight.

'Why do I like that?' Sophia mused. 'I hated your other birds.'

'I told you they were just experiments. This is the real thing.'

'What do you mean? What is the real thing?'

'Christ, I don't know. That's up to you, isn't it?'

'It's the light again, of course. You know, it's odd, but I get the feeling this bird is going to be killed by the sun, yet it can't help going there, and it also actually wants to go there. Did you think that when you painted it?'

Thomas grinned. 'Doesn't matter what I thought, does it? All I know is I *had* to paint that picture, and it had to be just like that, not any other way. Look, here's another. Birds in the sun.'

It was a brilliant, intense white and yellow haze — a mingling of air and fire — with the suggestions of bird shapes at its heart. Like the first bird painting, it was in oil; the paint had been thickly applied, but the effect was nevertheless of lightness as well as light.

'Birds in heaven,' said Sophia. 'Perhaps this is what happens to them when they reach the sun. Not death, but transformation.'

'Don't ask me; I don't know about all that clever stuff.'

There was a portrait of Allegra. 'She doesn't know I've done it; she didn't sit for me. I did it from photos and memory and imagination. I suppose I'll have to sort of ask her permission to have it at the show.' It was of her, head flung back, the sun in her hair. The likeness was true and unmistakable. In her laughing face he had captured her joie de vivre and generosity as well as her evanescent butterfly quality. There was more to her than just flightiness.

Most of the work was not from life but purely from imagination. The landscapes were dream landscapes, peopled by dream people; Dorset and Allegra may have been their respective starting points, but they suggested different worlds. Sophia sought for the right words to describe them.

'Pictorial myths,' she said at last.

'Do you like them?'

'Oh yes. I probably like them more than anything else you've done so far. I can't say now exactly why I like them, or how.'

'Don't. Let them be. I'm glad you like

them. I want to paint a picture of the Annunciation.'

'*Annunciation?*' Sophia started in amazement. 'Why? You're not interested in religious things . . . '

'I just like the idea, that's all. I'd love to do an angel. It'd be one up from my birds. Logical, isn't it? It'd be a huge canvas — huge for me, anyway. Biggest thing I've done. I've done some sketches. I'll show you one day, not now.'

* * *

They embarked on a period of peace and happiness. Each worked hard, but not too hard. Sophia had some business trips abroad. Sometimes she wondered what the next step was for her from being the head of research, but the question lacked urgency. Thomas attended and rejoiced in Royal Ascot with his parents, who had a runner there. They saw their friends and visited the theatre, opera and restaurants. Sophia had no more contact with Anthea or anyone else in her family, and Thomas did not press her on this point.

One day Thomas said to Sophia, 'I need a break. I miss Avondale. Can you take two weeks off?'

'I was thinking of going to Bayreuth, but just for a week.'

'Bit of a weird place, isn't it? Aren't they bombing it, or have they stopped there? The Palestinians — '

'*Bayreuth*, not Beirut. I always go. I didn't really think you'd like it.'

'I was just wondering if you'd like to crash out at Avondale for two weeks in August. Father and Herm always go to Scotland for the twelfth, and then after a few days of that they come down to York for the racing and stay with some friends there. They'd love us to house sit. We'd have it to ourselves. It'd be heaven.'

Sophia looked at him and smiled. 'Can I miss my Wagner?'

'Do you want to ruin my life? I'll be really bored at Avondale on my own.'

'Rubbish. The family. Not Richard and Hermione, but the children. Charles and Victoria and Jules and everyone.'

'The children will all be at Pony Club camp. Victoria does that. Jules is also going to Scotland — different party to Father's — and there won't be anyone around.'

'So just you and me?'

'Just us.'

'Do you know it will be the first time for

eight years that I shall have missed a Bayreuth?'

Normally Sophia always took two weeks off in August to attend the opera festivals at Salzburg and Bayreuth. It was the only holiday excursion on which she seldom felt lonely, because many of her fellow opera-goers, at Bayreuth especially, were also alone. She had, over the years, made tentative friendships with some of them. This year she had obtained her tickets, but had made no arrangements to travel, dithering uncharac-teristically because of Thomas. The idea of spending two weeks' holiday with him was entrancing. She had never been on a holiday with anyone else since she had stopped going away with her family.

Latterly she had found the need to take time off irksome. Except for the trips to Bayreuth and Salzburg, she disliked travelling for leisure by herself because all her fellow travellers seemed to be in couples. Even the unattached went with friends of the same sex. Occasionally she made friends with people on holiday and thus overcame the daily ignominy of dining alone; for the most part, she read hugely and went to bed early. Her preferred destinations were Aladdin's caves of culture such as Florence and Rome. Venice had nearly broken her heart. The thought of lying on a beach was anathema to her.

Sophia's seniority in the firm ensured that she could always take time off whenever she wanted; it was not as if she had ever had her full entitlement to holidays each year. She thought it might give her a wrench to send back her Bayreuth tickets, but when she had done so she felt strangely happy about it. For the first time in her life she was going on holiday with someone with whom she was in love.

19

They drove down on a Saturday morning, not wanting to get stuck in the summer nightmare of traffic leaving London on Friday evening. It was the first time Sophia had returned to Avondale by car since her first visit in January. In the light, and with Thomas by her, the journey was effortless.

As they came up the drive to the golden house, she exclaimed, with a shock of recognition, 'It's like coming home!'

'It *is* coming home,' said Thomas.

It was indeed a home-coming, but she had never seen Avondale in the light of such sun, surrounded by green trees and lawns and the bright soft pastel flowers of English summer. As before, the dogs rushed out to greet them, but now they were old friends, especially Bella.

Hermione and Richard spent the Saturday night at Avondale before setting off early in the morning on the first leg of their two-day trip to Sutherland. They left copious instructions, but in their absence Avondale was always run perfectly capably by the grooms, the gardener and the housekeeper. Thomas and Sophia hugged and kissed them before they drove away and waved them away from the gate until they could no longer see them.

Thomas put his arms around Sophia.

'We're all alone,' he said. 'It's all our very own for two whole weeks.'

'Nothing to do but enjoy ourselves,' said Sophia.

As before, they explored the place, but now it was changed by summer. The house smelt of flowers from the garden. Outside, the colours had turned from dark gold and iron-grey to bright gold and green. The placid brood mares that Sophia had helped lead out in winter now had foals, seven in total. The dogs were also increased in number by the addition of two delinquent hound puppies who were on walk. There was a small lake, hitherto unknown to Sophia, near a covert between two of the fields; here the Avondale children had always swum in summer, and there was even a rope still hanging from a branch over the water from which they used to jump into the deepest water.

Sophia was unexpectedly entranced by one of the foals. The smallest and last-born of the seven, a May filly, it was dark bay with a large round star on its forehead; she thought it the prettiest. Less wild for some reason than the other six, it would let Sophia pat and stroke it, and it had a way of licking her hand. Harry, the stud groom, expressed his doubts about it, pointing out that it was too small for its breed and weaker than the rest.

Sophia would spend time in the field simply watching this foal. The other, bigger foals did not greatly concern her. For her it chased butterflies, rearing and striking at them with its little forefeet, occasionally emitting in its exuberance a young, high-pitched squeal; it galloped teasing round its dam, wheeling and abruptly stopping; it crouched and lowered its head through impossibly bent forelegs in attempts to eat grass before giving up and suckling, its small starred head tucked under its dam. In her minutes of entrancement Sophia forgot nearly everything else in the world; seldom had she ever relaxed so completely.

However, after two days this idyll came to an abrupt halt. Thomas and Sophia found the mare with the foal in the stable one morning instead of in the big field with the rest. The vet was there. The foal seemed to have shrunk overnight; its eyes were half closed, its coat dull, its breathing laboured. Gastroenteritis was diagnosed. They gave the foal an injection in the neck and some pink medicine which they squirted into its mouth through a syringe.

That evening, it was worse. The vet reappeared. With the help of two of the grooms, he put it on drips for water, feed and medicine. When Sophia came to see what was going on, she found plastic tubes spouting grotesquely from the foal's neck and one of its nostrils. It was standing swaying, its head lowered. The dam seemed to have lost interest.

'What's that noise?' Sophia asked in a low voice. 'Sort of chewing?'

'That's the foal grinding its teeth,' explained the vet. 'It's in pain.'

The vet and the groom between them carefully fed water to the foal through the tube of the nasal drip. 'This is the last chance,' said the vet. 'If it doesn't pull through tonight I'm sorry, but we'll have to consider putting it down. I've seen them get better from there, though. Don't give up hope.'

Thomas and Sophia had an unusually gloomy supper.

'That foal,' said Sophia. 'I can't get over it.'

'I understand,' said Thomas. He touched her hand.

'You must do. I've never felt this about an animal. It was in such pain.'

'I know.'

'And it couldn't *say* anything. A human

would protest and try to get away from the pain, but it can't. It just has to suffer.'

Thomas stroked her face in an intimate gesture. 'Don't fret about it. I know it's hard. It's had a wonderful life so far. It's wanted for nothing. Everything possible's been done.'

They were up unusually early the next day. They went to the stables before thinking about breakfast. Bella the Doberman came with them, but when they reached the foal's stable Bella whined and sloped off.

The mare was no longer in the stable. The foal was lying down, eyes closed, its ribs pumping for breath. Harry was sitting in the bedding at its head.

'The vet's on the way,' he said in a low voice.

A car drew up in the yard, crunching on the gravel. Sophia found her eyes filling with tears and realised that Harry and Thomas were looking unnaturally solemn, being close to tears themselves. Gently and quickly the vet explained how he was to inject the foal to put it down, pointing out that the injection would not hurt it. Sophia was grateful for his consideration; Harry and probably Thomas would have known this.

'There,' said the vet a few seconds after the injection. 'She's gone.'

Sophia astounded herself by retreating

quickly to the kitchen, shutting the door and stuffing paper towels into her eyes as she shook with tears.

Both halves of the stable door were shut. Harry went to ring the hunt kennels to collect the corpse; then he joined Thomas, Sophia and the vet for some coffee and breakfast.

'It's mad,' Sophia said later to Thomas, 'but I did love that foal.' They were walking thoughtfully around the garden.

'It's such a *bastard* when they die like that,' Thomas said gloomily, kicking at Hermione's lawn.

'You know me, I never cry. Look at me. I could cry now.'

'We're tremendous criers in this family. D'you know, if I wanted to make myself cry right now I'd just think of the foal, or remember when Barney was put down. He was my Labrador. He was fifteen, and so was I.'

'I only cry when I go to the opera.'

'Oh, I understand all about that. You should have seen me when I went to Chartres cathedral for the first time. It was so staggering, all that blueness in the windows, and that tremendous building. It floored me. I wasn't sad or anything, just . . . Oh, it was awesome! The tears just came, I couldn't stop them.'

'God, you're soft. I do understand, though.'

'You aren't soft. You're hard as nails.'

Sophia began to smile. 'Don't you tell me I'm hard!' They reached a field where they found the dead foal's dam together with two other mares which had not had foals this year.

'Look at her,' said Thomas. 'You'd think she didn't give a stuff.'

'She does seem a bit unconcerned.'

'The milk just dries up. She's got her own life to get on with.'

To cheer themselves up and for distraction, Thomas and Sophia took advantage of the hot, sunny weather by driving to the coast, which was only about five miles away, and spending some hours on the beach. They took a picnic and swam in the sea and read as they sunbathed.

★　★　★

In the succeeding days, they experienced the best of an English summer. The sun rose every morning in a cloudless sky, and during each radiant day there was always just enough breeze to prevent the air from getting too hot. They saw no one and indulged themselves. They took to having drinks and meals out of doors. Every evening they would sit in supremely comfortable old cane chairs which were upholstered with sun faded cushions, and drink a bottle of white wine. The dogs lay on the lawn by them, and in the distance, beyond the bottom of the garden, they could sometimes see indolent horses standing nose to tail near the fence, their tails swishing gently. The setting sun sent golden stripes through the evening shadows on the lawn and glinted on the backs of the horses.

'You know when we first met?' Sophia said one evening before dinner, when they were enjoying a splendid bottle of Sancerre. 'You were working on Claire's portrait, and you didn't ring and didn't ring. I was beside myself.'

'Oh, were you?' said Thomas. 'I'm so sorry. I had no idea, then, you would have taken it so to heart.'

'It was worse than you think,' she said with a smile. 'You see, I actually thought I was pregnant!'

Thomas sat up. 'You *weren't*, were you?'

'Good God, no! As if I would be!'

'Really, Sophia, you make yourself sound as if you weren't like other women. Women do get pregnant, you know. It's quite usual.'

'Yes, well, maybe, but you can't imagine *me* pregnant, can you?'

He leaned over and touched her face,

inclining it towards himself so that he could look her in the eye.

'You didn't have an abortion, did you?'

Sophia started back from his touch. 'Of course not! I tell you, I wasn't pregnant! I just thought I was and got into a tizzy about it.'

'But you wouldn't have, would you?' He pushed his forelock back.

'Well, I don't know. Yes, I do. If I'm going to be really honest about it, yes, I would. What would I have done with a baby? And I hardly knew you.'

'And you wouldn't even have told me . . . ' He spoke with urgency. 'Sophia, promise me, if you ever, ever even suspect you might be pregnant, you tell me, do you understand? And you do *not* get rid of my baby.'

'Why, what is this? There's no question. I'm not going to get pregnant. I'm extremely careful these days, I thought you knew.'

'But I so long to have a baby one day,' Thomas said dreamily. 'I couldn't bear it if you got rid of it. I don't know what I'd do.'

'I can't just have a baby.'

'We ought to have one one day.'

'Are you serious?' she asked in astonishment.

He raised his eyebrows. 'But of course. Why shouldn't we have a baby?'

'What on earth would I do with a baby?'

'What mothers normally do with babies.'

'But I couldn't keep one; what about my job?'

'You'd give it up, of course. Where are your priorities? I'd keep you somehow. I'd probably be earning enough by then. I know, we'd live in the country. It's cheaper there.'

Sophia shook her head and interrupted: 'I don't believe we're having this conversation.'

'Do you mean to tell me you don't want to have *my baby*?'

She paused and frowned slightly. 'I just don't know. It's simply never occurred to me.'

Thomas leaned back in his chair and gazed at the garden.

'I've always loved children,' he said. 'I never really thought of having my own. I was too young when I was with Annie. I did once think Allegra and I could produce something wonderful, but that was pure fantasy. You and I, though . . . oh, Sophia, don't tell me you really don't want children and just want that bloody job, I just couldn't bear it.'

'I didn't actually say that. Everything just seems fine as it is, doesn't it? Anyway, what is this talk about babies? We're not even married!'

'Oh, well, *obviously* we'll get married,' said Thomas a shade impatiently. 'I'd rather like to get you pregnant first, though. Just imagine having a dear little bit of me inside you; wouldn't it be heaven?'

'Hang on one very large minute. I certainly don't want babies right now. Marriage has never even occurred to me. I'm not at all sure about that either.'

Thomas looked stunned. 'But I just thought . . . *of course* we'll get married.'

Sophia smacked her wine glass down on the table.

'There's no 'of course' about it!'

'Why are you so bloody *difficult*!' Thomas exclaimed in fury.

'Look.' She leaned forward to take his hands and spoke softly. 'I've never been so happy in all my life as I am with you now. This is something I've never said to anyone, and I don't expect I'll say it again to anyone else. We are fine just as we are. Why change it?'

He looked sadly at her. 'I really love you, Sophia. I believe you love me, though you never say it, and I don't know why. Will you marry me?'

'I don't know.'

He chuckled without mirth. 'I used to go out with these girls who actually wanted to marry me. D'you know, I've had two proposals.'

'Isn't that funny. I used to go out with

these men to whom it never occurred to want to marry me. I've never got close to having a proposal.'

'Until now.' He gripped his wine glass. 'Sophia. I really do want to marry you, and I desperately want to have children with you.'

'Give me time.' She sighed and looked away.

'We haven't got all that much. Your 'biology clock', or whatever it's called, is ticking away. You'll be thirty-four in November.'

'Oh for Christ's sake! I will *not* have you putting this kind of pressure on me! It's manipulative and — and I just can't stand it.'

They had dinner in near silence, but that night she clung to him, and their love-making had seldom been more passionate.

In the succeeding days the questions about marriage and children hung between them, unspoken. Daylight was full of companionship and sun, and the night-time of love; however, there was also a certain constraint, an unvoiced and vaguely threatening sadness which each refused to acknowledge.

★   ★   ★

'I've got an idea,' said Thomas at breakfast a few days later. They were drinking strong coffee on the lawn; the sun was up and the

262

birds high in the sky.

'Yes? God, Thomas, how could you get the newsagent to deliver the *Sun*? I don't think I've ever read such rubbish in my life.'

'Snob. Go back to your *Financial Times*. Listen to my idea.'

'You want to order the *Times Literary Supplement* on Fridays instead of the *Sun* every day.'

'Get real. Let's go riding.'

Sophia put down the *Sun*. 'I haven't heard you right. Did I hear you say *let*'s go riding?'

Thomas leaned forward and looked appealing. 'Listen. We'll get ancient Basil saddled up for you. We'll just walk. We'll only go a little way. We won't do a single thing you don't want to do.'

'Too right we won't. I'm staying here. Hermione told me to freeze hundreds of pounds of raspberries while she was away and dead-head a million roses. I have work to do.'

'Sophia. Trust me. I solemnly swear to God it'll be good. You'll really, really enjoy yourself. This isn't a ghastly riding school, and dear old Bas'll look after you. I promise.'

'I don't know.'

'So you will?'

'I didn't say that, you manipulative brute. I have raspberries to pick.'

'Brilliant. We'll do Herm's garden stuff in

the morning and go riding in the afternoon.'

Basil was nearly as old as Thomas himself. A remarkably tough bay gelding with a mouth like iron and unusual intelligence, he had successfully introduced several novices to hounds and had been a reliable schoolmaster; he was still ridden out, and sometimes Hermione took him cubbing. 'If we stopped working him he'd literally die of boredom,' Thomas explained. Sophia gingerly led him in from his field and helped Harry to saddle him while Thomas sorted out a horse for himself. She was wearing an old pair of Victoria's jodhpurs, slightly small boots and one of many spare hard hats found in the tack room.

Harry kindly put a neck-strap around Basil's neck and held him next to a mounting block. He looked enormous to Sophia, but once she was on the mounting block his size seemed to diminish to almost manageable proportions. She put one foot in the stirrup, swung the other over and sat still for a moment. This was nothing like sitting on the fat little ponies at the riding school. Basil's neck was surprisingly long and thin, and his pointly lop ears seemed miles away. Also, he was narrower. Now that she was actually on his back, her bad memories of riding dissipated. Even when Thomas rode up on a grey hunter and Harry let go of Basil's head, the horse reassuringly did not move.

'Gather your reins,' said Thomas, 'and let's go.'

Off they went at snail's pace, up the drive and through the gate, which Thomas opened and shut adroitly without dismounting. Vaguely remembered instructions returned to Sophia; she sat up stiffly, tried to put her heels down and gripped with her knees. 'Relax,' said Thomas. 'Whatever you've been taught, don't grip with your knees. Just keep your chin up and your heels down, and above all, don't worry about a thing. That's better. Feel the horse moving.' After ten minutes or so Sophia began to admit to herself that this riding was mildly enjoyable; she was not at all frightened. Basil did not stop and try to eat grass, like the riding school ponies of her youth; nor did he display any desire to go any faster than a walk, or to snap and kick at Thomas's horse.

'Try a trot?' Thomas asked.

'I suppose so.'

After a minute or two, she remembered how to rise to the trot and felt tremendously pleased with her rediscovered ability. Perhaps riding had not been such a disaster after all in her childhood. Basil trotted patiently alongside the grey hunter, apparently undisturbed by Sophia's flapping reins and her occasional crash landing in the saddle. In a very short time Sophia was red in the face and out of breath. Thomas slowed his horse down to a walk; in the absence of clear instructions from his rider, Basil slowed down too.

'How did that feel?' Thomas asked.

'OK . . . I think,' panted Sophia.

'You see, I told you it wasn't so bad.'

They were riding off the roads in beautiful country, following a grassy track along the side of recently harvested fields. It was all Avondale land. 'Look,' said Thomas, pointing to a pair of cottages in the distance, 'there's where I'm going to live one day.'

'Those cottages?'

'I wanted to show you. They need a bit doing to them, but the bigger one would be ideal. It's got a big room on the first floor with lots of light for a studio and two lovely bedrooms — one for us and one for the nursery, of course.'

'*What*?'

Thomas's face was bright and hopeful; he seemed oblivious of the threat in Sophia's voice.

'Isn't it an idyllic place? I've been dying to show you. That's why I got you to come out riding, it's such a brilliant approach if you ride.'

The view with the cottages was indeed superb, especially with the sun shining. Its charm was lost on Sophia; she deliberately turned her head away from it to glare at Thomas.

'You mean this whole riding thing was stage-managed so that you could show me this? Thomas, what are you *doing* to me?'

'What d'you mean?' Thomas said blandly. 'Don't you think it's lovely?'

'You're on about babies again, aren't you? If you think you're going to persuade me like this, you'd better think again. I can't believe you're doing this, I can't believe you can be so manipulative. I tell you, there's nothing I hate so much. I thought we'd dropped this thing about having children and getting married. Now just *stop it*! If I'd known I would never have come riding. You *know* that.'

He chuckled. 'You always say, 'You *know* that' when you're cross. And you speak very quickly, and get red in the face . . . '

'I'm not cross. I'm furious. I want to go home. Now.'

She turned Basil round and kicked him abruptly. In some surprise, Basil broke into a trot. She leaned forward to grab the reins and the neck-strap; the horse misinterpreted her action as a signal to canter and duly obliged.

The wind seemed to whistle past Sophia's ears; underneath her the old horse suddenly became a concentrated ball of uncontrolled, horrific energy; she bounced painfully in the saddle. Gasping raggedly for breath, she tried again to seize the neck-strap. Basil cantered easily along the side of the field, plainly enjoying himself and completely ignoring the plight of his rider.

'You idiot, stop! Turn him!' Thomas yelled, and, seeing that she was out of control, gave chase.

Basil was an old hand at gallops. Sensing opposition, he speeded up. Sophia's discomfort was superseded by sheer terror; Basil's gallop was far less bouncy than his canter, but to Sophia he appeared now to be travelling at the speed of light. Beyond panic, she clung on. Thomas's much faster horse drew level, and Thomas leaned out of his saddle to grab Basil's reins. Her world abruptly turned upside down; the sky swooped beneath her, and the green grass rushed up to hit her; there was a sudden, shattering thump, and the sky reappeared equally abruptly.

'Sophia! Sweetheart!' Thomas pulled his horse to a halt and flung himself off. 'Are you all right? Speak to me, oh please tell me you're OK.'

Sophia, having ascertained that the ground

and the sky had resumed their normal positions in relation to each other, croaked and struggled for breath.

'Darling, I'm sorry, I made you angry, I'm a pig, oh please be all right, please, please forgive,' gabbled Thomas, kneeling by Sophia and kissing her hand frantically.

'Aaahh — winded,' gasped Sophia at last. She sat up and shook herself cautiously. 'Nothing broken.'

'You're really all right? Oh, thank God! Thank God! Oh Sophia, are you sure? Let me . . . '

'I'm fine,' she snapped. She got stiffly to her feet. 'Oh God, I suppose it's at least three miles to walk.'

'Darling, if you possibly can, it would be much better to ride.'

'To ride? Forget it. You must think I'm a basket case. Just take your accursed horses and go. I'll make my own way back.'

Basil, meanwhile, had stopped dead as soon as he had ditched Sophia. During this exchange between the humans he munched some grass; now, ears pricked, he approached them curiously, wondering what they were going to do about him. Thomas took his reins.

'Sophia, sweetheart, don't be silly. It's very important for you to get back on. I know it's difficult. You must not let it beat you. Look, I'll give you a leg up. I'll lead you all the way. It'll be much quicker and much less painful, honestly.'

She was too shaken really to protest; however, the physical and mental effort of climbing back onto the unprotesting Basil was huge. She sat in the saddle at last, hunched over Basil's withers, hardly holding the reins.

'You leaned forward in the saddle, that's why he bogged off,' Thomas said helpfully, when he had remounted his own horse. He took Basil's rein, and they set off soberly.

'I don't want to know, and I don't want to talk about it,' said Sophia sulkily.

'Oh well,' Thomas said good-naturedly. 'You'll have one heck of a bruise and ache a bit tomorrow, but thank goodness there's nothing wrong.'

'Speak for yourself,' Sophia muttered between her teeth.

They trailed home in silence. Sophia was unwilling to admit when they got home that she felt almost completely better. Thomas was subdued.

After their arrival home, Thomas was solicitous.

'Let me run you a bath,' he offered. 'Then would you like to lie down? I'll put out the chaise longue, where do you want it? I'll do supper . . . '

'Oh, shut up. I don't want a bath. I'm going for a walk. Alone.'

Freshly ablaze with anger, Sophia stalked quickly off down the lawn, almost running. Presently she reached the fields, which she crossed, heading for a hill beyond them which had a public footpath to the top. She began to walk up the hill. The path was clearly discernable and in places quite steep. The grass on either side was close cropped by sheep, some of which could be seen grazing silently near her. After a minute or two, she was out of breath and slowed down; as she did so and carried on climbing, her anger began to dissipate. Gradually she became passively aware of a great stillness and did not hear the song of the birds, the faint hum of insects or the occasional bleat of a sheep. The sky was clear and cloudless and tinged warmly with the beginnings of a gentle twilight, but she, intent on her climb, barely noticed it.

Her exertion had made her pulse quicken. As she neared the flat top of the hill, she was walking and breathing easily; she rejoiced in the movement of her limbs and was exhilarated. She drank in the golden air, all anger now forgotten. From the top one could see, in a velvet haze, the distant sea gleaming softly in the setting sun, and stretched out before it the golden greenery of the country. In the momentum of her climb she barely paused at this view and carried on, striding down the other side of the hill into the sun.

Enmeshed in her solitude, she was only vaguely aware of the beauty of her surroundings. A feeling of the deepest contentment began to well up within her. This rapture was almost a physical sensation. Without thinking, she knew in the depths of her being, as this feeling rose, that she was completely happy, and that for the first time in her life she had the liberty to be herself. There was no need, indeed no room, for worries. All the anxious little considerations about her life melted away, nullified by the joy within her. She understood now that she and Thomas might try for a child, and she would stay with him wherever he might be, because she was completely free to do so. All the anguish of her earlier life had simply led to this.

When she got to the bottom of the hill, her surroundings came into focus, so that now she was conscious of the fading sun and heard the birds singing. She passed by the big field with mares and foals in it and paused to admire them. Her body felt warm and loose limbed.

She found Thomas sitting outside the drawing-room with two of the dogs, a bottle of wine and two glasses on the table beside him. He immediately saw that something had changed in her.

'Did you see the sea from the hill?' he asked, as they drank their wine.

'I think so.'

'Oh dear, that means it's going to rain.'

'No, I didn't see it clearly. There will be no rain.'

They sat in silence for a few moments.

'Thomas,' said Sophia.

He looked at her. His face was serious, his eyes full of apprehension.

'I love you,' she said.

Slowly Thomas began to smile.

20

They returned to London sun-tanned and relaxed; both had put on weight. After they had done so, summer abruptly ended; the warm fine weather was blown out by cold wet winds.

Almost unconsciously, Sophia began working slightly less hard. She tended not to stay at the office so late. Her management style became discernibly more relaxed; her subordinates mostly welcomed this. Without exactly worrying about it, she wondered how she would spend her time if she didn't have her job and the routine of the office.

The one thing she had no need to worry about was money. Ever since she had started work in the City, she had been personally interested in the stock market, and she had soon discovered that she had a flair not only for picking shares but also for selling them at the right time. She had in particular made a small fortune from new issues. Although she had considerably enriched the Inland Revenue over the years with capital gains tax and knew precisely the content of her portfolio and its individual stock prices at any time, she had never sat down to calculate what she was worth. Money by itself did not interest her; she played the stock market purely because she enjoyed the challenge. She guessed, however, that she could already retire whenever she liked and live comfortably for the rest of her life off the interest alone. There was also more than enough to buy and renovate the cottage in Dorset — without the need to sell the London house.

'There won't be a problem with the cottage,' she ventured somewhat timidly one evening over supper.

'What do you mean?' Thomas smiled at her over a lasagne he had made.

'I mean, I do have some capital.' She hated talking about money and did not even look him in the eye.

'Oh come on, we don't want to worry about that. The cottage is mine anyway. We'll have to have the work done to it gradually; I know it'll be a bit difficult at first, and we may have to rough it, but we won't be far from Father and Herm, and it won't be for ages anyway.'

'Thomas,' said Sophia, looking up at him, 'what I'm trying to say is that I have money. Actually a lot of money. We shan't have to rough it at all. This lasagne is delicious.'

'Thanks. Hey, you know I'm not going to

touch your money.'

'Well, you may as well. It's not going to do anything. It's just sitting there. We may as well spend it.'

Thomas grinned. 'Don't be silly. When we get married, I'll provide for you. I'm very old fashioned like that. Tell you what, if you're so rich, why not have real fun with the dosh and buy a racehorse? The yearling sales are happening now, let's ask Herm's advice and buy a cracker and send it to their trainer in Newmarket.'

'How much would that cost?'

'You could get a really nice yearling for twenty thousand, say, and then allow another twenty to twenty-five for a year's training and all the expenses, less if you don't go to Newmarket. Actually you could be frightfully clever and get a world-beater for less than ten. Father knew a man . . . '

'I could do that quite easily,' said Sophia gravely.

'What, buy a world-beater? You fraud, you never let on you're an expert on thorough-breds.'

'I mean I could afford it, cretin. It would have to be an awful lot of fun to justify forty-five thousand.' She spoke matter-of-factly.

'Good God, you're not kidding. I was just *joking* about buying a yearling. I had no idea you had money. Did someone leave you some?'

'Of course not! In my family? No, I work in the City, remember? I just play the stock market, that's all. I like new situations and penny shares — very high risk, not widow and orphan stuff. And it really isn't insider trading because we don't research small companies — though I do hear the odd helpful rumour in the market from time to time. I'm more or less barred from buying the major stocks because I'm involved with them.'

Thomas began to laugh. 'To think I actually asked you for a loan to take you out to dinner the first time!'

'It doesn't bother you, then, that I have this money?'

'Why should it bother me? It's just that I don't feel concerned with it. You know, if this show's a success I really should be able to manage. I make enough for myself now; if I get better known and can sell pictures as well as portraits I can make enough for you *and* babies.'

She put her hand on his. 'It's all a bit premature, isn't it? You haven't had the show, we're not officially engaged, I haven't handed in my notice at work, or planned to, for that matter.'

'So much depends on that show.' He sighed and for a moment looked anguished.

'You *know* you're good.'

'I do not. I'm just bloody arrogant, like all us upper-class twits. On good days I think my work's terrific, and the punters would have to be mad not to like it and buy it, and on bad days — oh, I'm just sweating.'

'Come on, your pictures are exceptional.'

'Oh, Sophia, you're very sweet, and you may be right, but you don't buy pictures for the Tate Gallery, you aren't an art critic, you aren't even a buyer.'

'But even if the show isn't an out-and-out success, you're still wonderful at portraits. They'll always be there.'

Thomas grew noticeably pale. He laid down his fork and put both wrists on the table. 'Listen,' he said. 'If the show is a flop, and I have to *fall back on portraits*, as you say, I think I'll just go and shoot myself. My life is in this show.'

A new intensity began to creep into Thomas's life. He did not work as frenziedly as in the spring, when he was driven simply to get his ideas onto canvas. Very gradually he became more abstracted as his pictures increasingly claimed him. His absences at the studio became more prolonged.

Autumn advanced; Thomas grew more and more preoccupied.

21

Thomas and Sophia were still not officially engaged, nor had they told anyone their plans. However, it became apparent even to Sophia that she could no longer put off introducing Thomas to her parents. It was almost the only thing not connected with his work for which he was willing to make time; accordingly, a Sunday in mid-September saw them driving to Epsom for lunch.

Sophia, who had hoped vainly to be let off just with drinks, was gloomy. Thomas sensed her mood. He neither understood nor approved of her attitude to her parents, but now that they really were on their way to the meeting he had so wanted, he said nothing to provoke her.

'At any rate,' he told her, 'you mustn't worry about me. I'm so charming; everyone always loves me.'

Sophia knew Thomas was absolutely right. Her parents would eat out of his hand. What dismayed her was that they, or rather, her mother would try to *out charm* him. She could almost hear the gush and the tinkle; she shuddered.

'Will Anthea or Edward be there?' Thomas asked.

'There's an outside chance he will be. If pop-eyed Anthea and her dreadful husband are there I might simply turn around and go home. I hope we'll be on our own. Edward's not too bad, though.'

She half expected her mother to summon Edward for moral support. She had not been alone with her parents for very many years; on the increasingly rare occasions that she saw them, one or both of her siblings was invariably present. Edward and Anthea had a normal, affectionate relationship with both their parents.

As Sophia stopped her car in front of her parents' immaculate detached house she did not, as Thomas would have done, merrily toot her horn to announce their arrival.

'Chin up, sweetheart,' said Thomas.

Susan White sat at a window looking onto the street and watched avidly but discreetly.

'She's driving,' she murmured. '*Typical*. Oh! He's *rather good looking*, but a little *unusual*, perhaps? Bernard, *Bernard*!'

She had thought her husband was with her, but he was in his study, stuffing tobacco into his pipe. In an unwonted access of apprehension, she bustled in to ferret him out.

'Bernard. They're *here*!'

He lit his pipe imperturbably, then put it down as the doorbell rang. There stood Sophia, dressed up as usual in a frighteningly expensive suit, and behind her the young man, who had a forelock of white hair, a large bunch of flowers and — in contrast to Sophia — an expansive, engaging smile.

'Darling!' tinkled Mrs White. 'Did you have a *frightful* journey?'

Sophia hid her irritation at this remark, which she had accurately predicted to Thomas not ten minutes previously.

'Hello, dear,' said her father.

Stiffly Sophia pecked each parent on the cheek and formally introduced Thomas. As she stepped across the threshold of their house she felt its pipe-tobacco atmosphere envelop her, automatically lowering her spirits.

'I've so been looking forward to meeting you,' said Thomas with evident sincerity. 'It's sweet of you to invite us to lunch.' He presented Mrs White with his flowers.

'*How* do you do,' said Mrs White in a passable imitation of a soprano Margaret Thatcher. 'Oh, what *heavenly* flowers. They're not for *me!*' (coyly). 'Now do come into the drawing room. Bernard! Give Thomas a sherry while I put these *lovely flowers* into a vase . . . '

The drawing room was grown-up territory at the Whites' house. It had always been Mrs White's show-piece room. She had not encouraged her children to use it; they had had a playroom beyond the kitchen. In Sophia's childhood it had been a remote, stiff room; she had not liked to sit on the sofas and armchairs for fear of disarranging the plump cushions which were always perched awkwardly on their points; Mr and Mrs White had sometimes used it in the evenings after the children had gone to bed. Now, as before, it was in a state of highly polished perfection. It was slightly less redolent of Mr White's pipe than previously because it had recently been redecorated in pink and pale green.

Bernard White poured amontillado sherry into small crystal glasses and asked Thomas, 'You must work in the City with Sophia?'

Thomas laughed. His laugh was so friendly, open and artless that Sophia's father and Sophia herself smiled. 'Good gracious, no. Didn't Sophia tell you? I'm an artist.'

'Now I hope you haven't been saying *frightfully interesting things* while I've been out of the room,' gushed Mrs White, fluttering into the drawing room with Thomas's flowers in a vase. 'You'll just have to say them *all over again*, because I don't want to miss a *single thing*.'

'Imagine, dear,' said Mr White. 'Thomas here says he's an artist.'

'An *artist*? Just fancy that,' said Mrs White, suddenly at a loss for words.

Thomas stepped gracefully into the breach. 'I do portraits and paint pictures. I'm having a show at Zoff's Gallery off Bond Street this winter; I hope you'll come. I'll need lots of support!'

'Oh dear,' said Mrs White with pleasure, 'that does sound frightfully *smart*.'

'It is,' said Sophia.

'Now, Thomas.' Mrs White leaned forward in her armchair towards Thomas and adopted an almost conspiratorial air. 'I want to know *all about you*. How did you and Sophia . . . '

She embarked on a litany of questions which saw them through drinks and into the small dining room. Here the furniture was reproduction and the cutlery ornate silver plate. Sophia thought of the massive antique table in the dining room at Avondale, which was used for dinner parties and large family meals, and of the ancient, unusually large items of solid silver cutlery that had been in that family for generations. She hated herself for recalling these things.

Thomas dealt with Mrs White's interrogation with ease and apparent enjoyment; in so doing, he charmed her. Mutely Sophia passed the plates of roast beef that her father carved and shuddered inwardly as her mother fluttered and bridled and grinned at Thomas. She was actually flirting with him. Sophia felt cold with fury and resolved not to utter a word. Then her father poured her some claret which, upon tasting, she found to be very good indeed. It was by far the best wine she had ever drunk in her parents' house.

'What lovely wine, Dad,' she said.

Mr White did not smile often, but when he did so he meant it. He smiled now and said, 'I thought a special occasion needed special wine.'

Sophia was touched and looked gratefully at her father. However, there was no let-up in her mother's tinkling torrent of conversation.

'Oh yes,' she was saying to Thomas, 'how *right* your stepmother is. I try to keep active too. Why, only last week I won our girls' golf tournament at the club! *Rather* a sweet little trophy, and I must admit I *was proud*. Does your stepmother play golf? Such a *sociable* game, Bernard simply *loves* it.'

She batted her eyelashes and smirked. Sophia winced and stared at her plate.

'Hermione's rather more into horses,' said Thomas.

'Oh my *dear*. I *so* hoped Sophie would take up horse-riding when she was younger, and we paid for lessons at quite a good school, you know, but she just *didn't*. Some more beef, perhaps?'

'Oh yes please, it's absolutely brilliant. This is such a treat. We haven't had a proper Sunday lunch for ages, have we, Sophia?'

Mrs White's dazzling smile included everyone at the table. 'And I've got your *special* lemon mousse for pudding, dear,' she said, looking at Sophia.

'Special lemon mousse?' Sophia asked vaguely.

'*You* know, darling. I always did it for your birthday when you were *rather* younger. And when you'd had the measles so badly.'

Sophia could barely remember enjoying a pudding, but when she tasted her mother's lemon mousse she realised that her mother was right. She had not eaten this pudding since before she had gone up to Cambridge. It was delicious, light and fluffy and very sharp with lemon. Mrs White was a competent cook with a few outstanding dishes in her repertoire. Again, Sophia found this gesture disturbing. She wanted to disapprove straightforwardly of her parents — her mother's gushing flirtatiousness, her father's undemonstrative greyness — but faced with the small extra kindnesses of the good claret and the special mousse she could not do so. Her disapproval, and her memory of Avondale, made her feel guilty.

When they adjourned to the drawing room for coffee, Sophia tried to express her thanks for lunch with genuine gratefulness. Her parents seemed to recognise this and almost visibly relaxed. Mr White became a little more talkative, Mrs White a little less. She stopped gushing, and, as her voice softened, the harsh tinkle went out of it. Thomas told them his father had a farm in Dorset where he had grown up and managed to draw from Mrs White the information that she too had grown up in the country.

'My parents had a little shop, you know,' she told him. 'It was a little general store in the village, and my mother was postmistress. We lived in Suffolk.'

'Really? What fun it must have been, growing up in a shop. I do envy you, I know I'd have been at the sweets the whole time.'

Mrs White laughed. 'Oh no, Mother was ever so strict!'

Sophia nearly gaped. Her mother was not proud of her antecedents and never talked about her past.

'And what happened?' Thomas asked. 'Do they still have the shop? Do they still live in Suffolk? It's a lovely country.'

Mrs White sighed. 'They died quite young.

Cancer. Sophie was tiny when my mother died. She lived about five years longer than my father.'

'How dreadfully sad,' said Thomas. 'I'm so lucky. My father's tremendously fit, isn't he, Sophia? My mother did die when I was little, but I was too young to remember much, and my step-mother's like a mother really.'

'Ah,' said Mr White, 'so you've met Thomas's parents, then, Sophie?'

Sophia fiddled with her coffee cup. 'Er — yes; we went down to Dorset.'

'*What* dark horse,' said Mrs White archly.

Sophia frowned almost imperceptibly, but she was unable to detect any disapproval in her mother. On the contrary, her mother seemed genuinely pleased with her, perhaps for the first time in her life. She knew that her mother would be scrutinising Thomas as potential husband and son-in-law material; she didn't put it past her to be thinking ahead already to a wedding.

A half hour or so later, replete with food and coffee, Sophia and Thomas drove back to London.

'That's over,' said Sophia.

'Your parents were sweet.'

'Yes, they were.'

'I have to say I wish I'd met them ages before.'

Sophia looked away. 'It was a wonderful lunch, and they tried very hard. They couldn't have been nicer. Now you'll wonder why I've always been so cranky and ungrateful.' Her voice was flat.

Thomas did not comment.

'What you can't understand is that today I did something they approved of for the first time in my life. Always before I completely failed them. I never enjoyed what they enjoyed. I seldom brought friends home as a child because I preferred to read books on my own. I didn't have suitable boyfriends as Anthea did. Instead of doing a secretarial course and finding a husband, I won a scholarship to Cambridge and got a high-powered job in the City. I earn more than my father's ever dreamed of, not that they know that, at least I hope they don't. Whatever. They haven't liked anything I've ever done or been. Now I come along with a personable, well-spoken man, and they're over the moon, I may actually be normal at last.'

'They were most frightfully tense to begin with,' said Thomas, 'as if they didn't know which way we were going to jump.'

'When Mum began telling you about her parents and the shop, I almost began to enjoy myself. I couldn't believe she was opening up to that extent. She never normally talks about it. I always had the idea she was a dreadful snob and ashamed of her background.'

'I thought that was all rather sweet, about the shop. You know, I liked your mother. I shall have to get to know your father better next. She doesn't give him much of a look in!'

'Well, thank God we've done it now and got it over with.'

Thomas laughed and squeezed Sophia's leg as she drove. 'They're not really such a problem. You poor little neglected kid.'

'It wasn't precisely neglect.'

'Doesn't matter. It's all in the past. Everything is all right now.'

Sophia hunched her shoulders over the steering wheel and said with irritation, 'God, you're so simplistic sometimes, Thomas.'

In bed that night, after they had switched out the lights, they lay awake and talked.

'Come off the Pill,' said Thomas suddenly, à propos de rien.

'Shall I? We must be mad.'

'It takes ages to get pregnant when you've been on it. After the show . . . '

'I bet that's not true, and how would you know, anyway?'

'You forget, I'm horribly experienced and I've known an awful lot of women.'

'Mostly biblically, no doubt.'

'Yes, as a matter of fact you're right on the

whole. The point is, I don't think we should hang about after the show, do you?'

'Thomas, I'm still not really sure about any of this.'

'Bollocks. You know it's all meant to be.'

'*Meant to be.* What a pathetic cliché, if you don't mind my saying so.'

Silence.

The Sophia, who was lying flat on her back and staring at the ceiling, said in a different voice, 'I may as well come off the Pill, anyhow.'

'What d'you mean, *anyhow?*'

'It's most unlikely I'll ever have children.'

'*What?!*'

'I have a feeling about it.'

'You *never* have feelings about things.'

'No, but I do about this.'

'Don't be ridiculous. You're in perfectly good health.'

'Yes.'

'You've never been anorexic or anything. In fact you've never had anything wrong.'

'You don't actually know that, but yes, you're right.'

'So what is this nonsense?'

He heard her sigh in the dark. Then she said quietly, 'Anthea's had children. Most of the girls I was at school with have had children. It's not something that's ever going to happen to me.'

'I don't believe it.' He turned abruptly, discombobulating the bedclothes. 'Sophia, this is just a bad joke, isn't it. I don't like it, I really don't. Anyhow — you thought you *were* pregnant last year. And at Avondale you said it would be all right. You were so happy. What's wrong now? I don't understand.'

'Oh, I was silly and overwrought over the pregnancy scare. There was no chance really. As for Avondale — I felt different there. I'm in London now. This my real life. I realise that now. Thomas, I'm not like other people. I never have been. I'm not like anyone in my family. Other women have children. I *can't*. How could I?'

She had spoken dispassionately, but he inferred a terrible sadness. He reached for her in the darkness, threw his arms almost convulsively around her and held her stiff body tightly.

There was a shaking; she stirred. 'Thomas,' she exclaimed, her voice tired, distant and infinitely tender, 'what's the matter? You're not crying — '

'Tell me, tell. Do you *want* children?'

'*Your* child? Yes. I really think I do. But . . .'

'Tell me you love me. Go on, tell me.'

She twisted round in his arms; their faces

were inches apart; she whispered, 'I love you. Of course I love you.'

'Sophia, my love, my love, you're not Anthea, not other women, but you *can*. You can have children. I *know*.'

'Hush . . . Stop now. Don't cry. I love you. Can you love me without babies?'

'Don't be silly. I'll love you for ever, my only love.' He covered her face in kisses.

'Oh, Thomas.' Her voice was dry and came to him as though over a distance. 'I'll disappoint you. I can't give you any more than this. Everything's lovely now, it's already beyond my wildest dreams, but don't ask the impossible.'

He kissed her; she entwined herself about him; slowly they began to make love.

22

The birthdays of Thomas and Sophia — thirtieth and thirty-fourth — occurred in late September and October and passed almost unnoticed: Thomas absolutely vetoed any presents on either side or even special meals.

'There's no time to do them justice. Let's have a lovely party after the show for both our birthdays,' he suggested. 'We might tell everyone then we're engaged — what do you think?'

'That would be fun,' said Sophia, 'but where would we give the party, and what sort of a party would it be?'

Thomas looked blank. 'I haven't a clue,' he said. Then he seemed to lose interest and said no more on the subject; he was thinking about a picture.

Pictures took over Thomas's life. Earlier in the summer he had planned to work steadily for the exhibition, not intensifying the pace of his work and spending every night at Sophia's house; he had an idea that this would be better for his health. His last surge of creativity had left him too drained. However, steady work was not in his nature. His work-load began to unnerve him; to a greater extent, his pictures possessed him. He could think of nothing else. It happened with increasing frequency that he would find himself painting away at three o'clock in the morning, when it would be too late to return to Sophia's. He began to leave his telephone off the hook at the studio, forgetting to be punctilious in letting Sophia know what he was up to.

His picture of the Annunciation held him in particular thrall. He spent days and weeks on it and kept coming back to it while he was working on other pictures, not satisfied until days before the show.

As his absences lengthened, and he grew increasingly abstracted and distant with her, Sophia missed him acutely.

'Thomas,' she ventured during a rare supper at her house in November, 'are you sure everything is all right?'

He was eating ravenously and very quickly. 'What d'you mean?' he asked between mouthfuls.

'You don't look well.'

'You wouldn't look well if you were working like me.'

'We hardly see each other, and we don't talk.'

'Can't help that. I do have this show.'

'As if I didn't know.'

'I always warned you artists are horrible people. This show's the most important thing in my life, you must see that.'

Sophia had rather thought she was the most important thing in Thomas's life. She had acceded to his request and, with his knowledge, had thrown away her contraceptive pills; although she still genuinely believed she was unlikely to fall pregnant, there was the feeling she had burnt her bridges.

'Well, I hope you can live without it when it's over,' she said tartly.

'Don't give me grief,' he snapped, shovelling in some more food.

Even in bed he had become more remote; he tended now to make love quickly and very intensely and go to sleep immediately afterwards, not always leaving her satisfied. On this occasion, however, he hugged her briefly in bed and said, 'I know I'm a pig. I know it's dreadful. I'm sorry. I do love you really. You do understand, don't you?'

'It gets lonely sometimes. I thought I was through with all that.'

'You are. Sophia!' He sounded for a moment as he had in the summer. 'I'm always with you really. We're *part* of each other, don't you feel that? It'll all be all right after the show.'

She laughed softly in the dark. 'It's just a bit difficultnow, before the show.'

'Come on, you're tough.'

'Of course I am! I just worry about you, that's all.'

'No point in that. I've got to do all this. I know it's a stupid way of going on, but it works for me. I do get the work done.'

After this talk, she missed him still but worried less; she felt more sure of him. The threat of loneliness eased.

He did not miss her while he was painting. Sometimes, if he was working at a female image, he thought of her, or, if the image demanded it, of Allegra and other women. Similarly, he hardly missed his food or sleep. He absolutely forbade Sophia or anyone else to visit him in his studio.

Sophia determinedly distracted herself. She had been meaning to undertake a major business trip and had kept putting it off; now she plunged back into her own work with all her old acerbic intensity. In a mad, exhausting but ultimately successful two weeks she went round the world, visiting the US, Australia, Hong Kong and Japan. She went west, starting in a sleety, grey New York, where she spent a day before travelling on to Chicago and Los Angeles. There were meetings and presentations every hour of every day and over breakfast, lunch and dinner; the occasional excruciatingly tiring evening entertainment; days and nights spent in the first class cabins of various aircraft; too much food and drink and too little sleep.

However, the trip contained a treat which she had long promised herself. She had become friendly with the head of her firm's Sydney office when he had visited London and had often entertained him and his wife, inviting them to dinner and taking them to the theatre. Don Clancy was a huge, bear-like man whose slow drawl and casual manner belied a sharp intellect; his wife Josie was his physical opposite, a tiny, sparky red-head. She ran an advertising agency and was the apparently improbable mother of two large, untroublesome teenage boys. Sophia found Don and Josie great fun; they made her laugh.

'It's great seeing you in London,' Don had said to her on his last visit, 'but how can you live in such a, pardon me, shit place? OK, the theatres and restaurants are good, but it's a bloody awful climate and too many people. When are you coming to Oz?'

When she rang Don to set up her visit, he boomed down the telephone, 'Fantastic!

Don't you bother about hotels and all that crap. You come and stay with us. We've got a nice place near the centre. You can stay the weekend, can't you? Guess you'll be on your own . . . no worries, we'll fix you up, invite some people over to meet you. Fax me your flight times . . . '

She flew from Los Angeles to Sydney overnight to arrive on Friday and was so tired that she fell asleep soon after take-off, eschewing all Qantas's offers of caviar and failing to write up her notes. She woke up only when they had begun the descent to Sydney, as she had asked not to be disturbed for breakfast. Tired, stiff and irritable, she pushed up the sliding shutter on her window. The light that hit her almost made her gasp; then she looked out of the window and forgot everything. Sydney, its harbour and the land and ocean surrounding these lay below, green and blue and shining in the sun. She had never seen or dreamed of such an exquisite commingling of land and sea. The aeroplane circled, tipping the land and seascape out of her vision, and the bright sky, palest blue and gold and white, rose to dazzle her; as the aeroplane curved back towards the earth she picked out Sydney itself with its extraordinary opera house, white wings on a blue sea, and harbour bridge.

Thomas would think he was in heaven, she thought. She glanced at the big, empty seat next to her own and wished fervently, against all reason, idiotically, that he were there.

The flight landed shortly after six. The queues for passport control were nothing like as bad as in the US, and she got her luggage quickly. When she emerged, pushing her trolley, into the arrivals hall beyond customs control, she was surprised and delighted to find that Don had sent out a driver for her. A few minutes later they were on their way to central Sydney, with Sophia sitting in front with the driver.

The drive through the suburbs of Sydney between the airport and the city centre was not inspiring, but she was entranced simply by the brightness of the sun, which was like nothing she had ever seen before. The driver was friendly and chatty; as they drew near to Sydney he gave a running commentary. There was little traffic at that hour, and she arrived at the Clancys' house by the ocean before seven-thirty. It was in Vaucluse, which she discovered was not only a part of Provence in France but also a pretty residential district of Sydney. Don and Josie welcomed her with hugs and kisses and bore her indoors to meet their unusually tall teenage sons.

'This is Matt, he's still at school, and

Louie, he's just finishing his first year at uni.'

The sun-tanned young giants pushed their sun-bleached hair from their eyes, grinned and said, 'Hi, Sophie, good to see ya,' as if they had known her well for years.

They had breakfast on what they called the deck and Sophia called the veranda. Sophia, having not eaten on the plane, was ravenous and devoured mangoes, toast and coffee. A couple of brilliantly coloured lorikeets flew up and perched on the rail of the deck.

'Are those parrots tame?' asked Sophie. The Clancys roared with laughter. 'I can't believe you have brightly coloured things like that just flying around,' she said. 'They'd be caged up in a zoo at home.'

The light permeated the house. It was in all the big rooms which seemed to Sophia to have fewer walls than rooms in English houses; it blurred the distinction between indoors and outdoors; it filled the gauzy mosquito nets hung more for decoration than protection about Sophia's bed and bounced off the pale furniture. Beyond the deck, it sparkled on the Clancys' blue swimming pool, their garden of tropical flowers and the ocean.

Invigorated by her warm welcome and the light, Sophia enjoyed her day at the Sydney merchant bank which was her firm's subsidiary. Everyone she met seemed to go out of his way to be helpful and friendly, and she achieved more than she had thought was possible. The centre of Sydney charmed her, even though it was, as Don pointed out, far more formal and crowded than the rest of Australia. In the evening, Don, Josie and Sophia had a barbecue at home so that Sophia could go to bed early. Matt and Louie had gone out.

Australia continued to seduce her during the weekend. The Clancys took her out on their boat on Saturday, showing her the whole of Sydney's harbour and stopping in a small, quiet bay with a beach for a picnic lunch and swimming. They were wonderful company; the three of them talked and talked. Except that she missed Thomas — the more because she felt he too would have fallen in love with the place — she was completely happy. 'I like this place,' she thought, 'and it likes me.' They returned from their boat trip mid-afternoon so that Josie could prepare that evening's dinner party to be given in her honour. She was not allowed to help, but dispatched to the pool to lie in the sun.

That evening twelve of them ate Queensland mud crabs under the stars and drank a great many bottles of wine. Don and Josie introduced her to a young man called Larry. He was good-looking, and she found to her surprise that she not only did not mind the obvious match-making, but also enjoyed his company. Everything in Australia, including social intercourse, seemed effortless, and whatever she said or did seemed to win instant acceptance.

On the Sunday she slept so late that they had to give up their plan to drive to the splendid beaches north of the city; however, she welcomed the chance to catch up on her rest. 'Promise us you'll come back,' they said. 'It's so gorgeous up there, you never saw anything like it.'

'Oh yes,' she replied, 'I do promise to come back, but maybe I won't be alone.'

They teased her good-naturedly, and she told them about Thomas. They seemed so pleased for her that it made her feel more than ever that she belonged. She could hardly analyse how she belonged. Perhaps it was only because she had someone at home, and she therefore wasn't really alone; as she was therefore no longer lonely, her new sense of security owed more to Thomas than to the unconditional kindness she had received in Australia.

She had to leave on Sunday night, flying on to Hong Kong. The departure was hateful, as was the thought of spending the night not in the beautiful white bed with its billowing mosquito nets, but curled up uncomfortably in an aeroplane cabin. Don and Josie took her to the airport. 'Come back on your honeymoon,' they said in farewell.

The rest of her trip was highly challenging: doing business in the US and Australia was easy, far less easy in Hong Kong and extremely tricky in Japan. She found it stimulating and loved it, though she was less certain of her success there than in the US and Australia.

It was Thursday evening local time when she flew out of Tokyo, and she returned to Heathrow Airport very early next morning. She had meant to have a shower at the airport so as to return home looking and feeling vaguely refreshed, but as soon as her suitcase had appeared on the carousel she suddenly wanted to go home so badly that she just grabbed it and rushed out for a taxi. There was a chance Thomas would be at home, not in his studio.

The taxi just missed the build-up of early morning traffic into London. Home before eight, she unlocked the door (only one lock to open — did that mean Thomas had been, gone and carelessly left without double-locking, or was he really asleep upstairs? Did he not know she was returning today?), dragged in her luggage and quickly ran over the sitting-room with her eyes. No brightly coloured knapsacks: her heart fell. She tiptoed upstairs, opened her bedroom door, nearly tripped over something.

'Stop kicking my bag about!' Thomas exclaimed sleepily from the bed. 'God, you do it every time. I know you hate my bags — too much colour, I know you.' He yawned and stretched and pushed the white forelock out of his eyes; he sat up in bed and held out his arms. His skin was warm and drowsy. She bent to kiss him.

'You're rumpled,' said Thomas. 'I like that. And you even smell a little bit of sweat. Mmm, I like that too. Just off the plane? Come on, get those clothes off . . . ' He unbuttoned her shirt.

Later, she said, 'I can't stand the way you're always engaged when you're working. I tried and tried to ring you. It was a bore.'

'What, bad trip?'

'No, not being able to talk to you. The trip was wonderful. We're going back one day.'

'When?'

'Soon.'

'Not America — where? Got to be Japan, all that ancient culture. I suppose I could find myself a geisha while you got on with the culture.'

'Australia, would you believe? I fell in love with it. You will too, I know.'

'Go on, not Australia. Not you. No culture at all.'

'It's the light. You have to go and see that. The people . . . I felt at home there. It's also incredibly beautiful.'

It was only in the evening, when she returned from work, that she saw how pale and tired Thomas had become. He had lost too much weight. They had dinner quietly. He had been working flat out and had seen no one. 'It's nearly all done,' he said. 'Good thing. If it hadn't been I'd have panicked and not come here to meet you from your trip, and then you'd have felt like killing me, and I'm not really up to rows at the moment. Besides, I really wanted to see you.'

'So you'll have time to rest before the show?'

'Get real,' said Thomas with the ghost of a smile. Next day he went back to the studio, and Sophia did not see him again until the day before the show, over a week later.

23

That day, a van came to take Thomas's pictures to the gallery. The paint was not yet dry on some of them. Left alone in his empty studio, he thought he might go to Sophia's house. He had not had a whole night's sleep since Sophia's return, and he had just been awake for over twenty-four hours, putting on his finishing touches.

'How do you feel?' asked Sophia that evening, frowning with concern. His appearance had disconcerted her a week previously; now it shocked her.

'Nothing,' said Thomas. He smiled tiredly at her, as if entreating her to ask no more questions.

He ate little at supper and went to bed very early. She soon followed.

'Oh sweetheart, I just don't know if I'm up to it,' Thomas said as she put her arms around him.

'At least hold me. I've missed you so much.' She ran her hands over him; she couldn't help it.

'Sophia, this'll *kill* me.' He sounded quite unlike himself, but he could not refuse her.

He went to sleep immediately afterwards, but at three or four in the morning he woke up feeling sick and tired. As quietly as he could, he got out of bed, intending to go downstairs to find a book to distract himself; however, Sophia woke up.

He came back to bed. They cuddled each other.

'What if the show flops?' Thomas spoke into the darkness.

'Zoff's saw your work. They wouldn't have given you a show if they hadn't known you'd be all right. They liked the first pictures you sent.'

'Those aren't a quarter of the show. They don't count. These others are different.'

'They'll be fine.'

Thomas shrugged her away irritably. 'You don't *know* that. God, Sophia, if no one buys them and the critics hate them, I don't know what I'll do. I won't have a future. There'll be nothing for me, do you understand?'

'And if they sell and the critics love them, we've got everything to live for. Don't be silly, Thomas. These gallery people are business-men. They have complete confidence in you; you'll make them money.'

'I won't be any good for you, either. You won't be able to live with a failure, Sophia.

You're so competitive and successful your-self.'

'Thomas, *I love you*, remember? I also happen to love your work, and I believe in you.'

'Don't be ridiculous, darling. What you say is very sweet, but how can I stay with you if I can't even make any money? You know very well I can't live off you. I just feel as if I've gambled my life on this, and I'm not likely to win.'

'Yes, you have gambled, but I think you *will* win. Thomas, you're tired and depressed, you can't see it. Come here.'

She put her arms around him again, and they were silent. It took him some hours to get back to sleep, but when she arose to go to work, he hardly stirred.

★　★　★

At five o'clock that evening Thomas and Sophia stood in Zoff's gallery off Bond Street with Walter Zoff, the owner. Zoff, an East German Jew who had shrunk his name to commercial proportions, was a small, sleek man in his late fifties. He had grey hair, very dark eyes and a feline manner; he spoke with a slight accent. They were looking at the large canvas entitled 'Annunciation'.

It was one of the most ambitious Thomas had ever painted. A woman in blue knelt or sat on the right. Her figure was the essence of humility and innocence, but her face was alight with sudden new understanding and joy. She was utterly feminine, just as the Angel was completely masculine, winged and robed in fire. His energy was a contrast to her stillness, but the picture was so full of expectancy that the stillness seemed to suggest yet more energy, albeit latent. His face had the unearthly calm of a saint in a Russian icon. The picture was vibrant with colour and movement.

'This is excellent — it so impresses,' Walter said, or rather purred.

'It's not for sale,' Thomas said quietly. 'It can hang here, but it must be made clear that it's not for sale.'

'Oh my *dear*,' protested Walter, 'this you can't mean.'

'This picture is for Sophia and me,' Thomas said.

'I suppose it will go down well with the critics, but I am not pleased. It's not as if it was the only one. There is that little one too.'

'Which one is that?' asked Sophia.

Thomas smiled at her; it occurred to her that she had not seen him smile for some time. 'Come and see,' he said.

It was a picture of her sitting sideways on in the comfortable wicker armchair at Avondale. Her head was three quarters turned, and she was holding a glass of white wine. She was smiling. The likeness was true. The picture had all Thomas's characteristic incandescence, but it was soft and muted, an evening light.

'I couldn't think of another present to give you,' he said.

'It's a picture of heaven at Avondale,' said Sophia. 'As long as I have that picture, how can I ever forget how happy I have been?'

However, the rest of the show preoccupied Thomas. He had already spent much of the day at the gallery and had managed seriously to annoy Walter and his assistants as they were hanging the pictures. Nothing, according to Thomas, had been right, and he was still anxious.

'For heaven's sake, my dear,' Walter now said with a sharpness quite at odds with his normal feline manner, 'stop fussing. Come and have a glass of champagne. It might — *hoffentlich!* — calm you down.'

Sophia thought the show was one of the most beautiful things she had ever seen. The white walls of the gallery glowed with the worlds represented by Thomas. Birds flew, and animals, real and mythical, pranced;

there were seas and mountains and flowers and trees; there were people too, and gods and angels, some vaguely recognisable (Sophia thought she detected a couple of Allegras and a Julian), some imagined; a few pictures were abstract. All shone with light, whether bright or muted.

'I feel very awed,' she said to Thomas. 'You created all this. I can hardly believe it. Aren't you proud?'

'I don't know. Are you going to have some champagne?'

'It's too early.'

'I think I might get terribly pissed. At least it'd get me through all this.' He emptied his glass in a series of quick gulps.

'That would be an extremely bad idea. Can't you have something to eat?'

'Walter's minions are doing canapés. They're not ready yet. Walter! Can I have some more champagne?'

'No, you can't,' snapped Walter, showing his claws.

'OK, I'll go and shoot myself.' He walked out of the gallery.

'Don't follow him,' Walter advised Sophia. 'It's just nerves. These artists are monsters,' he muttered to himself in an aside.

'Perhaps I will have some champagne,' said Sophia.

Six o'clock came. A young woman seated herself at a table with catalogues; two more, the caterers, made themselves busy with very superior canapés in a kitchen behind the gallery and began opening bottles of champagne and white wine. No one entered the gallery. Sophia began to get fretful and watched the passers-by in the dark street outside the window. Thomas did not appear.

At six-thirty a few people wandered in; by seven the gallery was beginning to look crowded; by eight it was impossible to see the pictures. It seemed to Sophia that nearly everyone she knew socially had turned up for the party. Dozens of young socialites came, headed by Allegra and Emil. She saw Richard and Hermione hob-nobbing with older, grander socialites of the kind that tend to be associated with the arts. Her own parents and Edward came and were bewildered, and thrilled, by the smartness of the occasion, the occasional well-known face and the lurking photographers. Her own friends came. She even thought she saw, among the socialites, the Kingsleys. For her own part, she made little effort to talk to people because she was worried about Thomas.

'My dear.' Walter purred up to her, wreathed in smiles and nearly inaudible in the roar of the party. 'Have you seen Thomas? I have people who want to talk to him.' He dropped the names of some well-known art critics. 'You mean he *still* hasn't turned up?' His voice rose, and his face darkened. 'Artists ... *schrecklich* ... ' He dismissed Sophia and turned back to the critics.

Sophia sought out Richard. 'Thomas has disappeared,' she said, or shouted.

'I bet he's in a pub,' said Richard calmly but audibly. 'God, he's wet, not facing the music. Damn fool. I think it's splendid, don't you? The show, I mean.'

'Look at all the little red dots,' said Hermione.

Sophia looked. Wherever she could see a picture past the throngs there was a little red dot signifying it was sold. She blessed Richard and Hermione for being so sensible.

'I've seen some old friends,' said Richard. 'One or two of them know about all this sort of thing. They're frightfully impressed.'

Emil came up to Sophia and kissed her on the cheek. 'How can I persuade Thomas to sell me the large picture?' he asked.

'Hi, Sophie,' said Allegra, giving her a hug. 'Lovely party. Have you seen my ring?' She waved her left hand, the fourth finger of which was adorned by an enormous diamond rock. 'Where on earth is Thomas?'

'Hiding in a pub. Congratulations, I'm so pleased.'

'Mmm, it's announced in *The Times* today, and the *Independent* and the *Telegraph*. They did a thing on us in the *Mail*, also the next *Tatler*. Such fun. Emil's set his heart on the big picture with the angel.'

'Thomas won't sell. The gallery owner is furious.'

'I'll persuade him,' said Emil. 'Money talks.'

'I know it does, Emil,' said Sophia, 'but I really don't think you'll get round Thomas.'

'Shall we go and get him out of this stupid pub? Come on, Sophie.' Allegra took Sophia's arm.

Suddenly Thomas was there. His hair was ruffled and his eyes a little unfocused, but he was not completely drunk.

'Ran out of bloody money,' he said. 'I could only get two doubles. Where's the champagne?'

'Walter's after you with a gang of critics,' said Sophia.

'I'm not talking to anyone. I want a drink. This is impossible, all these bloody people!'

'Thomas, they've come to see your pictures.'

'Crap. They've come for the party, they don't give a stuff about the pictures. I know these private views, they're utterly bloody. Where can I hide?'

'Well, someone's been buying. It's got to have made money, look at the dots.'

'Thomas — *endlich* . . . ' Walter caught them. 'Come with me. I want you to meet — '

'I'm not meeting anyone. I want a drink. I'm staying here with Sophia.'

'Oh no you're not,' said Sophia. 'You're going with Walter. The show's obviously a success, for Christ's sake. Go and chat people up. You're meant to be professional: act it.'

Walter shot her a look of approbation, took Thomas's arm and steered him away.

Sophia, temporarily abandoned, stood in a corner and took a breather. The noise was still a nightmare, but she fancied the crowd was thinning. She reckoned that whatever the critics thought, the show was a commercial success; she and Zoff had been right. Over half the pictures had red dots. She also guessed that, judging by the type of buyer at the show, it would have been a social success; Thomas would be set fair to become a fashionable artist whose work would go on selling. Even if the serious critics had nothing to say, his show might be reported in glossy magazines and gossip columns. She hoped such praise would be enough for Thomas, who dreamed of having a picture of his in the Tate.

Some people came up to her to say goodbye. Her parents and Edward were among them.

'It was *wonderful*,' said her mother. 'All the *people* . . . so *exciting* . . . such a frightfully *smart* place . . . and the *pictures* . . . so *beautiful* . . . not all this modern stuff but all so *pretty* . . . '

'I really enjoyed it,' said Edward. 'I'd have bought one if I'd been able to afford it. It was a pity not to meet Thomas, though.'

'Splendid,' said her father, 'splendid.'

'I'm sorry you didn't see Thomas,' said Sophia. 'He seems to be surrounded by critics — or he was. I can't see him at the moment.'

'Never mind,' said her mother. 'Please give him all our best, won't you? Tell him we thought it was simply *fantastic*. I don't think I'll ever forget it.'

Sophia kissed them with a warmth she had not felt for years. Then she went in search of Thomas.

She found him with his parents in a little office behind the gallery. He was sitting in an armchair looking dazed.

'Not feeling very well,' he said.

'He needs to go straight home,' said

Hermione, 'and I should call a doctor, Sophia.'

'I don't want to see a doctor,' said Thomas.

Walter, all his previous irritation with Thomas gone, crept noiselessly into the little room.

'My dear,' he said to Thomas, almost audibly purring, 'you are *un succès fou*. It is probably the best show I have had this year at Zoff's.'

Thomas looked blank.

'But you are feeling unwell? *Wie Schade!* I had thought we might toast your success with a little something special I keep only for these occasions.'

'I'm afraid we'll have to take him home,' said Hermione, and her round blue eyes looked, as they had when Sophia first met her, full of apprehension.

'Of course, of course, dear Lady Avondale,' purred Walter. 'Clara here will call a taxi, yes? Perhaps while we are waiting, a little drink . . . ?'

'Very kind,' said Richard. 'No, thank you.'

They escaped at last, Walter's girl having hailed a taxi in the street. On the way back to Kennington, Thomas fell asleep.

'He's exhausted,' Sophia said.

'He just needs a good sleep,' said Richard. 'Bit drunk too, I shouldn't wonder.'

'A couple of glasses of champagne and two double whiskies? Only slightly.'

Hermione and Sophia put Thomas to bed at Sophia's house. He stumbled in and up the stairs, barely regaining consciousness.

'I don't think a doctor is what he needs,' said Sophia. 'He just needs to rest.'

'I don't know,' said Hermione doubtfully.

They had planned for the four of them to dine in a small restaurant near the gallery after the show, but Richard had cancelled it. Sophia offered the Avondales a meal at her house, but no one was hungry. Presently they left to spend the night at the London flat of a friend.

Sophia went to bed immediately. In the bed beside her, Thomas slept soundly, undisturbed by her.

★   ★   ★

Next day, when Sophia woke up as usual at seven, Thomas was still asleep. She brought him a cup of coffee in bed when she had got dressed, but he did not wake up. She rang up her office and told them she would be in late.

Thomas came to at nine.

'God, I feel dreadful,' he complained. 'How long have I slept?'

She told him.

'Did I have too much to drink last night?'

'No, not particularly.'

'I don't think I made much sense to those people of Walter's. Those art critics.'

'I hardly think that matters.'

'I think the show was all right, don't you? God, I wish I didn't feel so awful.'

'The show was terrific. What is it you feel exactly?'

'I don't know. Just awful. Tired even though I've slept so much.'

'Of course you're tired. Don't worry about it.'

'Sophia — would you mind awfully if I just went back to Avondale with Father and Herm for a few days?'

'Of course not. It's probably the best thing you could do. Then I'll come down at the weekend — that's in three days.'

Richard and Hermione duly fetched Thomas later that morning after Sophia had gone to work. When she came home to her empty house that night she felt tired and anti-climactic, cheated of a celebration with Thomas. She rang Avondale and had the usual long wait for Richard to answer the sole telephone in his office. When she spoke to Thomas he still sounded tired and out of sorts. He told her Hermione had tried to get a doctor to see him, but he had refused.

Sophia put down the telephone receiver, suffused with longing. It was Wednesday evening; in less than forty-eight hours she would be with Thomas at Avondale. Never had she missed him so badly; this weekend all the difficulties and frustrations of the last few months would be resolved, and she would get her reward.

24

On Friday morning, the telephone by Sophia's bed woke her up. She switched on her bedside lamp and saw that it was six o'clock in the morning.

'It's Hermione,' said the little voice through the receiver. Sophia was immediately alert; her hand tightened on the telephone.

There was a hesitation; then Hermione continued, speaking levelly: 'Sophia, Thomas died last night. It was his heart. It was very peaceful.'

Silence; not even a hiss from the telephone.

In that instant, Sophia's world turned upside down. She went numb. A tiny part of her remained awake and normal and spoke for her.

'No pain?'

'He must have just passed out. He had been watching television in the television room. Richard and I had been in the drawing room. When we went to tell him we were going to bed, he was just sitting there . . . '

The tiny, conscious part of Sophia thought Hermione might be fighting tears. The voice continued, with an effort, ' . . . and he didn't move. He had stopped breathing. We tried all the first aid and called the doctor, but it was much too late. We couldn't have saved him.'

'Can I come and see him? Can I come now? I won't go to work.'

'There has to be an autopsy. He's at the local hospital. It's best if you come straight here.'

'I'll be as quick as I can.'

Hermione's voice wavered again. 'Please come, Sophia. We need you.'

'I'll be there. I'll get up now. Goodbye.'

However, when she had replaced the receiver she lay back in bed, staring straight up at the ceiling. Her mind was a blank. It continued to be very quiet; she did not hear the distant early morning London traffic. Her bedside lamp made a pool of light on the ceiling of her bedroom. She thought she could detect the beginning of a crack in the left hand corner and the hint of a cobweb, but it might just have been the shadow. Outside it was very dark.

A little more of Sophia's consciousness stirred, as it occurred to her that she had to do certain things. She would need to pack a suitcase with appropriate clothes; she must ring up the office on her way to Avondale; the car had very little petrol.

Presently she got up, had a shower and

dressed in a grey suit from the period before she had met Thomas. She never thought of eating. It was still dark when she left the house. When she switched the car engine on, the car suddenly reverberated with Schumann's piano concerto, to which she had been listening on the way home from work last night. As if stung, she shot her hand out and jabbed at the knob to shut off the CD player.

She got quickly out of London, driving against the heavy incoming traffic. On the motorway, she drove faster than ever before in her life, cruising at over a hundred miles an hour. The idea popped into her mind that it might be appropriate now for her to crash the car and kill herself; then, as she approached a bridge over the motorway she noticed crash barriers around its supports at the side and in the middle of the road. She remembered they were there to prevent precisely such an attempt. In any case, she was instinctively concentrating intently on her driving, just as she always did when she went fast.

Her mind began of itself to focus on what Hermione had told her; with a conscious effort she distanced herself, switching on the radio to hear the news. She could not listen to music. At eight o'clock she slowed down to use her telephone to let them know at work that she could not come in today.

On the narrow roads nearer Avondale, she drove too quickly into a bend, nearly lost her steering, veered onto the wrong side of the road and only just avoided a crash with an oncoming vehicle. The other driver shouted imprecations and made rude signs. She felt as if it was happening to someone else, as if in a dream, but she slowed down and drove the rest of the way more carefully.

As she came up the familiar drive, the gravel crunching under her wheels, she realised she was extremely tired. She wanted to go to sleep. Perhaps if she did so she would wake up later, and the news that Thomas had died would prove simply to have been a nightmare.

The golden house looked exactly the same, and as always it betokened Thomas, but when she stopped the car outside the back door none of the dogs appeared with loud barks and waving tails. She looked at the back door, as if expecting Thomas to come out. As she rose from her car, Hermione came to greet her, holding out her arms. They said nothing and hugged each other. Richard joined them and also hugged Sophia mutely.

Sophia was shocked by their appearance. Each had aged ten years in one night.

In the kitchen they sat her down and gave

her coffee and toast. She ate and drank automatically. They asked her about her journey, marvelling at the speed of her arrival. She answered in monosyllables and stared around herself, sensing that Richard and Hermione and the dogs and Alice the cat and all their surroundings — hitherto dear and familiar to her — had changed for ever.

'Would you like to come and say goodbye to Thomas now?' Hermione asked her.

'Say goodbye?' repeated Sophia dully.

'It's just that we have to go now. There won't be another chance, because of the autopsy.'

She acquiesced numbly. They went out to the Range Rover. As they were about to climb into it, Harry, the stud groom, approached them.

'Lord Avondale,' he said with urgency.

'What is it?'

'May I drive you, please? I don't think you should.'

'Don't be silly,' snapped Richard, but Hermione intervened: 'Thank you, Harry. You're very kind. It's a good idea. Come on, darling, move over. None of us are fit to drive.'

The drive took about half an hour. At the small local hospital they were kept waiting for two or three minutes; then a nurse came and took them to the little room where Thomas was lying.

It was very dimly lit and appeared to be a sort of subaqueous green. There were no windows. It contained nothing but a hospital bed and a plain wooden crucifix on the wall above the bedhead. Thomas had been laid under a sheet and blanket, his hands tidily set straight down by his sides. Sophia found herself the first to enter this room. She kept her eyes down as she went through the door; then she raised them and looked at the bed. The body on it was not Thomas.

Slowly she extended her hand and touched the still hand on one side. It was very cold. She looked at the head. It had Thomas's features, but it was diminished. The skin was waxy and yellowish. Her instant reaction was revulsion; then she could not tear her eyes away. There was the white-grey forelock she had loved to stroke, and she saw and knew again for the last time the long, curving black eyelashes. Not properly aware of what she was doing, she knelt and kissed the stone-cold forehead and slowly ran her hand over the cheek, caressing it. She felt the rise of tears; they streamed silently out of her eyes.

Sophia withdrew to let the Avondales pay their last respects. As they left, they held hands tightly, Sophia in the middle. No one spoke.

Back at Avondale, they found Richard's other children, Charles and Victoria; they had left their spouses behind with their children. There were more semi-silent greetings. Over coffee, which no one wanted and everyone seemed to think should be drunk, they discussed what had to be done.

Victoria, standing in for her shell-shocked father and stepmother, was the best organiser. The death had to be registered, the family solicitor contacted, the vicar to be seen and the funeral arranged, family and friends to be informed, announcements to go into newspapers. In addition to this, there was the normal routine of Avondale, its stud and estate. Sophia was almost relieved that this activity was forced on them. She needed to be told what to do and, having convinced the Avondales she was up to it, was set the task of letting people know.

Sophia went into Richard's office and got to work. She made a list. She spoke to Walter Zoff at the gallery; calmly she rang up her parents, got her mother and managed to keep it short; Allegra was next, and she was difficult because she cried on the telephone. She told her news calmly and dispassionately;

the numbness which had taken her over at the beginning had only temporarily deserted her at the hospital. To the shocked reactions of friends she murmured simply, 'I'm so sorry,' and when they tried to condole with her, 'You're very kind.'

That afternoon the vicar called. He was a young man and had only been at the Avondale parish for eight years. Hermione and Sophia gave him tea in the kitchen.

He looked at them with grief and frank bewilderment. 'I'm so very sorry,' he said. 'It's hard to take it in. I didn't know him all that well; but it's just like — like a light going out. I can't put it any other way.'

Hermione and the vicar discussed the funeral and burial and set a date for next week in the small church at Avondale. Sophia fulfilled her second allotted task of having the death and the funeral announced in the newspapers.

After the vicar had gone Hermione said to Sophia, 'Will you stay the night?'

'May I?'

'We'd very much rather you did.'

'Only would you mind terribly if I didn't have my normal room?'

Hermione understood.

Julian came before dinner. He shook Sophia's composure more than anything since she had seen Thomas. He wept as he hugged her.

'I couldn't get away. I never even got to say goodbye.'

Sophia and Hermione prepared a scratch supper, but by that time no one could bear to eat. Charles and Victoria went home to their families. Richard, Hermione, Julian and Sophia went to sit over the fire in the drawing room.

Richard addressed Hermione: 'My dear, I think we should tell Sophia . . . '

His voice trailed off, and Hermione took it up: ' . . . about what he — Thomas — left?'

Richard nodded mutely. Sophia tensed.

'He told us,' Hermione started, 'that he wanted to marry you. You were engaged and wanted to tell us all after the exhibition?'

'Yes,' said Sophia.

'He had got this ring for you,' Hermione continued. 'Oh! I don't know whether this is the right time to tell you this, or to show you. It's all so painful. I've got it here. He was going to give it to you this weekend; we weren't sure of the size. Look — '

She handed Sophia a little faded blue velvet jeweller's box. Inside, sitting in a bed of creamy satin, was a gold ring set with large rubies and tiny pearls. It was unusual and evidently very old.

'It was his mother's ring. Sophia, I don't want to make it worse. But it was right you should know about it. He loved you very much.'

Sophia gazed mutely at the ring; then she looked up and saw the three pairs of eyes staring at her, bright with unshed tears.

'It's your ring now,' said Richard; 'will you take it?'

The words came to her with difficulty. 'Thank you. It's very beautiful.' Slowly she took the ring from the box, but she hesitated to try it on her left hand; she replaced it. Again those eyes met hers.

They gave her a small, anonymous room on the top floor that night; it was nowhere near the bedroom in which she had slept during her first stay there and which she had subsequently always shared with Thomas. She took some strong sleeping pills, terrified of being unable to sleep.

Next morning she woke up early as usual. The room was pitch dark. Her sleep had been so deep that she was disorientated, expecting vaguely still to be in London. She reached out for Thomas and discovered she was in a single bed. Slowly and inexorably her mind emerged from unconsciousness, and as she began to realise where she was she desired, with increasing desperation, to stop and revert to not knowing.

However, this was a new day. Thomas was dead.

She tried and failed to go back to sleep.

She, Julian and the Avondales supported each other through the Saturday and Sunday. On Sunday evening, however, she insisted on driving back to London.

'You're *mad*,' said Richard.

'Sophia, I'm not at all sure that's wise,' said Hermione.

'I wish you'd stay,' said Julian.

'I've got to go back to work.'

Richard was suddenly furious. 'I've never heard anything so ridiculous in my life!'

'I'm sorry.'

'You really are set on going, aren't you?' said Hermione, much more gently.

'Please let me go. I have things I must do there. There's not so much for me to do here. It's not just work. I have to go through his things.'

'For God's sake, drive carefully,' said Richard urgently.

'I'll come back the evening before the funeral.'

She drove slowly, feeling the need to be careful if only because Richard, Hermione and Julian had wanted it. Her little house was warm when she returned because she had forgotten to switch off its heating on Friday morning. She welcomed the warmth and felt a very faint relief to be there. It was, after all, the place where she had been used to being alone, even latterly when Thomas had been working so hard for the show. However, she avoided her own bedroom because it was full of Thomas's things, even down to a paperback on his bedside table; similarly she did not feel up to coping with their bathroom. She managed to go to sleep that night without drugs, but in her spare bedroom.

25

On the morning of the funeral, Sophia walked to the church arm-in-arm with Julian. It was about half a mile away. It was intensely cold; the sky was a clear pale blue and the sun was just beginning to melt the hoar-frost. She wore a black fur hat, a long dark coat and boots, but when she sat down in the front pew of the church she soon realised they would not protect her from the even deeper cold that seemed to permeate the church, completely overcoming its ancient metal radiators.

The funeral announcements had specified family flowers only, but the family was generous in these tributes, and the coffin was covered in them. In the centre was her own wreath of white roses and lilies and, because Thomas had been fond of them, freesias. The scent of the flowers rose faintly above the cold. At first the flowers distracted her from the coffin in which Thomas lay, just a few feet away from her.

Having arrived early, she did not notice the people behind. There were so many that the church could not contain them all. They crowded into the back behind the filled pews and spilled out beyond the open doors.

The service was dry and formal but not without beauty; the Anglican ritual was, as nearly as possible, without emotion. Sophia had requested and been granted the use of the King James Gospels and the old version of the prayer-book. The hymns were *He Who Would Valiant Be* (Richard's and Hermione's choice) and *Teach me, my God and King* (her own). Determinedly she sang them both, her head held high. She and Julian each read a lesson; hers was St Paul to the Corinthians on faith, hope and charity. When she stood in the pulpit to face the congregation its size took her aback, but she refused to be moved because she had to read properly, and she intended to show no emotion before all the people. She looked above the heads of the congregation, not seeing or singling out any individuals; in the pulpit before them she felt isolated. The sobs and sniffs, muffled and open, that she heard did not reach her. Similarly, she heard but did not take in the words of the funeral service.

Julian had insisted on reading his lesson; it was his tribute to Thomas. He read slowly and clearly, with evident concentration, but he was almost blinded with tears afterwards and stumbled back into the pew.

Outside, Sophia felt as if she had frozen over, physically and mentally. As the coffin was lowered into the ground she withdrew further into herself. Automatically she threw earth onto it, the first to do so. It rattled on the lid. She stood back as the rest of the mourners followed her. They took a long time; she did not look at them. Then everyone went away, and she stayed on at the side of the grave, not looking down at the earth-spattered coffin or at anything in particular. She just stood there as if rooted to the ground.

It was Richard who came back to her and very gently took her arm. 'Come on, my dear, it's all over.' Almost beyond feeling, she let herself be guided back through the church-yard and into the Avondales' car. In the car, she found that she had been clutching Thomas's ring in her right hand throughout the funeral; she had not worn it.

*   *   *

Over a hundred people had drinks and a buffet lunch at Avondale after the funeral. Sophia had expected to help with handing food and drink round, but the efficient Victoria had had the meal catered; women in black dresses and white aprons saw to it. The

336

guests disposed themselves around the hall, the drawing room (where the furniture had been moved back against the walls), the dining room and, in the case of closer friends, the kitchen.

'What a wonderful service,' said some of the guests to her, 'and how beautifully you read.'

She supposed they must think her cold and unfeeling, as she had displayed so little emotion.

'Hello, darling,' said one of the guests; 'how are you feeling?'

'Are you all right, dear?' said another.

She looked dully at these guests and had a shock; they were her parents.

'It's so kind of you to come,' she said, at a loss. 'How . . . '

'Don't you remember, you told us you didn't know the date of the funeral, but it would be in the *Telegraph*? We thought we *had* to come, not that we knew Thomas frightfully *well*, but we liked him so and, well, it's so ghastly for you . . . ' Her mother petered out.

Her father touched her arm. 'We're so sorry, dear, so very sorry.'

'I can't believe you're here. It's lovely that you came . . . thank you . . . let me find Thomas's parents so that I can introduce you.' She frowned with concentration and looked for Richard or Hermione.

'That's all right, darling,' said Mrs White. 'Lady Avondale has been so kind. We met them after the funeral, and they told us to come here.'

'Why didn't you let me know you were coming?'

'Oh, we didn't know whether you'd be here or in London . . . We didn't want to upset you.'

'I'm so glad you've found her,' said Hermione, approaching. 'Sophia, are you all right? Aren't you eating or drinking any-thing?'

'I don't really feel like anything, thanks.' Sophia felt slightly sick.

'Do you want to sit down, darling?' asked her mother.

'Please — I'm all right.'

'Oh Lady Avondale, she's frightfully *pale*. Perhaps she should lie down.'

'Please call me Hermione, and my husband's Richard. Sophia, you really don't look well, what do you want to do?'

'I'd like to be alone . . . I feel rather sick, actually.'

She barely made it up the stairs to her top floor room; when she lay down she was nearly fainting. She took off most of her clothes, pulled the covers over her head and turned towards the wall, but although nothing of the funeral reception could be heard she could not lose consciousness.

Some hours later, as it was growing dark, footsteps were heard tapping down the corridor. She lay half asleep and half awake, indifferent as to who the visitor might be. Her door opened a crack.

'Sophie?'

She switched on her bedside lamp. It was her mother.

'I've brought you a nice cup of tea. Milk, no sugar, just like you always had it. Are you feeling any better?'

Susan White sat down on the bed, placed the teacup on the bedside table and stroked Sophia's head. Suddenly, for the first time since Thomas's death, Sophia completely broke down.

26

Like a nightmare, Christmas descended on the stricken Avondales. Having discussed it not only with Sophia but also with her parents, Richard and Hermione persuaded Sophia to spend it with them. She was almost, but not quite, beyond caring, knowing only that despite the new warmth between herself and her parents, she would have cast a pall over Christmas at Epsom with which she would have been beyond coping. If she could have spent the holiday just with them and maybe Edward, she would have done so, but she could not stomach facing Anthea and that family. However, she worried that she would spoil things for the Avondales.

'I'm not a good person to have around at the moment,' she told Richard and Hermione.

'What silly things you say sometimes, my dear,' said Richard in a surprisingly gentle voice.

'I mean, you'll be having the children and trying to make it happy for them, and I won't be much help.'

'Such nonsense,' said Hermione. 'You surely don't imagine that even the children expect or want a jolly Christmas? They're devastated too. You know how much they loved Thomas. We can't make it happy for them. All we can do is to be together.'

'I'm sorry I'm so hopeless.'

'Come on, that's not like you,' said Hermione.

Sophia kept wanting to cry. She was feeling generally unwell and sorry for herself. At the same time she tried desperately not to think of Thomas because she could not yet bear to do so.

The Avondales observed most of the conventions of Christmas. Only Julian and Sophia stayed at Avondale, but Charles and Victoria and their respective families spent Christmas Day there as they always did, opening presents under the tree, going to church and eating Christmas dinner. Sophia, who had had several days off work partly for compassionate leave and partly for holidays long owed to her, had gone to much trouble over her presents, far more than in the past for her own family. Some, such as a crate of wine for Richard, she had bought even before the exhibition; most she had planned to buy with Thomas's help and advice after it.

They were all desperately kind to each

other. Tears seemed always to be just below the surface. All the Avondales and their spouses and Julian had vivid memories of Thomas this time last year which Sophia noticeably avoided sharing with them. If any of them so much as started, 'Do you remember . . . ' she would find an excuse to leave the room; if such a remark was made during a meal, she looked at her plate and made a conscious effort to switch off. Apart from this she made great efforts to contribute to the family gathering. It was heavy going. From time to time she felt unwell, which she thought was probably just a physical reaction to the strain of Thomas's death and funeral.

On Boxing Day Hermione and Julian went out hunting with most of the rest of the family; Richard elected not to go.

'I'm doing less these days,' he said to Sophia. 'Would you like to come and watch a little of it with me on foot?'

'That would be lovely,' said Sophia, her acquiescence concealing indifference.

They drove to the meet. Richard tactfully arrived just before the hunt moved off, relieving Sophia of the need to greet anyone there. Then he led the way down a track to the first covert hounds were to draw, explaining to Sophia as they walked along how hounds worked and what the huntsman was doing.

For fifteen minutes or so they stood at the edge of the covert on the other side from the field of hunt followers. The undergrowth was alive with the sniff and crackle and occasional bark or whimper of hounds; from time to time a hunt servant cried out to encourage them, strange liquid cries that were beyond Sophia's ken. Richard went on telling her, sotto voce, what was going on. She was entertained and began to relax. Then a hound spoke in earnest, and the others took it up.

'Look!' hissed Richard. 'Don't make a sound.'

A fox broke covert yards away from them. Sophia, who had never seen a live one before, was struck by its neat elegance. It paused for a split second, failed to notice them and ran off along the side of a hedge and up to a ridge.

Hounds picked up the scent and poured out of the other side of the covert. The fox was nowhere to be seen.

'It's going for the stream at the bottom of the hill over the ridge,' said Richard. 'They'll lose it, but they might have a bit of a run first.'

The field followed the hounds at some distance. They saw them begin cantering and jumping over a hedge between two fields.

'There goes Hermione — can you see? Jumped that beautifully. And Jules. Tom was first class over this country.' Richard looked animated, almost as in the old days.

The fresh air and exercise had stirred Sophia's spirits; intent on the distant horsemen jumping the hedge, she took Richard's comments in her stride. 'Oh yes,' she said, 'I can imagine. I'm hopeless at riding, but I always thought Thomas looked wonderful on a horse — very much at home in the saddle.'

'He was actually quite gifted with horses,' Richard said.

'He loved hunting, didn't he?'

'Marvellous at it. Knew the country and knew how to trust his horse. Not silly, you know — not one for jumping everything in sight just for the hell of it. He couldn't come out with us last year — no horse for him. Pity. He stayed at home with Victoria's children. Loved children. Always said he wanted at least ten of his own.'

Sophia laughed. Richard looked sharply at her, because he had not heard her laugh for so long. 'Ten! He never quite got round to spelling that one out to me.'

'I still think it's a pity you never got round to riding.'

'Oh, Thomas once got me onto a horse. It was when you were away. I fell off.'

'*Really?*' said Richard, his eyes alight with humour. 'Oh dear, Tom was good at getting people to do things.'

Sophia paused and raised troubled grey eyes to Richard. 'Please, Richard. Don't remind me any more. I don't think I can take it.'

'Didn't it give you pleasure just now to remember how well he rode?'

'I feel,' Sophia said slowly, 'as if I had lost part of myself. I can't bear to be reminded of it.'

'Oh, my dear,' Richard said, 'can I tell you something? Let's walk along here. Take my arm. That's just how I felt when I lost Marie-Hélène, Tom's mother.'

Sophia looked at him with new interest. 'I remember your telling me he was only four when it happened.'

'She died in a car crash. It was in January — icy roads, you know. She skidded coming out onto a main road; hit a heavy lorry. A few seconds earlier or later it wouldn't have happened. The police came to Avondale. I'd been getting worried. She died instantly.' He paused and then carried on, speaking more slowly. 'I was beside myself for some time. I didn't know how I could go on. I loved her so much. My first marriage hadn't worked; I met Marie-Hélène after the divorce. My first wife ran off with someone rather richer and grander than myself — I'm not boring you?'

'Not remotely.'

'I was devastated. Then I met this beautiful girl. She was half French, and we adored each other. We had a wonderful marriage, so happy. Never believed such happiness was possible. Then Thomas was born, and everything seemed perfect. He was such a beautiful child. I hadn't much liked babies, even Charlie and Victoria, but Tom . . . I went to pieces when she died.'

'But everything worked out in the end. You met Hermione.'

'That was later, much later. You see, I could never really let myself go. There were the children — Tom, Charlie and Victoria. Couldn't let them down. I didn't feel much at the time, but I loved them too, you know. And then I became terribly, terribly lucky and met Hermione.'

'Lucky?'

'Oh yes, enormously. You see, I never thought I'd get another chance. It wasn't that I was old, or anything like that. But I didn't believe I could love anyone else as I loved Marie-Hélène. Odd, that — but true. Hermione is very different. I don't love her more or less, just differently — oh dear, I don't seem to be making very much sense.'

'Oh yes, you are,' said Sophia, staring up at Richard as they walked along.

'I suppose all I'm trying to say, my dear, is that I do understand how you are now, simply because something like that happened to me.'

Sophia looked at the ground in front of her.

'And d'you know, it was all worth it, and not just because Tom was born. Even though she died and it was hell, we'd still been happy. Now . . . I suppose the experience will help me to come to terms with losing Tom . . . ,' his voice suddenly became bleak, 'only I can't quite see how at the moment.'

He set his jaw and stared straight in front of himself. They did not speak again until they reached the car, and they drove home in silence. However, when they reached Avondale, Sophia touched Richard's arm and said, 'Thank you for telling me about Thomas's mother.'

'Always remember, Sophia, that Hermione and I care very much for you. You were going to marry Thomas. You will always be a member of our family.'

Sophia squeezed Richard's hand and went indoors.

It was impossible not to be reminded of Thomas. Wherever Sophia was in Avondale, his image could be summoned by an effortless but not always controllable trick of the imagination. Hermione, Richard and Julian really wanted to talk about him; for them such talk was consolation, not pain. Sophia took to reading in her bedroom, rather as she had a year ago at her parents' house. She cried off one or two meals on the grounds that she was feeling sick.

Hermione decided to take matters into her own hands. The day after Boxing Day, she sought Sophia out in her bedroom and found her engrossed in literature of some sort. She sat down on her bed.

'We're worried about you,' she began.

'I'm sorry.' Sophia sat up in bed. 'I'm not good company at the moment. I'm so very sorry.'

'I'm not on about that. Sophia, I think you should see a doctor. All this being unwell isn't right.'

'Oh, it's probably just a silly reaction. I read somewhere once you react physically to great emotional shocks. I know it's gone on a bit, but I'm sure it's just that. I'm sorry — '

'Stop apologising! It's not like you. My

dear, it's not just that you feel ill so much. What really worries us is that you're not coping.'

'Not coping?'

'With your loss. You're still as you were when Tom had just died. Oh, I can see how desperately hard it is for you, but you're turning in on yourself, it's as if you can't help yourself. No one can reach you.'

Sophia said nothing. Hermione found the gaze of her large grey eyes unsettling. She sat with her hand on Sophia's motionless one.

Eventually Sophia spoke. 'I do hear what you're saying. Please don't take it amiss, but I think I ought to go back to London. I promise to see a doctor when I'm there because you want me to. I find it . . . ,' she paused, ' . . . impossibly difficult to be where . . . where we were once so happy.'

She came down to supper that evening.

'When you're in London,' said Richard, 'will you do something for us? Will you go to the gallery, what's it called? I believe there are a few unsold pictures, and we'll need to take delivery of them. The show is probably over now. There are also two of yours, aren't there?'

'Yes — of course,' said Sophia, making an effort to appear normal.

'You know,' said Richard thoughtfully,

'what a wonderful thing that show was.'

'*What?*' Sophia almost cried out. 'How can you *say* that? It killed him!'

'He died because he had a weak heart,' Richard persisted. 'The show was an out-and-out success, *and he knew it.*'

'He *didn't*: he was utterly depressed and run down because of it!'

'But it was the best thing he'd ever done,' said Julian.

'The depression was nothing,' Richard insisted. 'I knew he was going to be all right, I knew it when he talked to us about you and the ring . . . '

'Richard!' Hermione interjected sharply. 'Must you remind Sophia . . . '

'I'm not trying to remind her of what she lost, I'm trying to say what Tom — and she — and all of us — what we all *had*. No one can ever take that away from any of us. Tom died completely happy, he accomplished what he had always wanted. What an achievement!'

Sophia, fighting tears, carried on with emotion: 'But he's dead, and it's not right, it was too early, it's obscene.'

'Oh my dear,' Richard said gently, 'don't you see, that doesn't mean his life wasn't wonderful?'

27

New Year's Day came and went. Sophia did not even reply to her New Year's Eve party invitations and spent that night in a drugged sleep. She was finding it increasingly difficult to sleep without such aids, which left her feeling sick and muzzy in the morning; it became harder for her to concentrate at work.

She spent more time in the office than ever before. Because she was becoming inefficient everything took longer. She avoided being at home for any longer than was necessary. She switched off her answer machine, and if the telephone rang when she was in the house she refused to answer it. At the weekends she stayed for hours in bed and tried to lose herself in books. The only constructive thing she did was to answer the dozens of letters of condolence she had received. It was only much later that she became surprised and touched at their number; she had heard not only from close friends but also from people she hardly knew. Her house stayed silent: she played no music.

Her health began to suffer; she was not eating properly; she felt and even was sick frequently. Her wan appearance did not escape the notice of her colleagues, and the mistakes she could not help making eventually alerted her senior directors.

The managing director asked to see her in his office. They sat down in leather armchairs at a coffee table, away from his desk.

'What seems to be the matter?' she asked coldly, brushing aside his polite enquiries about her well-being and offers of coffee.

The managing director was a thin, aggressive type only a few years older than Sophia, a brilliant strategist who was known to be ruthless. Because he and Sophia had plenty in common as professionals, they respected each other and normally worked well together. He now fixed her with an unblinking stare and said, 'Sophie, you're beginning to worry me.'

She took a deep breath. 'What do you mean?'

'You're letting mistakes happen. You're letting your people get away with sloppy, under-researched work.' He referred to a trainee's report which had somehow slipped out without being edited. 'It's nothing serious yet, but I want to avoid any serious cock-ups.'

She had seldom received such harsh criticism and had no excuses for the trainee's report. She sat stiffly, leaning forward with her arms folded, hunched slightly as if cold, and held her tongue.

The managing director softened his tone. 'I know how difficult things must be for you at the moment . . . ' he began.

'You can have no idea,' Sophia interjected.

' . . . We all think you're extremely brave . . . '

'May wenottalk about this?'

She wore her grief like armour. It seemed to him that anyone getting too close to her was liable to get cut or bruised. He frowned and said, with a discernible edge to his voice, 'Please let me finish. In short, I think you're taking on too much at the moment. You've had an enormous and very distressing shock. It's too much to cope with that and hold down a high level job. I want you to take time off. Do what you have to do to cover your absence here and then have a holiday. As long as you want.'

Sophia drew in her breath sharply and struggled briefly to contain a sudden surge of anger. Unfolding her arms, she pointedly put them on her knees and leant forward. Now she held the managing director's stare as she said in a low, level voice, 'You never were known for subtlety or tact, Stuart. Isn't this a rather heavy-handed way of giving me a verbal warning?'

'What on earth are you talking about?'

'I hadn't realised that I was becoming incompetent. I suppose I might just as well resign.'

His eyes registered shock. 'Don't be ridiculous! I never — '

Suddenly she was on her feet. 'Don't ever imagine I'll allow you the satisfaction of getting rid of me,' she hissed. He gaped as she stalked over to the door. 'You'll have my formal resignation today. I shall need to know what period if any of my contractual notice you will require me to serve.'

He almost ran to the door and seized its handle before she could leave.

'You fool, there's no way I'm accepting your resignation!'

Her face changed, her eyes widening; she seemed to shrink back into her invisible armour; she looked exhausted.

'Come here and sit down,' Stuart ordered. She obeyed mutely. 'Let me put it to you in words of two syllables. You're not well. I know that because your work at the moment is crap. I can't have that. But you're one of the best people I have and I want you to go on working here for me. So I want you to get better. Oh, and the time off's on full pay — however long it takes. Understand?'

She nodded.

'Am I being unreasonable?'

'No.'

'Good.' He grinned. 'God, you can't resign! How could I let you go over to the bastard opposition?'

She gave the ghost of a smile. 'Is that all?' She got up again; as she squared her shoulders he thought he saw in her the shadow of her old resolution.

'Sophie.' She paused; his voice was different. 'Good luck. Listen — if ever you feel like a sympathetic ear — you know, maybe supper one evening — you only have to call. Barbara and I would love to see you. You might find it really helpful to talk to Barbara . . . she's good at that sort of thing — '

'You mean, coping with sad people like me?' He was sure there was a glint in her eye, something of the old Sophia. She half smiled, then dropped her eyes and murmured, 'You're very kind,' her formula for the past few weeks. She returned to her desk, reflecting that such kindness on the part of her normally relentless MD. was indeed remarkable, so that the still small part of her that was not numb was warmed.

Sophia sat down at her desk, having closed her office door. She checked her screen of share prices, looked at her diary and contemplated the work awaiting her attention. A wave of exhaustion assailed her. Her outside line rang.

'Sophie,' said Anita. 'Where have you been? I've been trying to get you for ages.'

'Sorry. I know I've been elusive.'

'I so want to see you. Can you come over for supper tonight?'

'Oh Anita, I don't think so. I'm not good company these days — '

'I'm not looking for good company, you stupid woman. I want to see *you*.'

'You're very kind.' Sophia bit her tongue. 'I'm sorry,' she said in a brisker voice, 'I'm fed up with that cliché.'

'What?'

'Forget it. Do you really mean it?'

'Mean what?'

'About supper tonight.'

'Of course I mean it. Harold's still on at the Garrick, so it'll just be you and me. I'm longing to see you.'

'All right then. That would be lovely. About eight o'clock? Thank you for staying in touch. I really appreciate it.'

Suddenly Sophia felt hungry for the first time in weeks. She had always enjoyed supper *à deux* with Anita; there had been gossip and warmth and excellent food. She now had something to look forward to. However, she still had to make some kind of plan for her time off. It was clear that she must do as Stuart had asked, but she had no idea how to set about it. Dispassionately she gazed up at Thomas's picture of light, not really seeing it, and said out loud, 'What on earth am I going to do?'

'Pardon?' said a well-known voice. She looked up.

'Kevin! When are you going to learn to knock before you come in here! You *know* . . . '

'I *did*,' said Sophia's aggrieved colleague. 'I thought you said something, so I came in. About this new issue we were on about at the morning meeting — may I have a word?'

She looked at him in silence, holding him in suspense, and briefly considered chucking him out of her office, forgetting not only the new issue but everything concerned with her work, and, despite Stuart's words, leaving it for good.

Kevin shuffled and looked anxious. 'I mean, if it's OK . . . '

At last she smiled, breaking the spell. 'Sorry. Of course it's OK. Come in and sit down.'

Calmly and professionally, she discussed the business with him. When they had finished, she asked him to close the door of her office and to tell her department that she didn't want to be disturbed; she had some planning to do. She now began to think clearly. In her disciplined way, she drew up lists of things to be done before leaving and successfully distracted herself from the consideration of how to fill her unwanted free time.

'I don't want to do anything in particular,' she confessed later that evening to Anita. They were having a drink before dinner.

'Oh Sophie, a free holiday — on a plate!'

'But seriously, what could I do?'

'I don't know — go somewhere exotic, do something you've never done before.'

'I always hated holidays on my own. The best holiday I ever had was at Avondale. Oh, I don't want to go there!'

'But aren't you staying in touch with the Avondales?'

'Oh, I can't see them right now. Later.'

'I know problems always travel with you, but why don't you really consider travelling somewhere far away? What about those friends of yours in Australia — Don and Josie, d'you remember we met them, they were lovely — you told me they'd begged you to go back?'

Sophia frowned. 'Sure, with Thomas — on my honeymoon. No, Anita, I don't need that.'

'I think that's silly,' said Anita. 'It's a beautiful place, you were happy there, you have terrific friends there who have nothing to do with Thomas. Also, I know Australia a bit, I really think it's the easiest country if you're holidaying on your own. It's so informal, you can't help meeting people, and you know how nice the people there are. There couldn't be a better break, this one was made in heaven and is out there, waiting for you.'

'It's the middle of summer there now,' said Sophia in a different tone of voice.

'There you are. Promise me you'll ring them up tomorrow and ask.'

'Oh, I don't know.'

'*Promise.*'

'Anita! Shut up. I don't know. Stop bossing me about. I don't feel all that well, anyway.'

Anita leaned forward, took Sophia's hand and spoke urgently. 'If someone doesn't boss you about you'll fall apart. You look dreadful, you aren't well — go to the doctor.'

'Oh God,' said Sophia, drawing back, 'I promised Hermione I'd do that.'

'You've got to do something about yourself, Sophie, you really must. You haven't been in touch with the Avondales, and I bet not with your parents either. You can't go on like this.'

Sophia drew herself in and exclaimed in fury, 'Don't you *dare* . . . ' but then she stopped suddenly, and her shoulders slumped. 'Don't lecture me,' she said in a small voice.

Anita came over and put her arm around her shoulders. 'I so want to help,' she said.

Sophia pulled herself together and smiled. 'You do help. What's for supper?' she asked in a firmer tone of voice.

Anita had made a thick vegetable soup with home-made bread; then there was a carbonnade de boeuf. 'The bread's a new thing,' she said.

Sophia spread butter onto a thick piece which was still warm from the oven. The butter melted at once. The bread was crusty on the outside and doughy on the inside; there were sunflower seeds in it; it was gone in a flash, and she asked for more.

'Thomas meant to try bread,' said Sophia. 'You remember how keen he was on food?'

'A man after my own heart,' said Anita, laughing. 'I used to say you didn't deserve him.'

'He even taught me to cook a bit, after a fashion. My wine and his food — we made a great team.'

'Have some more soup.'

'Do you know, this is the first time in ages I feel hungry?'

Sophia ate that evening until she could eat no more, and she and Anita drank two bottles of wine between them. She spent the night at their house, feeling grateful that she did not have to drive back across half of London to her empty one. When she woke up the next morning, she did not experience the usual nightmare of remembering that Thomas was dead, and that she had somehow to get through a new day.

28

Don and Josie Clancy had written to Sophia before Christmas, because although Sophia had not told them about the change in her fortunes occasioned by Thomas's death, her boss Stuart had done so without her knowledge. When she had received their letter of condolence, she had felt obscurely grateful to Stuart for telling them, although she never thought, in the selfishness of bereavement, to thank him. In their letter they had offered their hospitality at any time she liked and had even set out their immediate plans so that she might, if she felt like taking them up on their offer, arrange her travel around them. She had written back to them just as she had replied to all the other letters of condolence; her letters had been brief, polite and impersonal.

Sophia now sent Don a fax; he replied almost immediately, urging her to come out as soon as she could arrange a flight. She found out about flights. Because it was nearly February there was plenty of space whenever she wanted to go. It was suggested that she might stop off on the way to ease the jet lag, so she read brochures on Thailand, Singapore, Malaysia and Bali; she might also like to explore Australia a little, perhaps by visiting the Queensland coast and Alice Springs. None of it seemed real, but it gave her something to do.

Having worked out a plan for travel, she refused to commit herself. At the office, she worked hard to get her affairs in order for her departure. At home, she found a message on the newly reinstated answer machine.

'How are you, Sophia? I'm going to be in London tomorrow, may I see you? Ring me up tonight if you can't . . . ' It was Julian.

She frowned and told herself she should never have switched the thing back on. However, it never occurred to her to get out of seeing Julian. She rang him up in his flat in Cirencester and arranged to meet him at her house tomorrow afternoon.

He came as he had before in his ancient Landrover, but this time it was not raining, and he was not late. It was a mild, grey day with the sort of heavy clouds that make you wonder if you will ever see the sun again.

Julian immediately noticed a change in Sophia which took him aback. He had always found her very attractive. When she had been with Thomas she had had a certain way of looking at her lover; also, all her movements about him had seemed graceful and gentle, as if in an unconscious response to him. Julian had sometimes fancied that he was half in love with her himself, even though he regarded her as strictly out of bounds. Now, although she appeared as poised as ever, there was a coldness about her he had never seen. There was something missing in her eyes. Having lost her mysterious beauty for him, she merely looked too pale and thin.

'I left really early,' said Julian, giving Sophia his usual bear hug. 'I knew I'd get lost.'

'Would you like tea or coffee? Did you in fact get lost?'

'It wasn't too bad, actually. Yes, coffee please, with loads of sugar. Funny, really. It was a bit easier on my own.' They went into the kitchen, where Sophia put the kettle on.

She smiled without looking him in the eye. 'No distractions.'

Great sadness clouded Julian's eyes fleetingly; then he smiled back and asked how she had been getting on. She shrugged. 'It's been pretty bad,' she admitted, 'but I've got a vague plan to take some time off. They don't like my sad face in the office.' She laughed without humour.

'You look all right,' said Julian. 'Too thin, but then you always were.'

'You haven't told me what's brought you to

London. You never come here if you can help it.'

'Ah. Well, actually, I hope you don't mind, but I've come about Tom's pictures.'

'His pictures? Here, you'd better put in the sugar. Biscuits?'

Julian stirred four teaspoons of sugar into his mug and ate some chocolate biscuits which had been there since Thomas's time, and which Sophia had forgotten.

'Mummy told me to see to the pictures. She said you'd been going to do it, but she didn't want to push you.'

She stared at her coffee mug. 'I'm sorry,' she said without looking up at him.

'I know it's hard,' he said mildly, 'but why didn't you do something?'

'I should have done it. I should have been in touch.'

'Yes, actually, you should.' She glanced up at him and realised she had never before seen him frown. 'Mummy and Richard know better than anyone else that it's awful for you, but it's awful for them too. They've missed you. They tried to ring, but you never even had the answer phone on. I was amazed when I caught you, I was going to write and just tried on the off-chance. They didn't like to chase you. You might have thought of them.'

Anger began to rise in Sophia, the same

that she had felt in Stuart's office, but far greater. It seemed to Julian that she became even paler, and her eyes appeared huge and clouded. She began to clench and unclench her fists and to walk up and down her kitchen. Mesmerised, he watched her.

There was silence for a few seconds; then Sophia began to speak.

'You can't begin to imagine,' she said, speaking at first in a low, level voice which rose and quickened as she got into her stride. 'None of you has any idea what this bereavement is for me. Do you know, before I met Thomas I had nothing. Oh, I know I had a high-powered job and made lots of money, but I wasn't close to anyone, I was out of touch with my family, I had no real hope of settling down with someone and being happy. Don't you ask me why, it was the way I was. Maybe it was my fault. It probably was, I had a difficult character. Thomas was — Thomas *is* — the only person who has ever known me through and through and still loved me. He really loved me, even though he knew how difficult I could be. He loved me better than I ever loved myself. He was like the most wonderful part of me, and yet he was outside me, an independent person who loved me as no one has ever loved me. Do you know what he wanted more than anything else in the world?' Julian's mouth fell open and gaped; he made no effort to answer this rhetorical question. 'He wanted a family! With *me*! Babies, marriage, all the things I had always known were impossible for me. They were impossible because I wasn't like other people. I never had been. I'd always been alone. He believed, he really believed I could do it, I could have a baby like an ordinary woman. I actually began to believe it myself, he almost convinced me. Then just as I was beginning to hope, just when all the happiness seemed so possible, so close, just when I was realising how lucky I was, how much I loved him, how I wasn't alone any more, not at all, never as long as he lived, even if we weren't physically together — he *died*! God! What a massive cosmic joke! What an arbitrary, stupid piece of dumb luck! What a total, pathetic nonsense! *That's* what bereavement is.'

She stopped pacing and banged her knuckles down on the kitchen table. Julian stared at her dumbly like a sparrow hypnotised by a cobra.

'Don't accuse me of bad behaviour, Julian. I'm not proud of how I've been to your parents, but so what? What does anything matter to me now? I tell you,' she leaned forward and glared at him, 'there isn't much point to anything I do now! I'm meant to be

367

going to Australia soon. Who cares? I don't.'
She seemed abruptly to have forgotten that it
was Julian who was her audience and
addressed the air. 'Life has become so boring.
There's nothing to look forward to, and every
day is an almighty drag. I don't know why I
bother.'

Julian found a voice and half whispered,
'Why, then?'

'I don't know.' In her anger she did not
look at him. 'I was never religious, but now I
am convinced as never before that there is
nothing, no after-life, no God, nothing like
that. Thomas really is dead; he's not out there
somewhere waiting for me. I don't have
anything to live for. I've thought of ending it,
but I can't seem to do it. Before Thomas . . . '

She broke off suddenly, as if recalled to the
reality of her immediate surroundings and the
presence of Julian. She saw him properly, as if
for the first time since he had entered her
house. His round, normally rosy face was
nearly as pale as her own, and there was
misery — for himself, but also for her — in
his eyes. He was even shivering slightly. He
was altogether so woebegone that Sophia was
jolted out of her passion. For the first time
since Thomas's death she looked beyond
herself and found someone else suffering.

'Jules,' she said gently, sitting down beside

him, 'what have I been saying to you? I went too far just now. I'm sorry. No one should have had to listen to that. I'm not a good person these days . . . I've been so *angry*.'

'It doesn't matter.' Julian spoke softly; he thought he saw in her now a flicker of the old Sophia, Thomas's Sophia whom he had loved. 'That's nonsense, what you're saying. You're a perfectly good person, you're just very sad at the moment.'

'I hate myself, but maybe I could be even worse. When I said I had thought of ending it — you know, I wouldn't. Do you know why? Not because Thomas wouldn't have liked it. He certainly wouldn't, it would never have occurred to him. He wasn't the type. I don't totally understand, but perhaps it's the idea that I don't want to die of a broken heart. I had all this happiness, and it doesn't seem right for me to die just because I can't have more. And yet every day is so hard, and waking up every morning and realising *again* that I'm alone, without him.'

Julian was staring intently at his coffee mug, trying not to cry. Sophia touched his arm.

'I'm truly sorry. This is shameful, but Jules, I could never have said those things to anyone else, and even though it's awful I think you've helped me a lot. I'm grateful. Don't be sad for me, please . . . Come on,' she added in a brisker but still gentle voice, 'shall we sort out the gallery? I'll ring it right now, and we'll go and see to the pictures. Would that be all right? You haven't even seen them yet!'

An hour later, they were at Zoff's. Walter Zoff seemed pleased to see Sophia and bowed as he shook hands formally with her and Julian.

'The show sold out in a week,' Walter told them. 'Imagine! Not a picture left — except, of course, my dears, the two that were *not* for sale. How angry I was with the young Thomas, and how strange it is that now I feel no anger at all, only I am pleased that you will have them. Of course all the others sold because of his so untimely death — scarcity value, you know.'

'Where are the two pictures?' asked Sophia.

He led her to a large room behind the gallery where a number of pictures and sculptures was stored. The large picture was leaning up against a wall; the little one had been temporarily hung.

She had forgotten the impact the 'Annunciation' had had on her. Now she gazed at it as if entranced. She thought she could see in the woman not only joy, humility and new understanding but also the faintest touch of fear, because the angel was taking her into the unknown. It was amazing to her that Thomas, with his purely instinctive approach, should have created a work of such psychological complexity. She lost herself in it as if it were a novel, a poem or a piece of music, a work of art beyond and greater than herself. For some moments she even forgot that it was Thomas's creation.

'What do you think of it?' she asked Julian.

'It's staggering,' he replied. 'I never realised he painted things like that. It's almost religious. I don't know if I actually *like* it, but I do think it's wonderful.'

'An imposing piece,' said Walter, padding up behind them. 'Not, perhaps, his best, but very fine, very original.'

'Oh, I don't agree,' said Sophia. 'For me this probably is his best.'

'Ah well. All beauty is — how do you say it? — in the eye of the beholder. I think perhaps the smaller of the two is the finer; but after all they are so different, the comparison is useless.'

'The little one is so beautiful,' Julian said.

Sophia looked coolly at the picture of herself at Avondale. On parade before Julian and Walter Zoff, she had no personal feelings about it. As portrayed by Thomas, the image of herself in the picture was from another age and as such irrelevant to her now.

'I agree,' she said, 'that it's very beautiful. Thomas was best of all, I think, at light. He captured the evening light perfectly in this. I find the big picture much more interesting.'

'Mummy said you planned to send the big one to Avondale and to keep the little one for yourself?' Julian asked.

'Yes,' said Sophia. 'I shall hang the little one in my bedroom at home and have it always. Don't you think the big one would look well at Avondale?'

'It'll certainly be different,' Julian said, and for the first time he smiled and looked to Sophia like his old self.

'Then I'll arrange for it to be sent and let your mother know. Oh!' she paused, raising her head as if suddenly just remembering something.

'What is it?'

'Your mother will kill me. I promised her I should see a doctor, as I hadn't been well. Do you know, I genuinely meant to, because I really haven't been myself at all, and I don't now believe it's only because of losing Thomas; I just never got round to it. Oh dear.'

Julian patted Sophia's hand in an awkward little gesture that still managed to be brotherly and kind. 'She won't be cross, I promise. Tell you what, why don't you make the appointment and then ring her up?'

Sophia smiled broadly. 'Bless you, Jules. Now then, where's Walter . . . ?'

★ ★ ★

The following day, Sophia rang up the Avondales. She told Hermione the arrangements she had made for the picture and apologised for not having been in touch.

'I'm deeply ashamed of myself,' she said. 'I didn't think.'

'Never mind, don't worry,' said Hermione. 'How are you in yourself?'

'You'll be even less pleased with me. I kept putting off seeing the doctor, but I've made an appointment, I promise, and I'm going this afternoon.'

'Oh dear, I so hoped that whatever you had would have passed over, and you were all right again.'

'I'm sure I'm all right really. I'm just not feeling — I can't quite say. Anyway, my health is very boring. How's everything at Avondale?'

Sophia proceeded to question Hermione minutely on the people and animals she had known at Avondale, so that when they finished speaking and Hermione was telling Richard about it, she said, 'She sounded so much better, almost normal.'

29

The next day, following the doctor's appointment, Sophia was galvanised into action. First she let her office know the exact date on which she intended to return and arranged that she would be in contact with it regularly during her absence. 'I have to keep up with the market even if I'm not there,' she told Stuart briskly, 'otherwise there really will be no point in coming back.' Then she booked her return flights to Australia via Thailand — first class all the way. 'After all,' she said to herself, 'I have a great deal of money, so I may as well enjoy it.' (She had made a fairly spectacular profit on a new issue the previous week.) Finally, she got into her car and went to see her parents.

'Darling,' said Susan White seriously as she stepped into the tobacco atmosphere of the tidy house, 'you look *rather* unwell.'

'Is everything all right?' asked her father.

Sophia smiled unnaturally brightly and answered quickly, 'Oh yes, really.'

Sleep had eluded her the previous night. She had come on a specific errand to her parents, and she was amazed to find it terrified her. There was nothing she could do to avoid it. She had thought at first her task would consist merely of telling them; now she knew she, after all the years of defiant independence, of living her life not only apart from them but also in spite of them, was desperate for their approval. She could not help it, because everything had changed.

'You're pregnant,' the doctor had told her the day before. 'I hope it isn't bad news.'

He was unprepared for her look of blank astonishment. 'That's completely impossible,' she said.

'I assure you I'm not wrong.'

'But my partner's been dead for at least two months!'

'And your last period, by your own account, was more than three months ago.'

'But that was just because I was upset. I wasn't eating properly.'

'Miss White, you don't strike me as being that naive. You are at least ten weeks pregnant. I must advise you that if you feel you must terminate the pregnancy . . . '

'Out of the question.' She didn't think, the words produced themselves.

After she had left the surgery, she sat down for a few minutes in the waiting room, as if in shock. Although she could not immediately take in the implication of the doctor's diagnosis, she knew that her whole universe had tilted, and that her life from that moment on would never be the same again.

She had spent the rest of the evening quietly at home, taking care to prepare herself a proper meal (the doctor had insisted that she should eat properly from now on) and listening to the sort of music that demanded absolute concentration. It was after she had gone to bed that thoughts of the pregnancy at last invaded her. She struggled with the panic, grief and wild elation that possessed her, one continually superseded by the other. Only in the last hour or two before dawn did she drop off to an exhausted sleep.

However, the morning has more sense than the night before. She awoke full of resolution and energy, though her plans were only short term: she found herself obsessed with the desire to visit Australia (the country of light, she told herself). Now, faced by her parents, some of the panic returned.

They entered the ever-formal drawing-room, where she perched on the edge of an armchair. Bernard White offered sherry; she refused. He poured some for himself and his wife, and they all sat for a moment in silence, looking at each other. There was a strange light in Sophia's eyes, which seemed huge now in her white, thin face, that her parents couldn't read; at the same time she seemed highly animated.

Her voice broke the silence. 'I have something to tell you.' She paused. 'I don't know how you're going to react.' She knew they suspected nothing.

'Well, go on, dear,' said her father.

'I didn't really know how to react myself at first,' Sophia ploughed on. 'But I think — I believe — it's tremendous. Oh, I do hope you're pleased for me.' She was twisting her fingers together, her eyes down. Then she looked up at both her parents. She was like a diver teetering in terror on the edge of the high board, about to launch himself head first into the distant water. Susan White suddenly understood her eyes: they were beseeching.

She took a breath and announced, 'I'm expecting Thomas's baby.'

They just stared at her for what seemed like a long time, looking at and past her unusually bright eyes.

'Oh, please be pleased for me. It means so much to me.' The words bubbled up and cascaded out from deep within.

They both spoke at once.

'Have you told . . . ' began Mr White.

'How do you fee-' began Mrs White. They both stopped and looked at each other.

'Are you very shocked?' asked Sophia, half

whispering and almost rigid with apprehension.

'Oh, darling . . . ' Susan White said hesitantly, and then she completed her question.

'How do I feel?' said Sophia. 'I feel good. I think so. I miss Thomas dreadfully.'

'Would he have . . . ' Bernard White started.

Sophia finished for him, ' . . . married me? Oh yes. This was to have been my engagement ring.'

She showed them the pearl and ruby ring, which she wore on the fourth digit of her right hand. 'It belonged to his mother,' she explained. 'She must have had thin fingers too, because it fits me perfectly.'

'Oh, darling,' said Mrs White, 'how are you going to *cope?*'

'I'll be fine. I'd like to go on working, because I don't know what I'd do otherwise. Obviously I'll hire a nanny. We'll see how it all goes. Maybe I'll move into a bigger house, though I probably won't need to at first.'

'Can you afford . . . ' her father trailed off in confusion and embarrassment.

'Oh yes. There may be things to worry about, but I promise you money isn't one of them.'

'Babies are . . . *difficult,* you know,' Mrs

White said. 'They're bad enough when you have a husband, but on your own . . . ' She too petered out.

'I'll be all right,' Sophia insisted. She glanced almost fearfully from one to the other.

There was a silence, broken by Mrs White suggesting, in the same subdued voice, that they should have lunch.

'Have you told Thomas's parents?' asked Mr White as they sat down.

'No, not yet. How could I tell anyone before I told you? I'm driving down to Avondale tomorrow to do so.'

Sophia's mother, having got over the initial shock of Sophia's announcement, asked question after question. Encouraged that she at least might be taking her news positively, Sophia answered her questions eagerly and ate plenty.

'It's wonderful, Mummy, and just what I need. The doctor ticked me off for being underweight. Do you know, if I'd gone on not looking after myself I could have lost the baby!'

This set off a string of questions about Sophia's current state of health: had she been sick, how was she feeling, when was it due? As the meal progressed, Sophia grew more and more cheerful and correspondingly garrulous. She discovered she liked talking about the pregnancy. For the first time in her life, she out-talked her mother. The baby was due in June. Yes, she had been sick a few times; it was the main reason she had visited the doctor. She had not entertained the faintest suspicion that she might be pregnant, having ascribed her missed periods to shock and insufficient food. She would have gone into far more detail about her gynaecological symptoms had her father not been present.

He managed one question. 'Why?' he asked simply. 'Why did you let it happen?'

Sophia turned her full stare onto her father; it seemed to her he almost quailed before her grey eyes and was diminished. Now she demanded rather than besought his approval and felt less sympathy for his shock. 'Because it was something Thomas wanted so dreadfully. It wasn't a mistake, you know. He wanted it first, then I did too. I didn't think it was possible for it to happen so quickly. He wanted babies even more than he wanted marriage, but we were going to tell you and then announce our engagement just after the show. No one knew. He told his parents only just before he died. We wouldn't have waited long to get married.'

Towards pudding Mrs White's stream of questions dried up. Sophia noticed that they were hardly eating. Silence fell again.

Sophia turned again to her father, now more gently. 'I've shocked you, haven't I? I'm sorry.'

'Oh, well, I wouldn't say — ' Mrs White began, but Mr White said, 'Yes. You have.'

He got up and walked slowly out of the dining room. Susan White, seeing Sophia's face fall, went over to Sophia's chair and put an arm round her shoulders.

'Don't you worry, dear,' she said. 'He's upset, but he'll be all right. I promise. Now how would you like to come for a little walk with me?'

'A little walk?'

'Let's just stroll on the downs, shall we? Come on, I'll do all this clearing up later. I'll just tell your father we're going.'

'No, darling,' she said later as, arm in arm, they walked along the downs towards the racecourse, 'I'm not upset. Isn't it funny, every parent who has a daughter dreads what you've just told us more than anything else in the world — pregnant out of wedlock, an illegitimate child . . . '

'But you can't think of Thomas's child like that!' Sophia burst out.

'No, you can't, can you? But it is, you know. I'm on your side, though. Darling, you know I've *worried* about you all your life

— much, much more than about Anthea and Edward. I worried more than ever after Thomas passed away. But now . . . ,' she paused, 'now I know you're going to be all right.'

They walked on for a few moments in companionable silence. They were going uphill, and Sophia soon got out of breath.

'I'm so unfit,' she confessed.

Her mother laughed. 'I'm not bad for my age. Now, darling, you're really going to have to *look after yourself.* You must start by eating properly, and yes, you really must get fitter, it'll be ever so much easier if you do. I don't suppose you'll want much advice from me, but always remember, I've done it all before — three times.'

'Of course I'll want advice from you, Mum. Where else would I get it? Oh, I know there's the gynaecologist and ante-natal classes and all that, but it's not the same, is it?'

'Well, no, it isn't, but oh darling, I'm *so* glad you really think so.'

When she took her leave later that afternoon, Sophia kissed her father and said, 'Everything will be all right, Dad, I promise.'

She thought he looked confused and old, but behind the confusion there was the kindness that had always been there. 'Oh, I hope so, dear,' he said. 'I do hope so.'

'I'll come and see you again before I go to Australia,' she promised them, and then she drove home. A tremendous, pure relief flooded through her. She knew this would probably be the last time that she would feel any sort of relief on leaving her parents' house, and that this present feeling had nothing to do with the enervated release she had experienced with such depressing regularity in the old days.

30

The dogs began barking as she drove round to the back door at Avondale, and when she opened her car door they leaped at her, Bella first, her huge paws making muddy marks on her jeans. Relieved by this distraction, she stretched out her arms in delight to pat them and found herself briefly in tears. Bella's stump wagged frantically, and she licked her face. Sophia briskly blew her nose and got out of the car. Richard and Hermione were standing at the back door.

They looked, at first glance, somewhat grim-faced; again, she thought they had aged. She walked firmly up to them, her arms open; they embraced her almost shyly.

'You're looking a bit more cheerful,' said Hermione; 'much better.'

'Far too thin,' said Richard more sternly. 'I don't believe you've been feeding yourself properly.'

'No; well, I've been very silly. I'm eating like a horse now, always hungry. Hello, Alice.' She bent down to stroke the cat.

They had lunch in the kitchen, and again Sophia, trying desperately but more successfully than she realised to hide her nerves, announced that she had news for them.

'I do hope you won't be shocked,' she said. Richard and Hermione appeared full of curiosity but neutral; however, at that moment they had never seemed more remote. For the first time she genuinely felt the weight of the difference she perceived between them and herself. She was an outsider to their way of life, and her news would surely represent a monstrous intrusion. She forced herself to carry on but could not be direct. 'My parents didn't know whether to laugh or cry — no, that's not it. My father *was* shocked. My mother was all right.'

'You're not . . . ?' Hermione began. Sophia sought her eyes and snatched, in their enquiry, hope.

'Yes, I am,' said Sophia.

Richard frowned and asked irritably, 'Are what?'

'Thomas's baby,' said Hermione and, 'Pregnant,' said Sophia simultaneously.

'Good God!' Sophia froze. Then Richard began to smile. 'You're . . . pleased about it?'

'Oh yes,' said Sophia, 'so pleased.' She began to look forward to feeling massively relieved and found herself dangerously close to tears again.

'Well,' said Hermione, who had begun to beam, 'I think that's simply splendid. Well, done, my dear! Will you get some champagne, darling? Oh dear, you probably don't feel like drinking, I know I didn't with Julian . . . '

Sophia succumbed to the tears. Both the Avondales rushed to her and began patting her shoulder and pressing handkerchiefs on her. She was astonished to find she was unembarrassed by these tears, and they dried up almost as soon as they had started; like the sun breaking through cloud, she smiled at them.

'How kind you both are, and how wonderful to be able to tell you. I was frightened you might have been quite upset.'

'Such nonsense,' said Richard. 'Thomas's child!'

He rushed off to the cellar for the champagne. 'Shed a quiet tear too, no doubt,' said Hermione. 'Oh, Sophia, I'm so, so thrilled for you.' She took Sophia's hands. 'Were your parents really all right about it?'

'Yes. My poor father was very taken aback at first, but my mother was rather pleased. In fact she was really good about it. They both adored Thomas, you know.'

'I couldn't bear to think they might disapprove and make things difficult for you, but then, you know, you've always got us.'

'Thank you so much! No, they were fine. Isn't it funny, Hermione, but Thomas brought me closer to my parents than I have been since early childhood, and now that I'm expecting his baby it cements it — I think.'

Richard brought up vintage champagne. 'I hate it when people say what a dead person would or wouldn't like when they're just talking about their own desires,' said Sophia, 'but I'm definitely going to drink some of this, because apart from the fact that I want to, Thomas would have been simply outraged if I didn't.'

'Oh, the relief!' she exclaimed after they had drunk. 'I was so dreading that you wouldn't like it — as I wasn't married to Thomas. I know it's silly. Without you I should have felt so alone — even with my own parents' support. Now it's all right. I'm not alone. But I've never missed Thomas as much as I do now. I keep thinking how thrilled he would have been, and I can't get over it.'

Over coffee in the drawing room, Sophia asked, 'Richard, I have a request about this baby.'

'What can that be?'

'The name. I don't want to appear presumptuous, but do you think it might be all right for the baby to have Thomas's name?

Avondale, I mean. Not for some silly reason such as trying to make out we had been married after all. It's just that it was Thomas's name, and I'd so like the baby to have it.'

The request pleased and touched Richard. The three of them sat and talked about Sophia's immediate plans and her tentative ideas about the pregnancy and birth. Eventually, Sophia said, 'Do you mind if I go out for a little? I just want to have a walk.'

She wrapped up and walked up the hill behind Avondale, where she had been on the evening after her quarrel with Thomas last summer. The sky was in its leaden cast of February, but it was mild, and soon she was sweating slightly with the effort of the walk. On top of the hill she paused and looked towards the sea, but it was barely visible in the greyness.

A rustle in the bushes behind her made her start. She turned in sudden fear, but then her face changed, relaxing into a smile.

'Bella,' she said.

The black Doberman trotted up to her, wagging her stump. Sophia bent down to fondle her ears, a favourite caress. Bella sat down, half-closing her eyes in ecstasy, until Sophia stroked her head and straightened up. When she realised she had lost Sophia's undivided attention, she found a fascinating rabbit hole nearby and dug at it.

As Sophia turned to descend the hill, the setting sun suddenly appeared in a chink between two grey clouds. It blazed, lighting up the edge of the clouds and making everything around Sophia pale gold. She paused again to look about herself. Her mind seemed to unfurl, and for the first time she had a vivid sense of the baby to be, urgently present and alive within her.

'Come on, Bella!' she called. 'It's time to go home.'

The dog ran back to her, and together they walked back down to Avondale in the soft light.

THE END

We do hope that you have enjoyed reading this large print book.

Did you know that all of our titles are available for purchase?

We publish a wide range of high quality large print books including:
Romances, Mysteries, Classics, General Fiction, Non Fiction and Westerns.

Special interest titles available in large print are:
The Little Oxford Dictionary
Music Book
Song Book
Hymn Book
Service Book

Also available from us courtesy of Oxford University Press:
Young Readers' Dictionary
(large print edition)
Young Readers' Thesaurus
(large print edition)

For further information or a free brochure, please contact us at:
Ulverscroft Large Print Books Ltd.,
The Green, Bradgate Road, Anstey,
Leicester, LE7 7FU, England.
Tel: (00 44) **0116 236 4325**
Fax: (00 44) **0116 234 0205**

GHOSTMAN

Kenneth Royce

Jones boasted that he never forgot a face. When he was found dead outside the National Gallery it was assumed he had remembered one too many. The man he had claimed to have identified had been publicly executed in Moscow some years before. The presumed look-alike was called Mirek and his background stood up. The Security Service calls in Willie 'Glasshouse' Jackson — Jacko — as they realise that there is a more sinister aspect. Jacko and his assistant begin to unearth commercial and political corruption in which life is cheap and profits vast, as the killing machines swing into action.

THE READER

Bernhard Schlink

A schoolboy in post-war Germany, Michael collapses one day in the street and is helped home by a woman in her thirties. He is fascinated by this older woman, and he and Hanna begin a secretive affair. Gradually, he begins to be frustrated by their relationship, but then is shocked when Hanna simply disappears. Some years later, as a law student, Michael is in court to follow a case. To his amazement he recognizes Hanna. The object of his adolescent passion is a criminal. Suddenly, Michael understands that her behaviour, both now and in the past, conceals a deeply buried secret.

THE WAY OF THE SEA AND OTHER STORIES

Stanley Wilson

Every story in this collection was written by Stanley Wilson with radio in mind. The BBC has broadcast all of them, and many have been used overseas. All have appeared in magazines or newspapers. The stories range the globe and beyond, from India to Canadian backwoods, from an expedition up the Amazon to a hundred years' journey to the planet Eithnan, from the Caribbean to a rain-sodden English seaside promenade, and from a fishing trawler to a hospital ward. There is frustration, there is tenderness, there is horror, there are tears, but there is laughter as well.